Lindos
Affairs

John Wilton

ISBN: 978-0-244-47976-3

PublishNation

www.publishnation.co.uk

Acknowledgements:

Once again I would like to say another big thank you to all my very good friends in beautiful Lindos. As with my previous Lindos novels - Lindos Retribution, Lindos Aletheia, and Lindian Summers – my warm thanks go to my good friends Jack Koliais and Janis Woodward Bowles, who both encouraged me greatly to get on and write these Lindos novels. Also, my thanks go to everyone in Lindos and beyond who has said and wrote such nice things about them. Finally, my endless gratitude goes yet again to Fiona Ensor for her tireless proof-reading efforts identifying my errors.

Needless to say, this story is total fiction. However, without the magical village of Lindos, and the people in it, it could never have been written. For that reason, as with my previous Lindos novels, I will always be grateful to the people there, my friends in that magical paradise.

Author's website: www.johnwilton.yolasite.com

Previous novels by John:

The Hope (2014)

Lindos Retribution (2015)

Lindos Aletheia (2016)

Lindian Summers (2018)

All available on Amazon and Kindle.

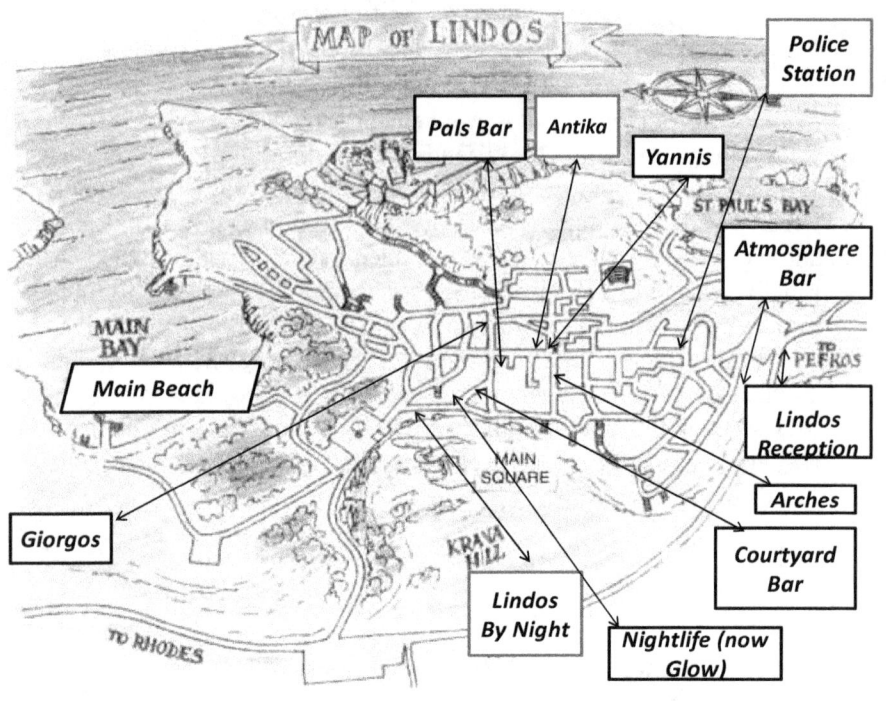

MAP OF LINDOS

Police Station

Pals Bar

Antika

Yannis

ST PAUL'S BAY

Atmosphere Bar

MAIN BAY

Main Beach

TO PEFKOS

Lindos Reception

Arches

MAIN SQUARE

KRANA HILL

Giorgos

Courtyard Bar

Lindos By Night

Nightlife (now Glow)

TO RHODES

Contents

Part One: First encounter

1

Wednesday 22nd June, 2016

What do people do during the safety demonstration by the cabin crew on a plane? Some people do actually pay attention and watch in silence of course, as the pilot requested a few seconds before. Others just carry on looking at their electronic devices, iPads and phones, irrespective of the request, and some even carry on chatting to their travelling companion seated alongside them. He was one of those who always felt obliged to watch it attentively all the way through, even though he had seen it many times before. Although as it was being performed impeccably by the steward or stewardess in the aisle in front of him he did think that if someone really did have to be shown something as basic and obvious as how to fasten and unfasten a seat belt should they really be allowed to travel on a plane? Of course, he had no idea just how many of his fellow passengers on this particular seemingly full flight needed such guidance.

Anyway, as he stared aimlessly ahead down the plane from his aisle seat in row thirteen he consoled himself through the boredom with the fact that at least the flight looked like it was going to leave on time, and its four hour duration would give him ample opportunity to get on with his writing. Although his aimless staring was forced to continue for just over twenty minutes more while the aircraft taxied out to the runway, took off effortlessly, and eventually the 'fasten seat belts' sign went off. Despite the considerable number of flights he took each year, for work and pleasure, he was never really very clear whether or not it was allowable to open up his small netbook and switch it on until the seat belt sign went off. He thought he vaguely recalled being asked by a stewardess on some previous flight to turn off the netbook as they were preparing to land, although that was probably a few years before when all airlines required all electronic devices to be switched off for take-off and landing. Being something of a creature of habit he just carried on with the same routine without even enquiring from a member of the cabin staff if it was still necessary.

Once the seat belt sign did go off he stood up, opened the overhead locker, and took out from his black rucksack the small soft fabric case enclosing his netbook. He returned to his seat, opened up the device, and turned it on. A few seconds later he clicked on and opened a folder, then a document within it, and was scrolling down it, scanning the first part of the text as he did so. He continued doing that for ten minutes or so, occasionally stopping and tapping away, editing to insert some further text into the existing or deleting some. He was now completely focused on the netbook and text on the screen in front of him, so much so that he never really even noticed the two women passengers who were sat in the middle row seat next to him and the window seat. He had been vaguely aware of a whispered conversation between them a few minutes after he had started to work on the netbook, not that he actually could make out what they said to each other, or was even that interested in doing so. He was far too focused on what was in front of him on the netbook screen.

His mind wandered a little at that point as he considered how strange it was that people on planes, strangers, can spend hours sat next to each other without actually exchanging even a cursory nod of acknowledgment of their existence, let alone a word or two. Even odder if they happen to be sat in seats by the emergency exits as their lives could be dependent on the swift actions of the person sat alongside them, or possibly two seats way, in the event of an emergency requiring the opening of the emergency exit door. But he was just the same. Just like everyone, or at least most, of his fellow passengers he never made any effort on any of the flights he took to engage those sat next to him in conversation, or even a basic hello.

At the point that he was reminding himself to focus and get back to the job in front of him on his netbook screen, the female voice

5

from the middle seat next to him demonstrated that she clearly hadn't signed up for the unwritten aircraft flight protocol of not engaging the person next to you in conversation.

"Excuse me, are you writing a novel?" she asked. "Only I hope you don't mind, but I couldn't help noticing that was what it looked like, there on your laptop." She pointed at the screen, and had referred to it as a laptop, although it wasn't, but he wasn't going to be so pedantic as to correct her when she'd been so brave as to break the unwritten aircraft protocol and speak to him. "I said as much to my friend here, but she obviously couldn't see from her window seat," she added.

As she spoke she pointed again, this time in the other direction, briefly to her friend with darkish blonde hair sat by the window, who just nodded slightly in agreement.

He turned his head away from looking at the screen in front of him and towards the face of the female voice as he replied a little hesitantly, "Err … yes, I am, although technically I'm editing, not writing. It's the first draft and my agent's editor sent me some suggestions about the story."

"How interesting, I wish I could write a book. I'd love to be able to," she told him.

"Well, you should do. Everyone has a book inside them, so it's said. I only started it as a hobby. Like you I always wanted to write a novel, so I did, and now this is a second one. You should try."

"Oh, I'm not sure I could. What's this one about, and the first one?"

He clicked the 'Save' icon on his netbook, and began to answer her with, "It's set at the time of the 'Velvet Revolution' in the former Czechoslovakia in 1989, and is about the relationships between two women and a man during those events. The first one is-"

Before he could finish though she had noticed him clicking the 'Save' button and interrupted quickly with, "Oh, Czechoslovakia … err … why there?" Her expression changed into something of a frown and she seemed to take a gulp as she hesitated briefly before adding much more pointedly as she changed the subject, "I'm sorry, you are trying to get on with it and I'm just stopping you."

He was a little confused, and taken aback, by her reaction to his mention of Czechoslovakia, but just told her, "No, no, that's ok. As I said, it's just editing. Plenty of time to do that while I'm on holiday, well, sort of holiday. I'm going to be on Rhodes for three weeks, so plenty of time, and that's what I planned to do anyway. That's why I booked it. And it's because I've spent some time there for my work, Czechoslovakia, or rather the Czech Republic as it is now, not Rhodes, in answer to your question. I'm Martin, by the way."

"Aileen, Aileen Regan," she told him and once again pointed to her friend sat in the window seat as she added, "and this is Sandra."

"So, with a name like that you must be Irish. I thought so straightaway, from your accent," he asked.

She smiled broadly and then let out a small chuckle before she told him, "Well spotted."

"What part?"

"Bantry, Bantry Bay, West Cork, do you know it?"

"Yes, well I know of it, my grandmother came from near Cork," he told her.

Where are you staying on Rhodes?" As she finished her question she lifted her hand to tuck her jet black shoulder length hair behind her left ear.

"Lindos, I go there quite a lot during the summers when I'm writing. I rent a small apartment from friends who live there. My first novel was set on Rhodes, to answer your question earlier."

"That's where we're staying. So, we'll no doubt bump into you at some point. I read that Lindos is not a very big place?"

"No, it's not, it's a village really. A very nice village though. It's your first time there then?" he asked, "You'll love it. Everyone does, and lots of people come back time and again. And yes, I'm sure we'll bump into each other at some point. How long are you there for?"

"Just the two weeks, we only booked it a couple of weeks ago," she informed him. "I just had to get away for a break. It's been a crazy time, lots going on, and I persuaded Sandra to come with me. Not sure how happy her husband was about that though."

She grimaced a little as she finished speaking.

"Workwise," he asked.

"Sorry?"

7

"You said it had been a crazy time with lots going on. Was it work?"

He was fishing, trying to find out what she did for work. But she wasn't responding in that way. After a slight sigh she simply replied, "Yes, that and other things."

He decided to switch the subject back to Lindos.

"Well, if you need a guide for Lindos I know a good one, and very cheap," he told her, allowing a slight smile to creep across his face.

"Oh … well … err-"

There was more than a hint of hesitation in her voice. She obviously hadn't picked up the humour in his voice. He put her out of her discomfort as he quickly added, a bit nervously, "Me, I'm sorry, I meant me. I didn't mean a guide as such, just me if you'd like to meet up for a drink one night I can show you some of the local bars in the village. I can give you my phone number if you'd like. And when I said cheap I meant free, of course." He added a small smile when he told her that last bit.

She glanced sideways at her friend Sandra, who just shrugged her shoulders and tilted her head slightly to one side in a very non-committal type of gesture, making no comment at all.

After a few seconds hesitation while she glanced at her friends face Aileen eventually said, "Yes why not, of course," and reached to the seatback pocket to get her phone from her handbag.

"So, Martin who?" she asked as she began to enter his name into her phone directory.

"Cleverley, Martin Cleverley," he responded and then rattled off his number while she entered it.

As she did that he couldn't help glancing at her face, trying to estimate her age. He reckoned she was in her late thirties. She already sported a bit of a tanned face on her smooth, bright skin, maybe fake, but he had no idea anyway how you'd tell. Her high cheekbones and full red lips were perfectly framed by her shoulder length dark black hair which was slightly curled at the ends, emphasising her delicate features. Her very striking dark brown eyes were darting back and forth from the keys of her phone to its screen as she entered his number. There was something immediately

8

extremely attractive about them, emphasised by their brilliant white surrounding her brown pupils. This was an attractive woman who was clearly interested in talking to him about his writing. He couldn't tell easily as she was sitting, but he thought she was probably about five foot six tall or so, and appeared to have a good, slim figure beneath the plain white t-shirt and light beige calf length cut-off trousers she wore. He had been instantly attracted to her, especially when she offered him a couple of sparkling smiles in response to some of his more flippant comments. As she held her phone in her left hand and tapped in his number with her right he took the opportunity to check for any sign of a wedding ring on the fingers of her hand holding the phone, or even anything that resembled an engagement ring. There was none, which, unnoticed by her, prompted a very slight pleasurable smile to himself.

His inner pleasure was rudely interrupted as he glanced up from watching Aileen entering his number and felt a much more, what can only be described as unfriendly glare, from her travelling companion sat by the window. Sandra's face was emotionless, and exhibited no expression towards him at all. She appeared disinterested, verging on hostile. He tried a smile across at her behind Aileen as she leaned forward to replace her phone in her bag, but that only provoked a continuance of the stony stare. She wasn't unattractive. Although she didn't quite possess Aileen's attributes, and she was exhibiting what was clearly a wedding ring on the third finger of her left hand, confirming her friend's comments about their holiday and her unhappy husband. From what he could make out she appeared to be equally as slim as Aileen and probably about the same height. Her, what appeared natural, darkish blonde hair, was somewhat shorter though, cut in a bob that actually only appeared to highlight her slightly chubby cheeks. There was absolutely no change in the far away distant look in her deep blue eyes though.

So, he decided to give up on trying to engage even visually with Sandra and just focus on her much more friendly travelling companion. As Aileen sat back after placing her phone back in her handbag he asked, "So, is it just the two of you going to Lindos?"

He was fishing, starting to check and try to confirm her marital or non-marital status.

"Yes, just the two of us."

As Aileen told him that she again briefly turned her head to face her friend looking for her to confirm it, but once more she was expressionless and unwilling to offer even the shortest comment. Martin took the opportunity to complete his fishing expedition.

"So, no husband or boyfriend joining you later then?"

She let out a slight chuckle that caused her head to rock back and forth once very slightly in her seat, then allowed a small grin to spread across her lips as she grasped the third finger of her left hand in an apparent reflex action and rubbed it briefly with the thumb and forefinger of her other hand.

"I doubt it," she began to answer him, "Not in my case at least. That would be a surprise, although not a very good one I think." She grinned once more as she turned her head to face him and said, "I got divorced almost a year ago. It's a long story, and I won't bore you with it. As I said before, Sandra's married, although her husband won't be joining us. It's just a girl's break, if you know what I mean."

Apart from saying briefly, "No, I'm sure it wouldn't bore me," he listened in silence, deciding it was best to just let her continue and tell him as much, or as little, as she wanted.

"I was married for twelve years. The divorce wasn't acrimonious, surprisingly amicable given the circumstances. I did wonder at one point if he was having an affair, but in the end I wasn't really that bothered even if he was to be honest. At least that's what I told myself at first, that's what I believed, until I found out the full facts later. We had grown apart, so I thought it was bound to happen at some point, and I actually thought at one time he thought I was having an affair. I wasn't, but that was irrelevant really. It's feelings that matter don't you think?"

As she explained to him what happened she had turned her head away from facing him and just stared aimlessly at the back of the seat in front of her as she spoke. As she said that last sentence she turned back to face him and looked straight into his eyes.

"Erm ... err, yes, I guess that's true," he agreed, feeling her deep brown eyes almost piercing through his, and simultaneously somewhat overwhelmed by the intensity being exhibited by this very attractive stranger he had only begun conversing with around twenty minutes earlier.

He was clearly disorientated by her as she asked, "And you?"

So much so that all he could respond with was, "And me what?"

"Married, divorced, single?" She gave him options.

"Oh, no, I see, err … divorced, ten years ago, and was married for six years before that. We'd grown apart too, just like you said with your marriage, so it was all fairly amicable. What about kids, any?"

This was getting a bit personal. He wondered if that was about to scare her off, but he needn't have worried.

"No, none," she answered in what seemed to him to be a slightly softer and lower tone of voice as she once again turned her head to look straight into his eyes, adding again, "You?"

"No, none either." This was definitely getting a little heavy now though he thought, and she seemed to be getting more and more intense. He should have been pleased with her interest and reaction, but far from that, something was making him feel a little uneasy. Maybe it was simply because he'd been on so many planes and flights where no one spoke to him at all, never said so much as a 'hello', and here he was engrossed in a conversation with a complete stranger about parts of his, and their, life.

He decided the best thing to do was to try and lighten the mood by telling her with another accompanying smile, "Perhaps we should have just given each other questionnaires to complete? That would have been simpler."

She smiled her sparkling smile once more and let out a soft chuckle. "Yes, I suppose it would," she agreed. "Let's move on down the list of questions on the questionnaire then. Are you an author full-time, or?"

"No, just a hobby really, well, that's what it started out as during one summer while I was in Lindos. I was in a bar late one night that a Greek friend of mine owns and was talking to him about possibly writing a novel. He suggested that I should write one about Lindos. There have been some written, but I came up with the idea of one with a twist about a murder. He thought that was a great idea, so I set about trying to do it, and eventually ended up writing it."

11

"Sounds a good hobby," she told him. "But what do you do that enables you to spend whole summers on Rhodes?"

Before he could answer one of the stewardesses with the drinks trolley asked if they wanted anything. Sandra broke what was obviously a vow of silence to immediately respond with, "A gin and tonic, with ice and lemon, please." To which Aileen added, "And for me please."

As the stewardess finished serving the two women and they paid he told her, "No, nothing for me, thanks."

Aileen opened her small can of tonic, poured some of it into the plastic glass containing the gin and the ice, and took a sip, before asking, "Well, where do you get all your money from then, Martin? Are you a bank robber or something?"

She looked a lot more relaxed now. Maybe it was the smell and taste of the gin and tonic. Whatever it was she was offering him another one of her captivating smiles.

"I'm a Professor," he began to explain, "At King's College London. So, I get long summer holidays. I used to do a lot more academic research stuff through the summers, especially in Greece. But now I prefer my hobby of writing novels."

"Professor of what?" she asked.

"Greek Mythology, so obviously Rhodes is ideal for some of that sort of stuff."

"Sounds interesting, I love Greece. But then why are you writing a book about Czechoslovakia?"

"I've been there half-a-dozen times or so for my work at King's, in connection with academic research and conferences on Greek Mythology. King's has some connections and student exchange programmes with some Czech universities, in Prague and in the second city of Brno. Each time I went I got more and more interested in what happened there in 1989 in the revolution, partly from talking with colleagues and friends at the universities there. So, I decided I'd try to write a novel, historical fiction based around that time and also on the relationships between two women and a man within those events."

He once again noticed a change in her expression at the mention of the Czech Republic in his answer. Her body language changed instantly as she folded her mainly bare arms across her chest. Her whole demeanour became much more rigid and less relaxed. He was perplexed, but just told himself that she had asked, even if he had no idea quite what had appeared to offend her in his answer. He decided the best thing was to quickly change the subject and to go back to asking about her work.

"So, what is it that you and Sandra do workwise that pays for holidays in Lindos then?"

"Nothing as important sounding as a Professor or as glamorous as an author, well not as far as what I do is concerned. Sandra's is a bit more glamorous. She's a fashion photographer, freelance, but with her own agency. I'm just a P.A. for an Advertising Executive."

He once again looked across towards Sandra as he repeated, "Fashion photographer," adding, "that sounds exciting." However, Aileen's friend wasn't interested at all in getting involved in their conversation and just continued sipping her drink and staring straight ahead at the back of the seat in front of her or occasionally looking out of the window. After her lack of response he decided to continue concentrating on his conversation with Aileen.

"But a P.A. to an advertising executive must also have its interesting moments too? Is it in London?"

"Yes, although I don't live in London really. Sandra and her husband do, St. John's Wood, but that's a bit too pricey for me. I'm in Cheam, near Epsom. What about you?"

"North London, Highgate, It's a bit pricey now too, but was a lot cheaper when I bought my flat after my divorce ten years ago. It's handy for work at the college. How do you two know each other then if you don't work together?"

"University, we met at Bristol Uni. We both did a media studies degree, became good friends over the three years and just kept in touch after we graduated."

Although Aileen didn't seem in the slightest bothered by his string of personal questions, and, in fact, appeared more than happy to continue their conversation, he could somehow increasingly sense that her travelling companion appeared to be growing more and more irritated with his questioning. He decided to once again try and lighten the atmosphere by telling Aileen, "Asking you all these

13

personal questions I guess you must think I'm some sort of Sherlock Holmes. Sorry, it's probably just the writer in me."

She turned her head slightly towards him and replied, "No, not at all. It's fine, as long as I'm not going to end up in your next novel though."

Her last comment was accompanied by a grin and a slight tilt of her head to one side, before she added, "And you certainly don't look like Sherlock."

At least he was grateful for that last comment, and hopefully he didn't look like the famous Conan Doyle detective at all. For a start he wasn't wearing a deerstalker hat on his light brown quite short-haired head, and his long face and smooth chin wasn't being partly concealed behind a large pipe. He actually had no idea just how old the famous detective was in Doyle's books. Maybe they were the same age though, forty-one, and, from what little he had read of those books, he always imagined Holmes was tall and slim for some reason, tall like him at six foot one although he couldn't claim to be overly slim.

"Not sure whether I should take that as a compliment or not, but thank you," he replied, returning her grin.

She just chuckled slightly and reached to pick up her gin and tonic and take another sip.

He was wary of turning their conversation back to a much more serious side, but he was curious about something she had said when telling him about her divorce, as well as her reaction to his mention of Czechoslovakia when she asked about the subject of his novel. Those two things were going over and over in his mind while they talked about what they both did for a living and where they lived. Eventually he couldn't resist asking.

"Can I ask you something about what you said when you talked about your divorce? You said, 'until I found out the full facts later'. Found out what? I don't mean to pry, but you also seemed a little disorientated when I told you my novel was based in Czechoslovakia and then the Czech Republic. I'm just wondering what it is about that country that you obviously dislike so much? Are the two things connected, your divorce and Czechoslovakia or the Czech Republic?"

She put her drink down on the seatback tray in front of her, turned her head to briefly glance at Sandra by the window, who sighed audibly, raised her eyebrows, and then shook her head slightly, making a bit of a face as if to say, "You asked for it," to her friend.

As Aileen turned back to face him she took a deep breath and told him quietly as a frown spread across her forehead, "He went off with a twenty-two year old Czech girl, my husband. Of course, he didn't tell me that at the time. He just said he thought we'd grown apart and he didn't love me anymore. Obviously I was shocked. I didn't have a clue, and the more and more I went over it during the next few weeks and months the more I convinced myself that maybe he was right and just accepted it. I asked him if there was anyone else of course, and he firmly denied it. Then two months after we had separated I found out he was with this Czech girl, and that he'd been having an affair with her for over a year. She had been working as an au pair in London. That's when I finally got round to divorcing him. Maybe up to that point I thought he would come back and we could sort it out, but when I found out about his cheating with that girl for over a year, and all his lies, that's when it sunk in I guess. So, I eventually accepted I had to divorce him."

Her face was a strange mixture of anger and resigned disappointment.

It was an unfortunate revelation. Certainly more information than Martin required and not exactly the sort of answer he was expecting. Her mood had changed considerably and he was now totally regretting having asked. No wonder she reacted the way she did when he told her about the novel he was editing on his netbook.

She was in full flow now so all he could do was to listen and try to not let any facial expression display his anxiety over the delicacy of the moment.

"He was never good enough for me anyway. I always knew I could do much better. There were lots of times in the marriage when he was a complete arsehole. He always had been, and I guess always would be, a total waste of space, always shallow and unreliable. All of my friends, including Sandra, especially Sandra, told me that plenty of times for years."

15

She once again turned her head briefly to nod towards her friend, who just shrugged her shoulders and nodded back in agreement as Aileen continued. "I never thought for one minute he was actually having an affair though. The thought never entered my head, even when he was being an arsehole. I should say affairs to be exact, because as I subsequently discovered the Czech girl wasn't the first, and I certainly doubt she will be the last, despite what she might think. Anyway, I'm sure the bloody Czech girl will eventually realise, discover what an arsehole he is, and dump him. After all he is forty-two and she is twenty years younger, what could they possibly have in common, plus he obviously can't keep his dick in his trousers. She'll no doubt discover that soon enough, if she hasn't already over the past year. I have no contact with him whatsoever now, but I'd bet money that's what will happen."

Her voice had gone up an octave or two as the result of her obvious anger. Martin was trying to show he was listening intently and attempting to just nod in agreement at the appropriate places as she spoke. In his head he was thinking differently, however. Why the hell did he ask that? How could he get her off the subject and back to something much easier to discuss? Above all he definitely knew that it wouldn't be the wisest thing for him to inform her that from the time he had spent for work in the Czech Republic, and from what he'd learned, seen, and heard from his Czech friends, the Czech girls and women mostly tended to treat their male partners like Gods, even in many cases no matter what they got up in terms of infidelity. They always looked and dressed immaculately and couldn't do enough for their men in the home. According to what his male friends had told him they weren't exactly slouches in the bedroom apparently, although he had no actual first-hand experience or evidence of that.

Thankfully, however, at that point in their conversation she didn't appear much interested in hearing anything he might add on that subject and she just took another deep breath, a sip of her drink, and told him, "Sorry, I get very annoyed about it, as you can see, mostly because he lied to me about why he wanted to separate. Anyway, that's the reason for my reaction to your answer about the subject of your novel."

"Yes, I see, I mean I understand, of course, very upsetting all those lies, and I see about the Czech connection," he told her.

He wasn't sure quite where to take their conversation now. He didn't want to appear cold and callous by just stopping it there and then; giving her the impression he had been scared off from even talking to her, let alone possibly meeting up in Lindos.

While he was wracking his brain for something more to say, a different subject, she let him off the hook by telling him, "Sorry, I have gone on a bit. It's still raw, you see, what happened. I should let you get back to your editing for the rest of the flight."

He tried not to show the relief in his voice as he told her, "Oh, ok, yes I suppose I should. I guess we'll be landing in about an hour and a half, so I'll get back to it."

She gave a slight nod of acknowledgement in relation to his suggestion, then turned her head towards Sandra sat alongside, although they never spoke, just exchanged glances.

Just over an hour and three-quarters later the three of them were standing alongside each other by a conveyor belt in the somewhat dated and basic Rhodes airport baggage hall.

While they waited for the first of their bags to arrive on the conveyor belt Aileen asked, "How are you getting to Lindos from here? I think the guide book said it's about an hour in a taxi. That's what we're going to take. Do you want to share one with us or do you have anyone meeting you?"

Very encouraging offer, he thought, as he replied, "No, no one is meeting me, so sure, that's a good idea, share a taxi. Where are you staying?"

"It's a two bedroomed villa, in the centre of the village behind the church it said on the site we booked it on. The contact person we have for it said they'd meet us in Lindos Main Square. We have to call them as soon as we leave the airport. Is the Main Square any good for you?"

"Yep, that's fine," he told her. "The apartment I rent is in the centre of the village too, and cars don't go into the village. So, the taxi can drop the three of us off in the Main Square."

Just over an hour later the taxi was depositing them there. Their contact, a local Greek, Nikos, which Martin knew as a nodding

17

acquaintance in the village, was there to meet the two women. So, the Englishman said a quick 'Hi' to Nikos, as well as his goodbyes to the pair of women, telling Aileen he would text her at some point about meeting up in the village one evening. Then he turned and made his way with his case into the fading Lindos twilight, across the square into the alleyway towards the centre of the village and the apartment he was renting.

2

Next day: first contact and a discovery

By early afternoon the next day the two women were relaxing on their sunbeds in the shade of the parasol between them on Pallas Beach, enjoying the first day of their holiday. The hot Lindos sun was burning down from the clear blue sky above the quite crowded beach, mostly populated with couples and groups of three and four men and women. The schools in the U.K. had not yet broken up for the summer, so there were very few children around. The tourist sun worshippers were predominantly British, although there was also a smattering of Greeks, Germans and Italians.

Sandra was reading, beginning a paperback she had bought at Gatwick airport, while Aileen flicked through a magazine she had also bought there. The two women's reading was interrupted by a couple of bleeps emanating from Aileen's phone inside her straw beach bag, and she reached in to rummage around the bag to retrieve it. The bleeps signified the receipt of a text message, a first one from Martin. It simply said, "How about meeting for a drink tonight at 9 at the Courtyard Bar?"

Eating a late lunch of omelette with a small Mythos beer outside Giorgos café bar in the centre of the village Martin had agonised over just how long he should wait before texting Aileen about meeting. Eventually he decided he had nothing to lose, so should 'seize the day' and send that first text.

"It's Martin, wants to know if we want to meet for a drink tonight at nine in somewhere called the Courtyard Bar. What do you think?" Aileen asked.

Sandra revealed very little interest or enthusiasm in both her actions and her voice as she continued looking at the pages of her paperback and simply replied, "It's up to you, if you want."

"I think he means both of us, not just me. We should go. Why not?"

Now Sandra put down her book between her legs on the sunbed, but continued to show little enthusiasm as she commented, "You think he means both of us? It seemed to me on the plane that he was only really interested in you. So, if you want to go you should go."

"No, I'm sure he means both of us, Sandra. Let's both go. I'll text him and ask where that bar is. The village is not that big, so it can't be that hard to find."

Still exhibiting resigned disinterest Sandra reluctantly agreed as she picked up her book to continue reading.

Barely minute after she sent a text confirming they'd meet him at nine he replied, "Great, see you there," followed by some brief directions on how to find the Courtyard Bar.

As Aileen placed her phone in the shade on the small plastic table between their two sunbeds Sandra looked up from her book with a quite dismissive, "He seems a bit pushy don't you think? At least, he does to me. You should have waited an hour or so before you replied to his first text. He'll think you're too keen."

Aileen looked a bit perplexed by Sandra's dismissive tone and comment.

"Maybe, but it's done now Sandra, so … Anyway, I'm too hot now, going for a swim. You coming?"

"In a bit, want to finish this chapter first."

Shortly after Aileen had headed down the beach and into the crystal clear blue sea her phone beeped once more. She had left it on the table between the two sunbeds, towards Sandra's side of the table and just below her eye level. She glanced over at the phone's screen as it beeped and was instantly curious at what she saw. The phone was in the shade, but the screen was still dulled a little by the penetrating effect of the bright daylight. From what she could make out without reaching over to pick it up, she thought the name on the screen looked like 'Richard Weston', her husband, plus there was the beginning of a text message. Before she did reach over to pick up the phone she sat up a little on her sunbed to briefly peer down the beach between the rows of parasols trying to locate just where Aileen was. When she recognised her head bobbing up and down some way out in the sea, swimming part of the way across the bay, she picked up the phone and clicked to open the message.

What she read in the long text message shocked her.

"Still missing you lots. I know you said we should stop, and we did, but we had four great months and I can't, don't want to stop. I've told you that over and over, and it's not any easier knowing you're there on holiday with her. Realise it could be difficult for you, but if I can get away from work I'm going to come and join the two of you the second week. She won't be too pleased I know. She was adamant before you booked that she wanted it to be just the two of you. We argued again, of course. Thought maybe she suspected something, but am sure now she doesn't. Will check flights and let her know I'm coming. Make sure you look surprised when she tells you. Miss you. xxx"

Sandra's emotions were a mixture of initial shock followed by mounting anger. She'd had her suspicions over some of her husband's recent actions, and reactions to her, for the past three months or so, wondering if, in fact, he was having an affair. She recognised the signs as he had 'previous', as they say. Five years into their marriage he'd had an affair - he called it a fling – with a young secretary in his previous job. After her suspicions grew, and then she was able to check some of them out discreetly through her contacts and channels in her own other 'secret life', she eventually discovered the truth and confronted him and the woman separately. He said it was only over a couple of months and of course told Sandra it meant nothing. She eventually forgave him, although never completely forgot what he'd done. That was not in her nature, not part of her character, or even her training, at all.

Now this text message revealed that he'd not only been having an affair, but one with her supposedly best friend. No wonder he wasn't very happy when she'd told him she was going on holiday with Aileen. They'd had a huge row. That must have made him very uneasy, although he basically just argued, falsely in effect on his part, that he was hoping he and Sandra could get away on holiday somewhere.

Fortunately Aileen continued swimming for a further twenty minutes or so, giving Sandra some time to calm down, try and gather her thoughts, and decide what to do; decide what her reaction should be, if any, at that point. She took some deep breaths, replaced Aileen's phone on the small plastic table, and went back to reading her paperback, deciding to bide her time before saying anything to her holiday companion.

"That's lovely in there. The water's completely clear and not even cold. Quite warm, in fact. You not going in?" Aileen asked as she slumped down on the sunbed.

"Soon, in a while, nearly finished this chapter," Sandra said.

"It certainly is a beautiful place, great beach and swimming, and the village is lovely. Very unspoilt it seems, despite all the tourists. That friend of yours who recommended it knows what she's talking about," Aileen added.

Inside Sandra was still fuming, so could only bring herself to reply curtly while continuing to peer into her paperback, "What?"

"Your friend, the one who recommended Lindos."

"Oh yes, of course, yes, Gill's been here loads of times apparently. More summer's than she can remember. Think she said she worked here for a couple of complete summers years ago, in one of the bars I think."

As Sandra finished speaking, while appearing to continue peering at her paperback out of the corner of her eye she watched Aileen reach over to the table and pick up her phone. She tried as discreetly as possible to watch the expression on Aileen's face as she saw and examined the text from Sandra's husband. Eventually, as Aileen quickly placed the phone in her bag Sandra couldn't resist asking, "Something wrong? Bad news from home?"

Aileen tried to appear relaxed as she laid back on her sunbed and replied as casually as she could manage, "No, no, just one of those junk scam texts you get from time to time. You know, usually telling you that there is a large sum of money in some Nigerian bank waiting for you. Why do you ask?"

22

Trying to look as equally relaxed and somewhat disinterested as she continued to stare at the pages of her book, Sandra told her nonchalantly, "No reason, just thought you looked a bit concerned. Anyway, I thought that's what the look on your face suggested."

"No, not at all. I'm fine. How could anyone be anything but fine here in this beautiful place? Don't you think?" Aileen thought it best to try and get their conversation back to the lovely relaxing hot surroundings.

But Sandra still needed some space and time to try and deal with what she had just discovered. She decided that the best way to do that for a bit was to go for a swim herself.

"Right, let's see if you're right about that water," she said. She put her book down on the table, stood up, slipped on her flip flops and headed down the beach towards the sea, hoping that a swim in the clear, calm water would have a similar effect on her and help her decide just what to do next about what she had just seen on Aileen's phone.

Sandra was not one to make instant decisions or exhibit immediate reactions. She was more disposed to cold, calculating, often ruthless, responses, whether in her professional work life or her private one. The people who worked with her and for her in her agency had experienced that side of her a number of times. Probably that was why she was so successful at what she did professionally. It was the same in her private life on the few occasions when difficult issues and problems had arisen. When she initially discovered her husband Richard's affair with the young secretary five years into their marriage she didn't immediately confront him. Instead she bided her time, found out as much as she could about the woman over the next two weeks through her 'secret other life' sources, and then deliberately confronted her at her work place, much to the woman's embarrassment. She calculated, and slowly and calmly decided, that she didn't just want to cause problems to the woman in her personal and private life, but also to cause problems and destroy as much of her employment and work life as possible. She wanted cold, calculated, nasty revenge. That was the sort of woman Sandra Weston was now; she'd been well trained to be that way. Richard no longer worked at the same place as the woman when she discovered the affair, but once Sandra had finished with her, exposed her affair with Richard in front of her work colleagues, nor did the woman. Sandra heard that she left that job soon after. Once she had engineered that Sandra eventually confronted Richard.

Now, as she felt the relatively warm, but cooling sea in Lindos Bay engulfing her hot body she turned over to float on her back and look up at the radiant, cloudless blue sky, thinking through calmly just what to do next about what she had just discovered about her husband and her best friend.

3

Martin Cleverley: insecurities and labyrinths

"Sure, tonight at 9 at that bar's good. Text me where it is. xx"

Martin allowed a slight, pleasurable smile to creep across his lips as he read the text from Aileen just as the Slovak waitress brought him another small beer. He quickly replied with the location of the Courtyard Bar.

Giorgos Café Bar was entering its quieter early to mid-afternoon phase in terms of customers and clientele. The lunchtime rush from the tourists coming to Lindos on the excursion boats from Rhodes Town was subsiding as they made their way under the hot afternoon sun back to the boats at the jetty in Lindos Bay, ready for the return sea journey having explored the souvenir shops and alleyways of the beautiful white walled village.

As he had done countless times before on his many visits to Lindos, Martin was sat outside the popular café bar at one of the small round tables. The bar was not only popular with the daytime tourists from Rhodes Town. It was also a regular late breakfast place for many of the young, predominantly British, bar and restaurant summer season workers following their many late night and early morning drinking and clubbing sessions. In addition, it had a regular older clientele of couples and families who frequented the bar in the evenings, sampling the range of excellent cocktails. Many of those returned year after year, sometimes two or three times a year. On that particular afternoon there was still a smattering of cosmopolitan customers – French, Italians and Germans, as far as he could make out from their conversations. There were also some Brits, although by the evening the customers would be almost exclusively Brits.

Despite his relatively successful professional life as a Professor, Martin Cleverley was a man prone to insecurities and doubts where women and relationships with them were concerned. In his profession in the lecture theatre, as well as in his writing, things came relatively easy to him, unlike his relationships with women. It wasn't that he was an unattractive man. He was tall, six foot one, with short light brown hair, and his angular face with its wide cheekbones was clean shaven, producing a pronounced jawline. He'd managed to avoid developing any obvious unattractive bulges around his waist as he turned forty, despite his fondness for the occasional beer, sometimes more. Despite a few women actually commenting to him when he was younger, and more recently, that he was an attractive guy, he could never seem to fully believe them and shake off his insecurities and hesitancy around women.

What he was engaged in now, sat outside Giorgos, was just another example of that insecurity. Staring at his phone, he was going over and over what Aileen had written in her text agreeing to meet that evening. It was as if he was some type of codebreaker at Bletchley during the Second World War. He forensically examined every word over and over, trying to convince himself it was definitely a positive sign, especially the two kisses at the end. Finally he reached for his second small beer, took a sip, and muttered to himself that he was, indeed, being bloody stupid.

Maybe he'd just spent far too much time embroiled in his academic work, trying to interpret and read between the lines of those Greek mythological texts to which he'd been exposed. As he sat there in the Lindos sunshine with his beer he simply couldn't stop himself wondering just what was that something that sparked between two people, particularly middle-aged ones, and in his case a man and a woman, which drew them together in a moment of uncanny recognition? That after all, and what usually followed as their relationship developed, was certainly a Greek labyrinth to be unlocked – the code of attraction, and ultimately love, were necessary if the clear correct path out of the labyrinth was to be discovered.

It was Daedalus, an inventor, architect and sculptor in Greek mythology, who built the original labyrinth for King Minos of Crete. From his studies, Martin knew that it was believed to be a diagram of the brain and a symbol of the imagination in Greek mythology. It represented the manner in which humans make associations, one thought following another in a long sequence, from the edge to the centre to the end.

The relationship labyrinth was something most people could not avoid entering at some point in their life. Once inside they could find that they may at times have no real idea where they were in terms of their feelings or those of the other person. They could feel lost, with no clear sense of direction regarding the relationship. Stuck in the labyrinthine maze of minute disparate, often contradictory, events and feelings they would increasingly never be able to see the whole design of the labyrinth; the bigger whole picture, the benefits, and the connections to the heart or centre of the relationship.

The King of Crete, Minos, ordered Daedalus to build a labyrinth to house the then half-bull, half-man Minotaur. The Athenians were then forced to pay the Cretans a regular tribute of seven boys and seven girls, who would be left in the labyrinth to be consumed by the monster. One year, Theseus, the son of the King of Athens, was sent to Crete as part of the tribute. Theseus and Ariadne, the daughter of King Minos, fell in love. With her help he killed the Minotaur, found his way out of the labyrinth, and they escaped over the sea.

So, in Greek mythology there was terror within the labyrinth, but ultimately there was also love. Perhaps, not involving actual terrors, but from his past relationship experiences the labyrinth of Greek mythology was a pretty good analogy. The centre and heart of relationships may not always be where you think it is or where you want it to be. Mostly people in relationships desire a clear pattern, shape and design to them – an understandable clarity and meaning. He knew he did.

Maybe it was the relaxing surroundings of Giorgos, together with the warm sun and the wonderful atmosphere of Lindos - that he always loved and instantly embraced as soon as he arrived - which had provoked his mind and thoughts to drift, and all over one small text message. That thought prompted a small chuckle before he reached to take another sip of his Mythos beer, deciding his time would be better employed just watching the 'Lindos world' go past with its myriad of cosmopolitan characters.

Part Two: The affair

4

London, 20th December, 2015

It started innocently enough. At least that's what she wanted him to think. Of course they knew each other through her best friend, his wife Sandra. Even so, they had met only a relatively few times, spasmodically, and always the three of them, her, him and Sandra. She met up with his wife more regularly, but always without him. Although they worked for the same company – an advertising agency - it was in different offices in different parts of London. So, workwise their paths never crossed, except that one fateful time at the lavish company Christmas party in a central London hotel four months after Aileen had started working for the company. He was the Senior Global Digital Project Executive, what Sandra always described as an ambitious high-flyer. Aileen's position was what she always described as a "simple P.A. to the company's International Legal Director."

The company was one of the leading and largest advertising agencies in Britain, possibly Europe. The party was just for the staff of their London offices, although that meant there were still over two hundred people present in the large, opulent ballroom.

Aileen was standing at the bar waiting for the barman to deliver her fourth gin and tonic of the evening. Although it was only just gone nine o'clock she'd convinced herself that as it was practically Christmas – another prospective Christmas she would spend alone – she should begin her festive celebrations in earnest that evening.

As the barman placed her drink on the coaster on the bar she heard a voice from behind her.

"That's a lovely red dress. You look stunning."

She recognised Richard's voice, but was a little surprised by his compliment. As she turned around, before she could reply he added, "Maybe I'll get another one of those and join you. I could do with a good drink after the week I've had."

"Thanks, about the compliment I mean. Bad week in the executive heights of the top towers then?" she asked.

"Yep, certainly was, and not exactly great at home either."

She tried to at least appear a little uneasy if he was about to cry on one of her very bare, fully exposed shoulders - fully exposed by her strapless "lovely red dress" - about her best friend, Sandra, and their marriage relationship.

So, she plumped for a very non-committal, "Oh well, we all have difficult weeks, especially at this time of year. I'm sure a few of these will help." As she told him that she held up her gin and tonic slightly towards him.

"Yes, a good few, I'm thinking," he replied, as he attracted the attention of the barman and somewhat abruptly ordered, "A large gin and tonic," without bothering with the curtesy of adding, "please."

He turned back to face her while waiting for his drink.

"Drinking alone, that's not a good sign. Where are all your new work colleagues? I know you've only been here, what is it, four months or so? Sandra told me when you started working for the company, but I'd have thought you would have made plenty of friends here by now, work mates. The few times I've met you with Sandra you always seem the friendly type, and I'm sure there must be plenty of guys in your department of the company who've noticed you."

She slowly took a couple of sips of her drink and glanced sideways at him a couple of times while he told her that, but remained silent, anticipating precisely where he was heading with all these compliments. He had no idea, but that was exactly the direction she was aiming for.

He ploughed on, clearly on a mission.

"Well, if they hadn't noticed you before, I'm sure they have tonight. As I said before, you look stunning."

Again, she merely fleetingly glanced sideways at him, but never responded. Indeed, she did feel "stunning" and was very aware of that. It was precisely the effect she was aiming for, on him anyway. The long satin strapless red dress hugged her still fine figure in all the right places, assisted perfectly by the broad matching fabric black sash type belt tight around her waist accentuating it impeccably. Her longer than usual dark black hair laid down to her bare shoulders either side of her head, framing her face beautifully, as well as halfway down her back. Heels of a certain height definitely always made her feel good, and not a little imposing. The ones that she wore tonight with their five inch heels, and new and red to match the dress, certainly achieved that. In fact, although he was two or three inches over six feet tall, in her self-satisfying heels she wasn't far short of his height at all.

He wasn't giving up. If anything, her silence was only intriguing and attracting him more.

"You can reply, speak to me, you know. Or is there some unwritten law between women friends that says you can't even engage in a pleasant conversation with your friend's husband?"

This time she took another sip of her gin and tonic and then turned to face him with a smile as she placed the glass back on the bar.

He took the smile as some encouragement, gave her a small smile in return and told her, "And if you were really daring and wanted to break that unwritten law you could even return the compliment, compliment me on what I'm wearing. At least then it wouldn't seem that my compliments to you were chauvinistic or patronising, or whatever, would it? It's new, a new suit. Nice dark blue don't you think? I thought, well it's a social evening, no need to dress up like a bank manager, or even an Executive, so no need for a tie, just a plain open neck pale blue shirt. I'm sure you've seen there are plenty of prats here dressed up in suits and ties like bank managers, don't you think?"

From his ramblings, and his animated hand and arm movements, she guessed that he'd already had quite a few drinks before the one he now reached to pick up and finish as he turned back to face towards the bar, rather than her.

She finished hers and then turned once again to look at him while he continued to peer towards the mirrored back wall of the bar.

"Yes, very nice, suits you, and a good fit, and yes, not good to look like a bank manager at these sort of things." She finished with a broader smile than previously.

It was, indeed, a good fit, and the dark blue colour highlighted his quite slim figure, although at thirty-nine his midriff was just beginning to spread a little. His clean shaven face and relatively good looks, together with his swept back, medium length brown hair masked his approaching middle-age, helping preserve at least some of his youthful good looks.

At times Richard Weston could be a quite unpleasant man; a bully, particularly towards other men he believed he was in competition with, especially where women were involved. It was a trait that for some peculiar, unfathomable reason, made him quite attractive to certain types of women.

He turned his head slightly to return her smile and told her, "Thanks. See, that wasn't difficult at all, was it?"

Before she could respond he summoned the barman and ordered another large gin and tonic, this time for them both.

While they waited for the drinks to arrive she asked, "So, tell me, just what does an Executive do in this large company? What is it, your official title? Digital Project Executive, or something, isn't it. I'm sure that's what Sandra told me it was."

"Senior Global Digital Project Executive, if you don't mind," he corrected her followed by an obviously not serious grin. "But let's not talk bloody work, and I promise I won't ask about yours. To be honest, I'm not really bloody interested at all."

The drinks arrived and he immediately took quite a large gulp. Despite his earlier compliments he certainly wasn't being the most tactful or polite of men. More than that, on this particular evening he appeared to clearly be an angry, unhappy man. She didn't recall being aware of his lack of politeness or tact on the few previous occasions their paths had crossed when she was in the company of both him and Sandra as a couple. But she decided not to rise to his obvious blunt rudeness, and instead just took a sip of her new drink –

her sixth of the evening. She too was becoming a little pissed, but so what, it was Christmas she convinced herself.

He wasn't interested in silence though. He wanted to talk. The drink in him was making him interested in anything but silence.

"So, what happened with your marriage then? Sandra told me some of it, something about a young Czech girl. Must have been a bit sickening for you, although to be absolutely honest I always thought he was a bit of a prat, your ex. Only met him a couple of times, of course, but that's what he seemed like to me, a prat. Anyway, as I said before, you can't be short of admirers, plenty of fish in the sea, as they say. You must be beating them off surely?"

"After we separated I eventually found out he'd been having an affair with a Czech girl for a year, an au pair in London, twenty two, so bloody stereotypical."

Now it was her turn to show some anger, something she thought she had completely disposed of, but in reality her nerves were still raw over what happened; being lied to for so long.

He just grimaced a little, but decided against commenting, not least because what was actually running through his brain was 'lucky bastard!'

"But no, I'm not 'beating them off' hardly," she continued. "Bit too bruised and battered emotionally for that at the moment, thanks. Definitely not sure about fish in the sea though, far too many sharks for my liking."

That brought a slight chuckle from him, followed quickly by, "Well, you have to get back in that sea at some point, and start swimming again. Maybe you need a harpoon for the sharks."

Now it was her turn to let out a small chuckle. She turned to face him as he leaned against the bar alongside her, deliberately contriving to let a small smile spread slowly across her face. She was feeling a lot more relaxed, more confident. To some extent her smile was a response to his 'harpoon' comments, but it was also because she now felt really good about herself; partly on the outside because of the way she looked on that particular evening - the effect of her long dress and new shoes – but also confident on the inside as it was all going so well. It was going exactly the way she'd planned it. His "stunning" comment and compliments confirmed that to her.

In fact, she now felt so relaxed and confident that she determined that it was the right time to go somewhere in their conversation that she had purposefully ignored earlier as she calculated it was too soon in their exchanges. Now though, she knew it was a good time to respond to his, "not exactly great at home," comment.

"Problems? Problems between you and Sandra? You said earlier that things were not exactly great at home this week," she asked, fixing a deliberate wide-eyed intoxicating stare on his face as she did so.

He looked more than a little stunned. He thought from earlier that she wasn't interested in getting into any conversation regarding her best friend, and her marriage."

"Oh, yeah, I did, didn't I," he agreed.

He reached to pick up his drink and take another swig, while she stayed staring at him in silence, facing him by the side of the bar, now no more than a foot away.

For a moment she thought that was all he was going to say; that the chance had passed and she'd miscalculated and missed the opportunity. But as he placed his drink back down on the bar he added, "And not just this week. For a while, actually."

She calculated that she had to prompt him a little more, not let him stop there. That wasn't what was supposed to happen. She tried the blunt direct approach, showing no mercy.

"I suppose it must have been difficult for Sandra after what happened before, what you did before, but I thought the two of you had put all that in the past, got over it. It always seemed to me that Sandra had. We talked about it a couple of times, of course, but to me, she seemed to have put it all behind her."

He rubbed the back of his neck with the palm of his right hand in obvious discomfort at being reminded what he did, of the affair he had before.

"I thought she had," he started to say. "No, that's not right, I think she has. I do really think she has, but lately something isn't right. I don't know what, but there's something. We argue a lot, and sometimes over the smallest of stupid things, and-"

"Richard, you hogging and monopolising all the good looking beautiful company women here tonight, as usual?"

33

A man who was wearing a tie and did indeed look like a bank manager, who looked in his early fifties with slightly greying hair, suddenly appeared on Richard's shoulder and interrupted just as her conversation with him was seemingly about to become deep and serious, and go in the direction that she was aiming for. Richard though was definitely not interested in engaging in a conversation with him. He was far too interested in, and was concentrated on, Aileen. She was also not interested at all in engaging this guy in any conversation. She had her own specific reason for that.

"What? Oh yes, err … I mean no, not really, Tony. This is a friend of my wife Sandra. She's a P.A. in the International Legal Department. This is Tony, a colleague in our department."

The man said, "Hello," but the body language of Richard and Aileen displayed no inclination on their part to turn around completely from the bar to face him, and neither of them attempted to engage him in conversation. Clearly Richard had no intention whatsoever in engaging him in a conversation between the three of them as he had pointedly not even introduced Aileen to him by name. For reasons only known to her, that was something which she was initially concerned about, but ultimately relieved over.

After an awkward few seconds the guy got the message and simply said, "Ok, well, I'll leave you to it, Richard." Then he turned to Aileen and told her, "Nice to meet you, must get off and circulate," and walked off.

No sooner had he left them at the bar than Aileen said, "That felt awkward. Don't you like him? Although, to be honest he didn't seem the sort of guy that'd I'd have much to say to either. Difficult I suppose, these Christmas do's, and having to make pleasant conversation with people you work with, but some you definitely wouldn't normally want to socialise with. Can't avoid them staying in here I suppose, instead of going somewhere else for a drink."

She was dropping a big, not very subtle, hint, and he took it as he asked, "Look, shall we get out of here? To be honest, I agree with you completely, although I work with a lot of these people they are not exactly the sort of people I want to socialise with much at all. There's a more private and comfortable bar just off the hotel lobby. What do you say?"

Once again for reasons only known to her, she was very pleased and somewhat relieved that he took the hint, but she merely told him in a quite matter of fact way, "Sure, let's go."

The hotel had a few bars, three in all. The main one was quite large and busy, but the one he suggested was much smaller and almost empty, with comfortable leather backed armchairs and even an open fire. They found a couple of chairs near the fire with a small dark wood coffee table between them. Within a few seconds of them sitting down the barman appeared by where they sat to take their order. He wasn't exactly busy as there were only two other people in the bar, so he was probably glad of the custom.

"Another gin and tonic?" Richard asked her.

"Yes, thanks, but no more doubles please." She had begun to lose count of the number of drinks she'd had, but decided on one more, a single, adding, "With plenty of tonic and ice please."

He ordered the same.

"So, you and Sandra, it's not good at the moment then?"

She was determined to pick up the conversation from the point at which they had been interrupted.

"No, not really, we're arguing a lot. She seems really unhappy, and I get angry, but she always knew that was what I was like. I even thought at one point a few weeks back that maybe she was now having an affair. Revenge perhaps?"

"Surely not. I'm sure she's not, Richard. I've known her a long time and I've never thought of her as someone who would do that. After all, what happened, what you did, was years ago now. I'm sure she's completely forgiven you. Why would she try and take some revenge now, after all this time, by having an affair herself?

Not exactly overrun with customers at that point the barman returned with their drinks. Richard reached in and pulled a small cardboard folder from his inside jacket pocket and handed it to the barman, telling him, "Charge it to my room, 415."

It contained the plastic electronic room key. The barman nodded, saying, "Certainly, sir, I'll be back in a moment for you to sign for it."

Aileen tried to look a little surprised as she asked, "You're staying here tonight, but you don't live that far away. What, a mile or so? I thought you'd just be taking a taxi?"

"No, thought it'd be easier to stay here, and thought that as I might end up getting pissed anyway that'd be better. Easier to stumble up in the lift rather than roll about in a taxi, even assuming I could get one at this time of year in the centre of London that would just take a short fare of a mile or so. Nice room, nice hotel, I've stayed here a few times before. Told Sandra I'd stay over. She didn't seem that bothered one way or the other actually. It's been a lot like that lately between us, as I said before. And anyway, I get breakfast in bed here, ordered it."

He smiled again as he finished speaking and reached for his drink.

"Oh, I see, just thought … anyway, you and Sandra?" she asked again, determined once more to get him back on the subject.

5

Room 415

Half-an-hour later the two of them were eagerly entering into the hotel lift. The doors had barely closed after he pressed the fourth floor button when he pinned her against the back wall of the lift and planted a long, passionate kiss full on her inviting red lips. As he finished kissing her and went to pull away she grabbed the lapels of his jacket with both hands and pulled him back into her for another lingering kiss.

This time as they separated she told him, "You do realise these things have CCTV cameras?"

"Good, so what? It'll give some poor bored sod in hotel security who has to sit and watch them all night a cheap thrill for a change. I'm sure they will have seen worse, or maybe better if you're a bored all night viewer."

He smiled as he told her that and the doors of the lift opened for the fourth floor. He grabbed her hand and led her down the corridor thirty yards to the door of his room, 415. Not that she noticed once inside as she firmly pushed him down onto the large King-size bed after yanking off his Jacket and shirt, but it was a very large, beautifully furnished room, what the hotel described as an 'Executive Room'. Not only was there the King-size bed, but also a sofa, an armchair, and a desk.

She wasn't interested in, or about to sample, any of that though. All she was interested in sampling was the bed. As she'd pulled off his jacket and shirt he'd kicked off his shoes. Now she was standing at the end of the bed above him reaching up her back to pull down the zip at the back of her long red dress. She slowly seductively allowed it to fall to the floor, exposing her sheer dark hold up stockings, skimpy red lace panties, and five inch red high heeled shoes. Above all that sat her firm, round, well-proportioned exposed breasts and excited nipples.

In the past, in her younger life before she married, the rigmarole of undressing for sex with a new lover could feel like a foolish awkward masquerade. But now she was older, wiser, and indeed much more experienced. This time it didn't feel at all awkward. This was no longer the young girl taking nervous pleasure at being stared at by a man as she undressed awkwardly. It was as though she was well practiced in the art, the performance. She wasn't, of course, but there was no nervousness at all on her part. In fact, she surprised herself at how relaxed she was, how at ease with what was happening, what was obviously about to happen. She was actually enjoying her tantalising seductive undressing performance. It was making her excited. Just a few minutes previously in the lift it had fleetingly crossed her mind there might be just that, nervousness and awkwardness. After all, this wasn't simply undressing for sex with a new lover. This was undressing for sex with her best friend's husband, and for a reason. How could that all be so easy? But it was, and she liked it, loved it even.

Yes, what was happening between her and him was emotionally messy, dark perhaps, but the erotic, and erotic urges, is always connected to that, whether with your own faithful partner, or between two individuals being unfaithful to their partners. Over and over eroticism can be the unstoppable force that plunges individuals headlong rapidly into the chaos of their strongest feelings, while simultaneously revealing a heightened sense of their own self, of their own individual identity. Maybe it was the alcohol, the gin, maybe it was the glamorous clothes, the underwear and the shoes, maybe it was her finally shaking off the anger over her ex-husband and the young Czech girl, the deceit, the lies, or maybe it was all of that and her at last feeling good about herself from his obvious attention. Or maybe it was simply, mostly, because she knew what she had to do, planned to do, and was doing it perfectly.

Whatever it was, all that combined had produced a sense of her own self, a belief again in herself. Right now, that evening, right at that moment in his hotel room, standing almost naked before him, she felt alive again. She was a beautiful woman, full of confidence, and bloody good at what she did. She had her identity again, a physical freedom from her re-found self-confidence, and this time she was sure she had a determination of her own. Whatever it was that her new determination and freedom was based on that night, at that particular moment, she told herself sod it; she'd planned it to be like this. Now she was going to get what she wanted when she wanted, and she wanted it now, all of it.

So, while he fixed a stare of pleasure on the delightful inviting image before him she slowly and deliberately leaned down to unfasten his trousers, pulled down the zip, and then pulled them off him.

Seconds later they were both completely naked rolling around on the large bed exploring each other's bodies. She wasn't thinking at all now. She was just acting on impulse. She was just focused on her anticipated pleasure with Sandra's husband, and she was determined that she would have it now, have him now.

She tried to roll on top of him, but he was equally as determined to be on top and he wasn't giving way to her. For a few seconds, maybe half a minute, they tussled on the wide bed, locked together in a grip like two Greco-Roman wrestlers, neither giving way, yet still managing to exchange passionate kisses and touches.

Finally, his greater strength told, and he managed to firmly sit astride her, lean forward towards her face that was now exhibiting a confused look, and pin her down, holding her wrists back towards the side of her head, with her arms bent at the elbows. She tried to wriggle free from the clamp of his hands on her wrists, but his force and the weight of him on her lower body prevented her from moving.

She started to say, "What-"

But he instantly moved both of her wrists held in his gripped hands up to above her head on the bed and then transferred both wrists to the tight, strong grip of his right hand, placing his left hand over her gaping mouth.

"Wait, just wait," he instructed her. "You'll see."

She felt very uncomfortable about what was now happening, uncomfortable and disconcerted over what had happened over the last few minutes. This was a man with what appeared to be some serious inner demons, uncontrollable perhaps? For those brief moments, totally unsure of what he might do next, she wanted him to stop.

"No, you wait, I don't want to see, not like this," she shouted at him as he removed his hand from over her mouth.

But he wasn't waiting. No sooner had she finished shouting that at him than she took a sharp intake of breath and let out a short gasp as he entered her. A low, deep moan of pleasure followed immediately from her gaping mouth. Now slowly, but surely, she realised that much to her surprise there was a feeling growing inside her of enjoyment and she was getting wet, very wet between her legs. Strangely, and disconcertingly, she was actually beginning to enjoy it. She preferred to be on top, always to be in control, but now she was experiencing something different, and was liking it more and more. So much so that when he released her wrists from the grip of his right hand above her head on the bed she immediately firmly instructed him, "Don't, don't let go, stay there. Wait for me, just wait …"

He returned his grip on her two wrists as his penetration started to get deeper and faster. The only part of her upper body she could move, her hips, began rhythmically thrusting upwards beneath him, similarly getting faster, less intermittent, more constant, and taking him deeper into her.

Her moans were getting louder and longer, interspersed with pleas of, "Wait, wait for me … but don't stop … faster, harder, deeper …"

He loomed above her writhing lower body, only intermittently lowering himself down to pleasure her now erect and firm nipples with his darting wet tongue. That succeeded in eliciting even longer moans of joy and satisfaction from her increasingly gaping and gasping wide full red lips.

Finally, she gazed up at him above her, displaying a pleading fixed stare as her penetrating brown eyes started to glaze over from a deep feeling of gratification rising up from between her firm thighs, and then racing through her whole body as she let out a piercing scream of, "Now! Now!"

He inhaled deeply as she contorted in seemingly endless waves of pleasure beneath him, her firm breasts rising and falling with every

40

convulsion from what was happening between her legs as that special part of her body gripped his manhood firmly, and she yelled, "Yes, yes!"

Almost simultaneously he exploded inside her, grinning into her face below him as he did so. His eyes were wide open with satisfaction and that indescribable feeling. Now it was his turn to make sounds, sounds of contentment. "Hmmm … hmmm."

Within seconds of being satisfied he quickly pulled out of her, without displaying any tenderness or delicacy whatsoever.

They both lay there on the still undisturbed, almost made bed, staring up at the ceiling for a couple of minutes in silence. She felt relaxed, peculiarly contented. It had been a while since she had felt like that, not since her separation and divorce. Yet this wasn't relaxed, tender sex. It was hard, rough, on the edge sex. No caressing, no stroking by either of them, most of all him, just his tongue occasionally flicking on and around her nipples making them hard and firm, and increasingly sensitive. Even so, much to her amazement, shock perhaps, ultimately she liked it, loved it. Not initially, but gradually she grew to enjoy it. Despite the sexual pleasure and gratification - good though that was and how it made her feel – as she lay their alongside him she knew that a large part of her enjoyment over what had just happened was because that was precisely what she wanted to happen, had set out to do that evening from the very start. It was exactly what she had planned and it had gone perfectly.

Now she was already thinking of the next stage as the words came out of her mouth, "Well, we can't stop there. We definitely have to do that again sometime, don't you think?"

He turned towards her saying, in an almost matter of fact way, although by no means displeased, "Yeah, sure, of course we should."

6

Again and again, including Vienna

So they did do it again – and again and again – regularly at least twice a week for over three months, sometimes at the same hotel and occasionally eventually at her flat in Cheam. A couple of times they even went out to dinner together in Cheam, to a little Italian restaurant in the village.

One time, after just over a month, as they had just finished their by now regular sexual encounter in the London hotel room and were both dressing, she started to make a big thing about it all beginning to feel a little sordid and dirty, sneaking around in the hotel cheating on her best friend. She deliberately made it appear a bit of a guilt ridden emotional outburst, but it wasn't that at all. It was a calculated move and she knew precisely what she was doing. It had exactly the effect on him that she desired.

He was clearly uneasy over it, not least because he was beginning to wonder if she was starting to take what was happening between them much more seriously than he did. That worried him. It wasn't at all what he wanted. Not at all, for him it was just fun. When she made her "sordid and dirty" comment his response was cold, detached, and very non-committal. He gave no impression whatsoever that he understood her concerns or shared them particularly. That was by no means out of character for him. That was him – cold, selfish, ruthless, both in his personal and professional lives, and at times totally arrogant. She was well aware of all that about him and his character, and that she could play on it for her own ends, which is just what she did.

His uneasy feeling over what she said wasn't eased at all by her reaction to his response, or rather, his lack of response. She got upset, or at least that's what she wanted him to think as she told him convincingly, "We sneak around this place, even arrive and leave the hotel separately. You never even stay the night, and I'm left here alone. Even dinner is room service. We don't go to the hotel restaurant because you're so frightened someone you know from the company might see us. It feels sordid." She even allowed her voice to break up a little in places for effect as she spoke.

Now she was purposefully trying to expose any guilt he might have. He stuck to character though and wasn't responding positively at all, very much the opposite in fact. His response was very 'matter of fact', giving the impression that he didn't really care how she felt, or what she felt. It was of no consequence to him whatsoever.

"That's because it is sordid," he started to explain as rising anger was portrayed in his voice. "Stop beating yourself up over it. It couldn't be anything else. That's the way it is. You love the sex, you know you do. I know you do, that's obvious. I love the sex. That should be obvious too, I would've thought. If you want someone to go out to dinner with maybe you should call an Escort service."

It was just the response she hoped for, wanted to provoke from him. Not that he had any clue, but she was toying with him, actually playing with and provoking his anger. She was like a kitten playing with a ball of wool, and he was at the end of that particular loose strand.

"Fuck you!" she exploded in feigned anger. "Is that what you really think? If it is. Really? Then maybe we should stop, stop this now."

But that outburst from her wasn't enough to penetrate his cold response and persona in quite the way she hoped.

"If that's what you want," was all he told her, again in a very 'matter of fact' non-committal way.

She tried to look shocked over his casual 'take it or leave it' response. She wasn't at all however, as she knew that was the way he was. She'd been told to expect it and accommodate it within what she had to do. That was precisely his character and attitude to relationships. They were all about what he wanted, when he wanted it. What satisfied him was all that mattered. Ultimately, however, he did actually quite like and enjoy what he had with her, but certainly didn't want to take it to another level, take it any further. Sex with her was fine, more than fine actually, bloody good. So, he didn't really want to give that up. Equally though he didn't want to get to a stage with her where she started looking for more, wanted more than just the sex. What they had was a hermetically sealed type of affair, carefully and completely sealed off and detached from any intrusion from the outside world and the reality of other relationships, particularly his marriage. That was the way he preferred it, wanted it, demanded it to be. So, that was always the manner in which he controlled it. This outburst from her challenged that it seemed to him. But, unbeknown to him, that was just what she wanted him to think.

When it came to relationships Richard Weston was a calculating manipulator, used to getting exactly what he wanted for as long as he wanted it. He had a particular attitude, outlook and approach to relationships between men and women. He had always been clear about that in his mind, even with his wife Sandra throughout their marriage, as well as even before they were married. He had to be in complete control. Relationships were not about equal partnerships in his world. Even when they at times appeared to be equal to the particular woman he was involved with, it was actually him who was in control, subtly manipulating situations and their relationship in ways that he desired. He was good at that especially, in total control, but appearing not to be to the woman. That was the way he liked it. It was actually the only way he'd ever known, ever experienced. It was a confidence thing, and he had plenty of that. It spewed out of him, often in a very intimidating fashion. He never particularly bothered finding out about them, the women, their background, what made them tick. He just wasn't that interested. It was his safety belt; a process and approach he applied almost automatically to prevent himself from becoming too interested in them, too interested in and entwined in their lives. That was never on his agenda, not part of his life or ever likely to be.

That was what he did when Aileen had her "sordid and dirty" outburst. He knew exactly what he was doing with his initial cold, casual, 'take it or leave it' response. As he also did with his calculated wait through a couple of minutes silence between them as

44

she stared aimlessly out of the hotel room window. He thought he knew precisely what she was doing; tussling in her mind with the obvious torment of not wanting to give up what they had, the very good sex, but feeling increasingly unable to cope with the betrayal of her best friend, his wife Sandra. He was wrong of course; it wasn't that at all that was going through her calculating mind.

He'd anticipated that what he now believed was a moment of torment would eventually arrive for her. He had no such qualms, of course. He wasn't that sort of person. Unlike her, he was more selfish. Ethics and morals were not in his vocabulary when it came to what he determined to be his best interests.

He reckoned that she wasn't like that at all; despite what she'd been doing with him that deep down he knew would destroy his wife, her best friend. She wasn't the first, though. So, he rationalised it on the basis that she was well aware that he'd done it before a few years ago, with a young secretary at his previous job. Aileen had said to him that night they met at the company Christmas party that Sandra had told her all about it. So, he'd convinced himself that she'd entered into this affair with him with her eyes wide-open to what he was really like.

What he wasn't aware of, however, was that Aileen was convinced that Sandra wasn't always the most faithful of wives anyway. She'd seen her flirting with guys, especially young guys, whenever the two women had been in some bar or other together in central London on a night out.

In fact, Sandra had only been able to tell her about that one time he'd been unfaithful in their marriage because that was the only time that she found out about, knew about. There had been more, quite a few more. The pattern was always the same. After a couple of months he tired of them and manipulated them one way or another into ending it.

At the end of his deliberate couple of minutes silent wait while Aileen tussled with her desires, her pleasure, and her guilty conscience, he believed he had manipulated her nicely into agreeing just what he wanted, which was to continue his pleasure, but on his terms. That was what she wanted him to think, though. He thought he knew precisely what he was doing when he offered her a lifeline, a small concession, deliberately designed to suggest he didn't want to stop their affair, not then at least. It enabled him to believe he was still in charge, as did her response, just as she wanted. The truth was though that he was enjoying himself too much to stop it there and then, although he always believed he would eventually want to. But it would be when he wanted, with as little collateral damage as possible, that's what he believed.

She was still staring out of the window as he told her, "Ok, what if I come to Cheam next week," calculatingly breaking the silence at precisely the point he thought would get the reaction he wanted from her.

"Really? You will?" She turned to face him as he stood at the foot of the hotel bed.

"Sure, no problem. I'll tell Sandra I've got a company dinner entertaining prospective clients, and I'm sure there must be at least a half decent Italian somewhere in Cheam?"

He presumed that did the trick, as he calculated and knew it would. She let him believe her mood changed immediately as she walked straight across to him to kiss him passionately, adding as she finished, "Of course there is, and it's very nice actually."

So, that's what they did. A week later he told Sandra he had a company dinner with clients in central London, but went to Cheam. He was a little disconcerted when Sandra asked if he would be staying over after the dinner.

"What? Err …-"

"Staying over, staying over in a hotel?" she explained. "I know you. You usually easily have too much to drink, so I just thought you may be staying over in a hotel."

"No, no, I won't be drinking that much. They are Japanese, the prospective clients, not big drinkers, and it's best if I keep my wits about me on this one."

For a moment he actually initially thought Sandra might have thrown the "staying over" question in because she was perhaps letting him know that she had an inkling about him having an affair, although not necessarily with Aileen of course. It threw him for a second or two. Then it did even very briefly cross his mind to take advantage of her assumption and tell her, yes, he would be staying

46

over in a hotel. However, he quickly decided that going to Cheam to go out to dinner with Aileen was one thing, and that was certainly enough to keep her happy for a while longer, but he didn't in the least want to stay over the night at her place. That would only give her more ideas, more expectations, he reckoned, and he didn't want to go down that road at present, or ever in fact.

He went to Cheam, and they had dinner in the 'nice' Italian restaurant. Then they went back to her flat in Cheam Village, where within minutes they couldn't keep their hands off each other and the obvious happened. She was much calmer now. He presumed that all her guilty conscience had been locked away for the moment. She was even okay when he told her just before midnight that he had to go. This time there was no anger from her.

He got back to St. John's Wood just after one and slipped quietly into bed alongside the already deeply sleeping Sandra. The next morning she asked him briefly how the dinner went and he told her, "Fine. It looks like we're going to get some good business from them, but you know the Japanese, the evening wasn't exactly a bundle of laughs, serious people when it comes to business." He was a good liar. He'd had a lot of practice where women were involved.

As far as he was concerned his pleasure and enjoyment with Aileen was back on track for a bit longer thanks to his little trip to Cheam, for as long as he wanted it to be anyway. He realised, however, that for as long as he wanted it to continue he would probably have to not only make another trip to the small Surrey village for dinner and extras with her, but offer her another little titbit to keep her happy. He was still telling himself, of course, that he could control their affair, was in total control of their affair.

He did have some feelings of unease on reflection though after he suggested a couple of weeks after his first Cheam visit that he and Aileen go away for a weekend somewhere. In fact, she'd carefully strategically planted the idea in his mind over that first dinner in the Italian in Cheam. She told him that she, "Realised it was difficult, but it was a pity he couldn't make a night of it and stay over at her place that night." She stared intensely across the restaurant table at him with her smouldering deep brown eyes as she reached over to take hold of his right hand and added, "But maybe we can get away

47

somewhere nice for a weekend soon. It'd be good to spend some more time together, rather than merely the odd evening here and there, at that bloody hotel or even at my place here."

It took a couple of weeks, but eventually he took the bait, just as she wanted and planned. Although he had no idea what she'd been up to when she planted the 'weekend away' idea in his mind, he was starting to wonder if, in fact, he was still in control or was he slowly losing it? Was he being pulled into some sort of relationship with her, maybe through enjoying her company and the rest, the extras, a little too much? He wasn't really quite sure now what was happening to him, or between them.

Nevertheless, at his suggestion they went to Vienna for a Friday to Monday weekend at the beginning of March. She seemed more than happy when he suggested it, and let him know very much so in amorous fashion. He told Sandra it was a weekend conference for work on digital advertising processes and techniques. It got a bit awkward for Aileen when Sandra told her that he was going to be away over that particular weekend in early March and that they should do something together – "Go to a health spa perhaps?" However, Aileen quickly 'thought on her feet' and told Sandra that she couldn't as that particular weekend she had promised to visit her cousin in Marlborough in Wiltshire for a family birthday celebration, so maybe they could reschedule for another weekend? Sandra appeared happy to agree to that.

Richard booked a smart, expensive hotel in central Vienna, near the imposing St. Stephen's Cathedral. The Ambassador Hotel on Kärntner Strasse in the historic old town was an impressive building in the Habsburg Empire style, although the interior had been modernised and furnished to an excellent very high standard. He'd booked a suite, which included a large King-size bed, of which they made full use. The hotel, surrounded by charming cobblestone streets and alleys, was perfectly situated amidst the Imperial Palaces of the Habsburgs and a number of gilded theatres where composers such as Mozart and Beethoven premiered their works. In fact, after strolling arm in arm through the picturesque streets admiring the buildings in the crisp early spring sunshine on the Saturday, interrupted only for stops for coffee and lunch in various attractive cafes, she insisted that on the Sunday afternoon they visit the Mozarthaus, Mozart's apartment on Domgasse, where he composed most of his music during his ten years in Vienna.

How they fitted it all in when they also spent some considerable time writhing together, enjoying each other, in the large hotel bed over their Vienna weekend was a bit of a mystery, or maybe a triumph, as far as she was concerned. Nevertheless, they covered most of the key sights, or at least the ones she wanted to see. He wasn't actually in control now at all when it came to that weekend and sightseeing. To his surprise, pleasant surprise, it increasingly didn't seem to bother him over that weekend. She seemed very happy though.

Late on Saturday afternoon in the Viennese twilight they rode the giant Prater Ferris wheel, with its distinctive gondola wooden cabins. In 1897 it had been one of the earliest Ferris wheels ever built. Again, she insisted they visit it because of it featuring in Carol Reed's 'The Third Man' movie based on Graham Greene's story. She told him she loved that movie. He was totally ambivalent to that, as well as the Mozart House visit, but went along with it, just to keep her happy.

He was much more disconcerted about being somewhat removed from his usual in control situation when she told him as they reached the highest point of their ride on the Prater Ferris Wheel that, "The view of the twilight over Vienna, the sparkling lights of the city stretching below, and the two of us together on this iconic landmark, is so, so romantic."

She followed that with one of her long lingering passionate kisses.

All that now definitely made him feel distinctly uneasy. He was increasingly out of control of what he could see was a rapidly developing situation, on her part at least. He began to conclude that he had massively miscalculated by suggesting their weekend away, especially in Vienna, a city with which she appeared so enamoured. Why had he let himself be so sucked in? It wasn't what he usually did. It was at that point, on the Ferris Wheel, at the height of the most romantic moment for her, that he realised he had to soon put a stop to it, end their affair. Her pressure had worked, just as she hoped it would.

He'd suggested earlier on Saturday that they should go for their final dinner on the Sunday night to the historic, beautiful Café Central. He'd read in one of the guide books in the hotel that it was famous for its links to Sigmund Freud and Leon Trotsky amongst others, who used to take their coffee and lunch or dinner there during their time residing in Vienna. Very apt, he thought – a favourite haunt of an Austrian psychoanalyst and a calculating scheming Russian revolutionary – perfect for beginning to plant some seeds undermining what he thought was her optimism about what was happening between the two of them.

When late on Saturday afternoon he asked the hotel Concierge about Café Central, and directions to it, he fortunately suggested that it would be best to make a reservation if they intended to dine there on Sunday evening. So, that is what the Concierge did for them, calling and making the reservation for eight o'clock on Sunday evening. It was fortunate because when they arrived outside the café just before eight o'clock there was a long queue of tourists waiting to get in. Richard guided Aileen to the front of the queue and then up the few steps, where he informed the doorman they had a reservation, and he proceeded to open the dark wood and glass panelled door to let them in.

The place was packed, mostly full of tourists it seemed. The rich aroma of the Viennese café flooded into Aileen's nostrils as soon as they came through the door. The impressive opulent interior was old-style traditional Viennese. It had arched ceilings, padded fabric benches around the walls, and a multitude of small round light brown marbled tables with dark wood straight-backed deep red patterned fabric covered chairs either side of them. In the centre of the large room were six beige marble round pillars supporting the various arches in the roof and surrounding a grand piano, at which the pianist was playing a medley of pleasant music from a bygone Viennese age.

A waitress led them to their table towards the centre of the café and handed them menus. After they studied them for a few minutes they ordered their food and a bottle of Italian red wine. As the waitress departed with their order, followed by a couple more minutes of her commenting on how beautiful and atmospheric the place was, he launched his strategy, designed to try to cool their relationship and her developing enthusiasm for it. He was very blunt about it, seeing no need to even try to gently guide their conversation round to it.

"How do you deal with it, with all this?" he asked, interrupting her eulogy about the place, Café Central.

She looked bemused as she responded, "With what? What do you mean?"

He had no intention of being delicate. In fact, he was quite brutal, as was deliberately his way.

"The guilt, the guilt about what we're doing and Sandra."

She feigned shock, as well as surprise at his timing, although she anticipated it would be coming before the end of their weekend. Anyway, that's what she hoped.

"What ... err ... what? Why now? Why bring that up now, Richard?" she asked, trying to make the sound of surprise ring in her voice as much as possible.

"I'm sure you must feel very bloody guilty, after all she is your best friend and you've known her for years." He thought his comments had just the effect on her he desired and he wasn't letting her off the hook.

However, she was resolute in appearing to play along with his perception of what was happening. She gulped, then took a deep breath, before asking with a deliberate mixture of a hint of both anger and disappointment in her voice, "Why now? Why are you asking me that now? I really don't want to think about that now here with you in this beautiful place."

He knew precisely what he wanted to do however, and knew that at that time he could push it, the doubt, and her, just a little bit more. He thought it was all about laying the ground for what he eventually intended to do, wanted to do, to in a week or two finish the whole affair. His aim was to sow the seeds by working on her guilt over Sandra and then tell her at that point – in a week or two - that he couldn't handle it or deal with it either, what they were doing and the guilt, so easily anymore. As far as he was concerned it was all about firstly managing her expectations, then manipulating her to come around to his way of thinking, and finally into mutually agreeing they would stop, using the guilt argument to achieve all that process. In that way there would be no possibility of her getting upset and angry if he just broke it off, and then running off to tell Sandra everything in some sort of monumental blood-letting exercise. He would be back in control, was already starting to be back in control. She let him think so for now, but she certainly knew differently, and he had no idea whatsoever about that.

He'd done as much as he wanted to do for now at that point in Café Central, put the doubt in her mind. So, he agreed with her, but with a small caveat.

"No, you're right, not here. Sorry, it's just that I've been thinking about it quite a lot lately, and I'm finding it more and more difficult to deal with, the guilt."

He'd achieved his desired effect perfectly, or thought he had. She allowed her expression to change and a worried look to spread across her face for effect. Seeing that, he quickly added, "But, yes, you're right, let's not talk about it here. Forget it, I'm being silly. Just forget I even mentioned it. I won't bring it up again."

After they returned from that weekend in Vienna he found a way to carefully drop the 'guilt' issue into the conversation every time they met up for sex. It was just a brief mention, but enough to implant it in her mind and leave it nagging away at her, he assumed. Again, she knew exactly what he was doing. Little did he know that she'd achieved her aim and now was just waiting for the end to arrive to this part of her plan, so she could move on to the second part.

Three more weeks passed towards the end of March. They'd met up five more times, a couple in Cheam and the rest at the usual hotel. By that time he was convinced that his strategy had left Aileen wracked with the guilt. She encouraged that belief by telling him a few times that she was finding it more and more difficult to deal with, especially every time she met up with Sandra for drinks or coffee. That was when he seized his moment, sympathised with her over her dilemma, and then almost casually told her that he thought Sandra was getting suspicious.

"I think she is starting to suspect something," he dropped into their conversation after sex in the hotel one night at the end of March.

"About us?" Aileen asked, trying to look worried and alarmed.

"No, I don't think about us, but I am getting a feeling she is beginning to suspect I'm having an affair, although not with you. Just a couple of things she said about all these late night work meetings and dinners I'm having, or I'm telling her I'm having."

That was enough for him to achieve what he wanted. Not there and then, but he thought that over the next few days Aileen would dwell on that last thing that he told her. He also knew that she was scheduled to have dinner with Sandra a couple of nights later on one of their girls' night outs. He'd worked out his timing to perfection, he believed.

So, although it was now him who feigned surprise, even appearing a little upset, he thought he'd got exactly what he wanted three days later when Aileen called him at work that afternoon and told him she couldn't go on with it anymore. Now it was her turn to get her timing right. She told him, sounding as convincing as she could, that the guilt was too much for her to handle. To something of his surprise, and what he thought was a bit deep, she even told him the fleeting moments of erotic arousal, which she definitely enjoyed, weren't worth all the damage it generated, or could generate if they were discovered by Sandra. She couldn't resist that philosophical embellishment. She knew it would unnerve him somewhat. Anyway, she said because of that they had to stop. He thought that he tried to convey as much disappointment in his voice as possible without it causing her to change her mind. But, in fact, she had no intention to whatsoever, and he got precisely what he desired. That's what he thought; that he was back in control and he had put a stop to it because he wanted to, not because she wanted to. She knew otherwise though. She knew that little did he realise that the next part of the game playing was only just about to begin, and she would be very much in control of that part.

Ending the affair is what he thought he desired at that time, but as it turned out, despite that, it wasn't entirely what he wanted. Soon, after two weeks he began to miss the good sex. So, he ended up

53

pestering her with calls and texts, as she knew he would, wanting that, the good sex. He didn't want any emotional involvement of course, just the sex. She resisted his calls and texts, telling him firmly a number of times in text replies that she was determined not to get dragged back into the deceit again. So, it was over and she couldn't do it anymore. That was precisely what she wanted him to believe. In any case, she knew that she didn't require his involvement in that way any longer. She'd manufactured precisely the situation she wanted, and got him in exactly the place she wanted him in mentally. She knew his character well, and that he wouldn't be able to leave it. His ego wouldn't be able to cope with what he saw as rejection. And that's what she banked on.

It didn't quite go as she expected, however. Instead, it did actually go relatively quiet between them after another month. The texts messages from him got more and more infrequent. That was when she decided she needed to push things along a bit. She casually mentioned to Sandra one night while they were out drinking together in London that she really needed a holiday. "It had been a tough couple of months at work," she told her, and she, "really needed a break."

Although Sandra took her bait, her response included a little more information than she anticipated. She was a bit taken aback when Sandra just came straight out with it, telling her, "Sounds good to me, and I could definitely do with a holiday in the sun somewhere, just you and me. Only the other day I told Richard I'd felt something hadn't been right between us for a few months now, and that perhaps I should get away for a couple of weeks as that would give both of us a chance for some space to try and work out what was wrong. Of course, he chose to think I meant the both of us, away together, which I didn't. So, I quickly put him right on that. I told him that perhaps I'd ask you if you fancied a couple of weeks in the sun. So, you must have read my mind. I was talking to my friend through work, Gill, about getting a break, getting away, and she recommended a place called Lindos on Rhodes. She's been there loads of times apparently, says it's great."

"Sounds a good a place as any, some Greek sun," Aileen agreed, before not being able to resist asking, "So, Richard was okay with that, you going away with me and not him?"

In fact, she was sure that he would be desperately worried about it. What if both women got very drunk one night and Aileen didn't realise what she was saying, and just exposed their affair by mistake; gave Sandra some clue or hint by mistake about what they had been up to. Surely she wouldn't choose to deliberately tell Sandra what had been going on, but once they'd both had a drink, were relaxed and pissed on holiday, who knows what might happen. She was certain that those were the sort of things that would be scrambling his brain no doubt. Perfect, she thought, couldn't be better. Although she obviously couldn't show it, inside she was feeling very smug and amused.

While she was thinking about that Sandra answered her question about Richard's response with, "Well, he wasn't exactly happy about it at all. He kept saying things like, 'But surely if you feel there are things we need to work out between us it would be better if we went away, just the two of us, not you and Aileen.' I was just adamant that I need some space, just for a couple of weeks that's all. I told him I'm sure I'll feel better about everything after a couple of weeks in the sun. So, he had to accept it in the end. What choice does he have?"

"Suppose so," Aileen agreed briefly, although she was once again concerned over what Sandra told her next.

"He did seem to be coming round to the idea after a while. Although he got a bit more agitated again when I suggested I might talk things through with you about me and him."

"Really? How did he react to that? Some men aren't very happy when their partners start discussing their relationships with their women friends." Aileen was fishing for more information.

"I just explained that it's usually good to talk these things through with a female friend, rather than just between us, just with your male partner. He seemed to accept it, a bit reluctantly perhaps, judging by the tone of his voice. But eventually he did say, 'Yes, maybe that was a good idea.'"

55

Aileen knew she had deliberately lit the blue touch paper of Richard's reaction through her response to Sandra's holiday suggestion. As she anticipated, the next day he called her. On this occasion she did answer, although glibly.

"I thought I'd hear from you soon. I know what you're calling about. Should be fun don't you think?"

"You're going? Don't you think that's-"

"A bit dangerous, Richard? But I thought you liked danger. You always said you did when we were rolling around in bed together. It never seemed to bother you then, the danger."

She knew that now it was her turn to have the upper hand and she was enjoying having him dangling, exposed to whatever she chose to do. She was playing with his mind, although she liked to describe the process she was employing by using a much stronger phrase that still included the word 'mind', but came attached to another less acceptable word beginning with 'f'. That had been her aim all along, and she wasn't about to give up that power easily. He could sweat over it for a few weeks, and certainly during the actual two weeks that she and Sandra would be away.

"But you won't say anything to her, you can't. Don't be stupid." His anger was seeping through.

"Stupid? That's an interesting word, Richard. You mean like you were, by having an affair behind your wife's back with her best friend?"

"Look, you can't-" he tried again to reason with her.

"No, Richard, you look. I can, of course I can, but you're just gonna have to sweat on that for a couple of weeks while Sandra and I are sweating in the Rhodes sun aren't you?"

With that she rang off. His initial reaction was to try and ring her back and reason with her, but he realised and decided that it wasn't the best time. He was angry, and he just thought that she was obviously angry at how he finished their affair, playing on her guilt. He would wait a day or so for them both to calm down and then try to call her again, maybe even suggest meeting to talk about it.

However, when he tried to call her two days later all he got was her voicemail three times. He left a message suggesting they meet and talk, but she never called back. He texted asking to speak with her, but she ignored all of them and never replied.

A week before the two women were scheduled to go on their Lindos holiday he tried again declaring to Sandra that he would go with them. He was panicking by that time, and thought that maybe the only way to prevent the secret of the affair being revealed was for him to be there all the time, with Sandra at least. If her and Aileen were never alone he could prevent them having any conversations that might lead to the affair being revealed. It was crazy and not logical at all, but by that time he was really worried and desperate. However, Sandra flatly refused and they had quite an argument. She was still adamant that she wanted some space and that she would get that with just Aileen, and not with him also there on the holiday. So, the two women set off to Lindos together for two weeks, alone.

Part Three:
Lindos, the first week

7

Thursday 23rd June, 2016 – Courtyard Bar and Pal's Bar

As he glanced at his watch for the third time in as many minutes he saw now that they were over ten minutes late. He'd said in his text nine o'clock and now it was just gone ten past. He was trying to relax and not get too perturbed as he sat on a stool by the bar. He'd decided beforehand that he should be quite cool and not appear too eager as far as Aileen was concerned. At least he wouldn't get hot under the collar when they eventually turned up as he'd plumped for wearing a pair of plain white shorts, a dark blue polo shirt and dark blue boat shoes.

"You expecting someone, meeting someone, Martin? That's the third time in quick succession you've looked at your watch and then over to the door to the courtyard," the owner of the Courtyard Bar, Jack Constantino, asked.

The décor of the bar was old style traditional Lindian with its usual fair share of dark polished wood. The bar itself ran all along the length of the back wall, except for a few feet at the end where there was a doorway and narrow steps down to the toilets. At the opposite end was the music console, together with a larger and wider area with some tables and chairs and room for dancing, as well as some stairs up to the open terrace.

Jack Constantino was a most convivial friendly bar owner and host. A lot of his customers were repeat ones who returned to Lindos, and particularly the Courtyard Bar, year after year and sometimes twice or three times a year. They spent a lot of time in his welcoming bar. It was particularly popular with families, not only because of its host but also because of the courtyard, which made it perfect for them to sit outside the bar through the warm evenings and yet still be able hear the music drifting through the bar's open doors. Some evenings there was live Greek music and dancing as Jack himself entertained the customers with his considerable various musical instrumental skills. He was a stocky, dark-haired, quite tall man in his forties. Born and bred in Lindos, he could relate many stories from his youth in the village in entertaining his customers. He'd also spent some time in America a few years before he married back in Lindos. Besides his bar, or maybe as well as is a better way of putting it, his passion was his music and he was a great fan of Cat Stevens, or Yusuf Islam as he now called himself. Jack would regularly entertain his customers with renditions on his guitar or bouzouki of the songs of his favourite musician.

On that particular Thursday evening the bar was already quite busy, with a few more couples also sat outside in the courtyard that gave the bar its name. The 'changeover days' as the tourist company holiday reps called them, were Wednesday and Saturday. They were the days when most of the charter flights, and flights in general, arrived from the U.K. with their hordes of sun-seeking tourists. So, Thursday evening was usually one of the busiest nights of the week in Lindos, if not the busiest. It was the first night of most of the British tourists' holiday. Consequently, it was likely that the place would get even busier that evening as it wore on. At that time, just gone nine, many of the tourists – those newly arrived and those who'd been there a week or so already – were still finishing their evening meal in the many rooftop restaurants. He consoled himself with that fact. No doubt that's what Aileen and Sandra were doing also.

"So, did you vote before you came away?" Jack enquired.

Distracted by having one eye almost constantly on his watch and one eye on the entrance to the bar, Jack's question took Martin by surprise.

"What? Sorry, Jack, what?"

"The referendum, it's today isn't it? Just wondered if you had a chance to vote before you came away? What would it be, some kind of postal vote?" Jack asked. "The two couples at the other end of the bar were talking about it earlier. Seems to be quite a split opinion on it in the U.K. from what I can gather from my customers."

Martin definitely wasn't too keen on getting embroiled in a conversation over the EU referendum at the best of times. As someone who travelled quite a bit in the EU for his work of course he had an opinion, but he had his mind on other things at that particular moment, such as where Aileen and Sandra were. Also, he knew enough about what had happened between the EU and the Greeks a few years before during the Greek Euro crisis to fully realise that the EU wasn't exactly a popular subject to get into discussion about with many Greeks. Besides which, he certainly didn't want to come all the way to Lindos on holiday to spend his evening discussing the merits or otherwise of the 'Leave' and 'Remain' arguments in the UK EU referendum with other Brits. He'd seen enough in the campaign to realise that the country was completely split over it, and that those divisions wouldn't be easily or quickly healed whatever the result.

"Oh, yes, of course, sorry Jack, was miles away. Yes, yes I did have a postal vote, so I voted before I came away," he confirmed.

He knew what was coming next, exactly what the next question from Jack was going to be.

"So, which way-"

"There you are. I was beginning to think you'd stood me up."

Jack's awkward question was interrupted, and he was saved from answering by the two women entering the bar.

"Sorry, no, of course not, the restaurant was really busy, and dinner took a bit longer than we anticipated," Aileen responded. Her holiday companion simply offered him a weak smile of acknowledgement as the two women took a seat on the stools next to him.

Aileen had obviously come to the same conclusion as him as far as what to wear that night was concerned. She'd also chose not to look too overdressed. She had decided on what she described to Sandra before they left their villa as 'effortlessly smart casual', consisting of an expensive looking pair of very dark blue designer shorts and a quite tight fitting plain white t-shirt that showed her figure off to its best. Sandra was also wearing a t-shirt, although pale green, and a shortish white skirt. The days sunbathing on Pallas Beach had already produced a healthy looking glow and slight tan on their faces and the exposed parts of their legs.

As they sat down on the stools Martin introduced them to Jack, informing them he was the owner, and proceeded to ask what they'd like to drink. They both told him, "Gin and tonic, with ice and lemon."

"So, where did you go for dinner?" he asked.

"That place you recommended, The Village House. It was very good. As you told us to, we told the owner you recommended it to us, Aris isn't it?"

"Yes, nice guy, nice food, nice restaurant. Good day on beach?" he asked.

To his surprise it was Sandra who actually answered him while Aileen took a sip of her drink that had just been placed on the bar in front of her by Jack.

"Yep, lovely beach, and an interesting day, the sea is lovely, so clear."

Aileen looked sideways at her friend as a slightly bemused look spread across her face. She was obviously as bewildered by the "interesting day" part of her reply as Martin. Neither Aileen nor him were able to dwell on it though and ask what she meant as Jack returned to their end of the bar and asked, "Is it the first time in Lindos then for both of you?"

"Yes, Sandra's friend Gill recommended it. Apparently, she's been here a lot, and we met Martin sat next to us on the plane. He gave the place a great recommendation," Aileen replied.

"Well, you've got a perfect guide with Martin. He's been here lots of times too. I even persuaded him to write a novel, a story based in the village."

As he finished speaking the bar owner half turned to point at a copy of Martin's Lindos novel on a shelf on the back wall of the bar behind him.

"So, you're the one, he told us about that, someone who owned a bar here suggesting it to him late one night over a few drinks," Aileen said, as she half turned on her bar stool to smile at the author.

"I'll have to read it now," and she quickly added, "on the beach on my Kindle, perhaps?"

"Yep, it's on Kindle," Martin confirmed.

"What about nightlife here though? Sandra and I like to have a few drinks and some fun on holiday," Aileen asked.

Jack smiled as he told her, "Don't worry about that. You've also got the perfect guide for that in Martin here. He knows plenty of places for a late night drink, including here. The local by-law means we have to turn the music off at one o'clock, but if we keep it low and the police in the village don't come by we can keep it on later. Plus, there are a couple of clubs in the village that I'm sure Martin will take you to, where the music can go on till five or six in the morning as they are soundproofed."

"Sure," Martin interjected, "Arches and Glow. We can make a start later if you feel like it. Maybe not till five or six tonight, although it's not really worth going to either of them till around two. Should be busy tonight though, the first night for those people like us who arrived last night. They usually are."

Sandra frowned slightly as she commented, "Five or six in the morning, definitely not tonight. Maybe another night, although I don't want to lose a whole day of the beach the next day. And I will certainly need to if I'm out drinking till then."

"We'll see, I know you once you get started, Sandra," Aileen commented with a grin.

"Ok, well maybe not tonight, but perhaps another night," Martin suggested.

"No, no, don't take too much notice of her, Martin. Wait till she gets a few more of these inside her." Aileen lifted up her now half empty gin and tonic, and then continued, "She'll change her tune then I'm sure. I've heard all that from her before, and then after a few G & T's she changes her tune. Either way, I'll be up for it for sure. I'm on bloody holiday and I'm determined to enjoy myself after the last few months I've had."

Before Martin or Sandra could comment further Jack had obviously picked up some of the comments and with a slight mischievous smile on his face aimed towards Martin he placed four shots he had prepared on the bar, one in front of each of the two women and Martin, and one for himself.

"Yammas, welcome to Lindos," he told the two women as he lifted his shot and drank it down, followed by Martin and the two women, although by Sandra somewhat apprehensively.

An hour-and-a-half later, after more Gin and tonics for the women and bottles of Mythos beer for him, the three of them moved on just over thirty metres down the alley to Pal's Bar. Martin had suggested it and the two women readily agreed.

Pal's was situated on the corner of the main alleyway through the village and the alley running at ninety degrees to it going up to Jack Constantino's bar. It was a very small, but very popular bar, with two sets of double folding doors on each side through which the drinking clientele spilled out into the alleys. Outside on one side were some more comfortable padded benches and seats, and around the corner were some more usual small tables and stools. Its clientele varied, mostly tourists, but some Greek and Brit ex-pat regulars from time to time, and they tended to be middle-aged or even older. It was very popular with British couples on holiday, and many of its regular tourist customers of all ages, who returned to the village year after year.

That particular evening, by now around ten-thirty, it was just as packed inside as usual, so much so that a quite large number of people were standing, as well as sitting, outside in groups of four or five or more. There was never much room inside the small bar once the evening wore on as it became busy. As the three of them approached it the loud sound of happy, partying, drinking tourists inside the bar hit them, especially the number of them who were singing along to the music.

Seeing the tight squeeze inside Martin asked the two women what they wanted to drink followed by if they wanted to wait outside or venture in. Once again they both plumped for Gin & tonics, Aileen saying she'd go with him into the bar to get the drinks, while Sandra was more reluctant and told them she'd wait outside.

No sooner had he and Aileen started to squeeze their way through the tourist bodies inside than one of the guys behind the bar, Lou, a Brit, leaned down below the bar, picked up a bottle of Mythos and a glass and handed them over a couple of people at the bar to Martin.

The barman tilted his head a little to one side, raised his eyebrows slightly, and grinned when Martin quickly told him, "And two Gin and tonics, Lou, please, with ice and lemon."

Standing just behind him Aileen reached up and placed her right hand gently on Martin's left shoulder and then leaned in to say in his ear over the music, "You obviously really are a regular. He knew what you wanted, that beer, before you even said anything."

He partly turned his head around as she told him that and was greeted with a lovely smile from her, followed by a long lingering look into his eyes. Pleasantly surprised by her stare, he eventually managed a stammered, "Err ... yes ... err ... he does, and I am a regular, yes, I suppose I am."

Not his most inspiring response, but her look and smile had certainly had an effect and disorientated him somewhat. So, much so that his mind was totally elsewhere when the barman leaned across the people sat at the bar and tapped him on the shoulder to get his attention, pointing to their drinks on the bar. If he wasn't very aware of what was going on around him though, the other barman, a Greek, Stelios, was as he stood next to Lou and grinned at Martin, then added sarcastically, "You ok, Marty boy? You look a bit preoccupied there."

Martin shook his head slightly and threw a small grin back at Stelios as he picked up one of the Gin and tonics, turned slightly and handed it to Aileen. She took it from him, but just placed it back on the bar. Sarah, the owner's wife, was blasting out her usual selection of good music from the console at the far end of the bar. Most of the clientele obviously liked it as they tried to move and dance a little in the crowded bar. Sarah was always adept at reading her particular clientele on any one night, playing music that she thought would suit their tastes.

At that point she was blasting out nineteen-seventies disco classic 'Burn Baby Burn' in the bar. Much to Martin's pleasure, after she placed her drink back on the bar Aileen reached around his waist from behind with both her arms and started moving close to him in time with the music, telling him, "I love this one."

He was definitely in no hurry to disentangle himself from her arms around his waist. So, it was a few more minutes, until 'Burn Baby Burn' finished playing and the music moved on to Michael Jackson's 'Billie Jean', before he picked up his beer and turned to face her saying, "Shouldn't we be taking her drink out to Sandra?"

"Oh, yes, of course, with the great music I clean forgot about her drink," Aileen told him.

They squeezed their way once again between the gyrating crowd of customers doing their best moves, or trying to in what space they had in the now packed bar, and emerged through one of the sets of the open double doors into the alleyway outside.

There were three separate couples outside that side of the bar, two sat at the small tables and another couple leaning against the wall just along from the crepe shop, still open and doing a good trade with late night takeaway crepe eaters. There were also a couple of groups of four people, tourists, stood drinking and talking in the alley by the bar. Sandra was standing by the white wall opposite the doors, surrounded by, and engaged in conversation with, half-a-dozen young British guys who appeared to be in their early twenties. She let out quite a loud laugh at what one of the guys said just as Aileen went to pass her drink to her between two of the young men. She was clearly enjoying the attention.

"Thanks, these guys are here for the first time too, from south London," she informed Aileen, who simply said, "Hi guys," and then moved back slightly to stand next to Martin as the circle of six men opened a gap for them to join it around Sandra.

Martin glanced at Aileen, raised his eyebrows and gave her a slight smile, signalling his curiosity at what Sandra was up to. It was obvious to both of them that the young men were honing in on Sandra, and equally obvious that she was lapping it up, giggling and laughing at their slightest comical comments. Intermittently, she took a sip of her drink and then with her other hand flicked her hair back behind one of her ears. After about the third time she did so in just a few minutes Aileen reached up to once more place her hand on Martin's shoulder and whisper in his ear, "This is very interesting. I've seen her do this so many times before on nights out in London, and with young men. She loves it."

The competition was at its fiercest between the two young guys who had positioned themselves either side of Sandra, leaning side on against the wall and facing each other across her. Both were dressed in designer holiday gear, being in smart shorts and Ralph Lauren polo shirts.

The entertaining competition went on for around another thirty minutes or so, with Sandra continuing to enjoy herself and lap up the attention, obviously fully aware of the competition between the two guys. At one point one of them offered to buy her a drink, which she accepted, but when he offered to also get drinks for them Aileen and Martin thanked him, but both declined.

Eventually, the other four guys got bored and wanted the group to move on. One of them suggested, "Let's go and check out Antika."

While one of the two guys leaning against the wall beside Sandra asked her if she wanted to join them in going to Antika, Aileen discretely asked Martin, "Where's that? Is it any good?"

"In the centre of the village, about forty yards up that alley," he started to tell her as he pointed around the corner of Pal's. "It's good, yeah, but all the bars here are good in their own way, plenty of variety. Antika is one of the larger ones, combines the old traditional stone of the building with more modern interior furnishings, and there's an outside seating area at the back. It usually gets busy for the last hour or so of music, from around twelve. Music's good there also."

"Should we join them then?" Aileen asked.

Before he could reply Sandra decided for them, telling the guy next to her, "No, it's ok thanks. I'm probably going to have one more here and then call it a night. We plan to go to Rhodes Town for the day tomorrow, don't we, Aileen. So, I don't want a late night tonight boys. Another night maybe?"

As Aileen nodded in agreement about the Rhodes Town trip the next day one of the competing guys told Sandra, "Sure, no problem.

We'll look out for you in the village another night. Bound to bump into you somewhere, it's not that big, and we're here for a couple of weeks."

Now it was Aileen's turn to raise her eyebrows at Sandra and tilt her head slightly to one side as a smile spread across her face and the six guys headed off around the corner towards the Antika bar.

"How do you do it? So many times I've seen it, you and young men I mean, like flies round a jam pot," Aileen asked. "Left you alone for one minute while we got the drinks and we come out of the bar to find you surrounded."

"No, they are just being friendly. They are on holiday Aileen, having a bit of fun, why not?"

"Well, whatever, you definitely had a couple of competing admirers there. It was obvious from their body language, and yours wasn't exactly discouraging them from what I could see."

Sandra allowed herself a small self-satisfied smile, but decided to change the subject with, "Right, who's for one more? Beer, Martin?"

"Yes, thanks, a bottle of Mythos."

"That was entertaining. Does she do that a lot? Ever take it further, only you said on the plane that she was married," Martin asked as Sandra disappeared into the thronging crowd inside Pal's to get the drinks.

"No, as I said before, she loves it, the attention, the games, and I've seen it so many times before in bars in London. Don't know why, but she seems to have this attraction for younger guys. Never known her take it any further though, or at least, if she ever has she's never told me about it."

"Doesn't appeal to you then, with much younger guys? I'm sure you must have had the opportunity."

He was fishing again, and this time she was well aware of it. She turned towards him and deliberately slowly lifted her wide dark brown eyes to focus on his. Simultaneously, she appeared to bite on her bottom lip a little while tilting her head slightly to one side.

"You think so, Martin?" she asked somewhat mischievously. She knew exactly what she was doing. She didn't know why she was doing it, but for whatever reason she was enjoying it. Now it was her who was enjoying playing games, although not with young men, of course. She was enjoying disorientating him.

"I ... err ... I ... err, no, I mean maybe, well I don't really know do I? I guess, yes, you must have had the opportunity. I mean you're a beautiful looking woman. So, yes, I'm sure you must have had plenty of opportunities."

He was floundering. His self-acknowledged insecurities and doubts over communicating with women were being fully exhibited. But she was enjoying her game and wasn't letting him off the hook easily.

"Plenty? That's an interesting word, Martin. So, you think I've had plenty of opportunities, plenty of younger men?"

He was so flustered he failed to notice at all the slight grin on her lips as she finished speaking or even the look of mischief in her eyes.

"No, no, not plenty, I didn't mean you'd had plenty of younger men." He was desperately trying to dig himself out of the hole. "I just meant ... look, you're bloody attractive and even at your age you must get plenty of young men try to chat you up."

He should have put the shovel down. He just made the hole a lot deeper.

"Even at my age, that's sort of a backhanded compliment, thanks." This time though he couldn't fail to notice the broad smile spreading across her face as she finished speaking.

"Ok," he started to tell her, "I see. You've been playing a game with me. I realise that now."

This time she just stood smiling up at him, and then offered him a slight nod of recognition.

"Anyway, I definitely need another beer now after that. Where's Sandra with the drinks?" He was trying to change the subject.

"But, no Martin, just in case you're still confused, just to put you straight, there haven't been plenty of younger men, or even plenty of opportunities with younger men," she explained, ignoring his attempt to change the subject.

"Of course not, but I-" he started to say.

"Stop", she told him, smiling again, "Just leave it now. No younger men, just the one, around the same age as me."

"Oh yes, your ex-husband, of course."

"No, since then, since my divorce, but that's all finished now, been like that for a while."

"Oh, I see, when did-"

Before he could finish his question Sandra finally appeared with the drinks.

"Bloody nightmare in there," she interrupted. "Jammed, and even more people trying to dance. Music's bloody good though. I managed to get as close to the bar as possible to try and ask for drinks and then this guy grabbed my hand from behind and started trying to dance with me. Then three women, Brits of course, got up and started dancing on the bar, so nothing was being served while they were doing that. Manic! Bloody good though, Martin. Good choice, great bar."

"Yep, great, thanks," Aileen instantly agreed, grateful for the diversion from what she felt might have been an awkward moment approaching in her conversation with Martin.

He was a bit disappointed not to learn more about her and the man around the same age as her, though. However, he took the obvious hint from her comment agreeing with Sandra about how great Pal's was that she didn't want to go on talking about that and tell him anything more. So, he left it at that and took a swig of his new beer.

Approaching midnight he suggested they move on to another bar, Lindos By Night, adding that, "There were great views from it of Lindos and the lit up Acropolis at that time of the evening."

"Yep, sounds good, why not? Is it far," Aileen asked.

"Just up there, past the Courtyard Bar, up a few steps and about thirty yards along the alley," he told her, pointing up the alleyway to his right outside Pal's.

"Not for me, thanks," Sandra told them. "As I told those boys before, Martin, early-ish start for us tomorrow if we're going to Rhodes Town."

"Well, it doesn't have to be too early does it, Sandra? It's only just twelve, so another drink won't hurt, surely," Aileen suggested.

Although he desperately wanted Aileen to go to Lindos By Night with him Martin decided it was best to not intervene, and instead leave the two women to sort it out between them. To be honest he preferred Sandra not to come, so that he could get Aileen alone.

He needn't have worried, Sandra wasn't budging.

"No, maybe not, but I'm feeling quite tired, so it's ok, you go. We've both got a key to the villa so you can just make your way back later and I'll see you around nine in the morning. I'm sure Martin will look after you, and can show you the way back to the villa if necessary, but I'm off to bed." She didn't wait to give Aileen any further opportunity to try to convince her and just added, "Night, Martin, no doubt see you tomorrow evening in the village somewhere."

With that she kissed Aileen on the cheek and whispered in one of her ears, "Be good," before turning around and heading down the alley to their villa accommodation behind the Greek Orthodox Church towards the Main Square.

As she disappeared around the corner opposite Pal's Martin said, "Right, the Lindos night is young, LBN then, just for one"

"LBN?" Aileen asked.

"Lindos By Night, but everyone calls it LBN," he explained.

"Right, I see, let's go then, which way?"

"Up here past Jack's, follow me," he told her as he tentatively reached out and took her hand. She never refused it and seemed more than happy for him to continue holding it. A good sign he thought as they climbed the three steps at the end of the alleyway and made their way along another short alley past Jack Constantino's Courtyard Bar.

As they were halfway along she pointed and asked, "Is this one of the clubs that Jack mentioned earlier? It doesn't seem very busy?"

"Yes, that's Glow. It's good, but it has only just opened, opens at twelve, and it won't get busy for another couple of hours. Up here," he said and then led her up a few more quite big steps opposite the night club. At the top they turned right and walked the thirty yards or so down another white walled alley.

8

Lindos By Night and Arches – 'just for one'

The entrance to Lindos By Night was up an initial flight of a dozen steps or so. It had two bars. First there was a long narrow bar to the left at the top of that flight of steps, with an area full of tables and chairs outside to the right. Further up another flight of steps, there was another open seating area with tables and chairs and a small bar against the rock face. A key attraction of the top bar was its wonderful view of the Lindos Acropolis, especially when it was lit up at night.

As they turned into the doorway to climb the first flight of steps a good looking, dark haired young Greek guy in a smart white shirt and light blue jeans standing at the top let out a shout of, "Marty," followed quickly by a grin and, "Who's your friend?" as he spotted the couple still hand-in-hand.

Martin shook his head and let out a slight laugh. As they reached the top of the flight of stairs he let go of Aileen's hand and exchanged a warm hug with the young guy, adding as they parted, "This is Aileen. We've come just for one."

Now it was the Greek guy's turn to laugh. "Aileen, pleased to meet you, I'm Angelos. Be careful when this guy says 'just for one'. He can't count, and I've been on lots of 'just for one' nights in Lindos with him. They usually don't end till the sun is coming up."

As the Greek finished he exchanged grins with Martin, and then asked, "You going upstairs, or do you want to stay down here?"

"Up, I want to show Aileen the view," Martin told him.

With that Angelos led them up the second flight of stairs to a table and a comfortable cushioned double seat at the front of the seated area, with a great view of the lit up Acropolis. After he took

71

their drinks order, while she sat down Martin went to say hello to the disc jockey at the music console ten feet behind them, exchanging another warm hug.

When he returned to sit beside her he said, "Sorry, that's Mike, I've known him for quite a few years. He's a good DJ, usually plays in one of the club's later."

She obviously wasn't too concerned at his momentary absence though, being too busy gazing at the view. "That's okay. You obviously know lots of people here. Anyway, this view is amazing, wow!" she told him. "The Acropolis is beautiful. I have to come back here with Sandra another night to show her."

"Yes, it's quite a view," he agreed, although she never realised that the view he was referring to wasn't just the lit up Acropolis, but one that also included her against the background of it.

They spent over an hour sitting there talking, with her occasionally turning slightly to stare at the Acropolis and tell him again and again how beautiful it was. At one point Angelos came over to talk to them for a few minutes and get them another drink.

By approaching one-thirty, after their second drink and the music had finished, he told her the time and added, "I guess I better let you go to back to your villa and your bed, with that early start you and Sandra have."

But she wasn't in the mood for calling it a night. The alcohol had well and truly kicked in, the effect of by now multiple Gin and tonics.

"What? No way! You promised me a club, remember," she responded firmly.

He was pleasantly surprised, as he didn't really want to end the evening at that point.

"Okay, let's go to Arches then. It's in the centre of the village. We can go along the back alley outside here and cut down through one of the side alleys. It's only a couple of minutes, and it should be beginning to get busy around now."

She offered, but he insisted, so he paid Angelos for their drinks and said, "Goodbye," to him as they got up to leave. The Greek couldn't resist a, "Goodbye, enjoy just the one," to Aileen, which made her smile.

72

As they walked along the dimly lit deserted back alley she once again took hold of his hand. He was reading this more and more as a good sign, although he also wondered if it was simply because she was just a little unsure of her footing on the rough path in the dim light, especially after the multiple G & T's.

After about a hundred yards they turned left and went down a few well-spaced small steps into another alley that led to the centre of the village. They had gone barely twenty yards down it when a Greek voice boomed out, "Mr. Martin."

The voice belonged to a well-built guy who was standing by the small archway that led to the courtyard in front of the Arches club.

"Oh, good evening, Chris, my friend," Martin replied as he and Aileen approached him. After the two men hugged, Martin introduced him to Aileen, telling Chris, "You had better be nice to her, it's her first time in Lindos, so her first time in Arches."

"Of course, Mr. Martin, I'm always nice to people, you know that," Chris told him, followed by a grin.

As he finished another Greek voice from a man coming around the corner from inside the courtyard said, "Well, you'd better introduce her to the boss then hadn't you, Martin."

Another hug, and then Martin said, "This is Valasi, Aileen, he owns the place. He's the man I've given all my money to in this place over the years."

"Welcome, Aileen," Valasi greeted her, adding ironically, "Yes, as you can see all Martin's money has made me rich."

That caused Martin to chuckle a little before he asked, "Is it busy inside?"

"Getting busy, but not packed," the owner told him.

"Okay, let's go in and give Valasi some more of my money then and get some drinks," Martin told Aileen as he took hold of her hand and headed across the courtyard. "See you later, boys," he added to the two Greeks with a smile.

As all music in the many bars in the village had to stop at one a.m. because of a local by-law, for the tourist nightlife seekers, the Greek locals, and the Brit ex-pat workers, the two soundproofed nightclubs, Glow and Arches, were the only options after that for music.

Consequently, when Aileen said as they walked across the courtyard, "But I thought you said there was music? I can't hear any." Martin told her, "Wait, you'll see."

Arches had a soundproof entry system, whereby the inner entry door was only opened by the Arches' employee operating it once the outer entry door was closed and those people coming into the club had made their way into the sound vacuum space between the two doors. The process was reversed when people left the club.

As an Arches worker opened the inner door for them the volume and sound of the music hit them, and Aileen reached up and put her hand behind Martin's neck, saying in his ear, "Now I see what you mean."

He took her hand once again and led her through the groups of people to the small bar opposite the entrance door, asking her once they got to the bar, "Gin and tonic?"

"Of course," she confirmed, as he caught the eye of one of the two young Greek barmen and shook their hands as they both came over to say hello. While one of them made her drink and got Martin's bottle of Mythos she reached up again to say in his ear, "More people here you know?"

"Yes, Dimitris and Yiannis, they may be young but they've served me a few drinks over the past few years in here."

They got the drinks and made their way across the club to a space by the far wall, with him again taking her hand and leading her through the growing crowd of people. Talking wasn't much of an option due to the loud music, even though they were by now standing very close facing each other. Periodically Martin was approached by, and said hello to, a few of the various people in the club he knew that worked in the bars and restaurants in the village, including the waiter who had served Aileen and Sandra their dinner earlier in the Village House restaurant. They just had the one drink, and approaching two-thirty she told him that she thought maybe she should actually get to her bed for that early start in the morning. He agreed and again led her by the hand towards the exit and through the two sound vacuum doors. Once more he was pleasantly surprised that while they passed through the first open door, waited between the two, and then emerged through the second one and into the courtyard she kept hold of his hand, and at one point he was sure he felt her squeeze it slightly.

They said a quick, "Goodnight," to Chris - still on duty at the courtyard entrance - who gave Martin a smile and a wink, and they made their way hand-in-hand this time to the right and down the alley twenty yards to the centre of the village. As they reached the small, now deserted square opposite Yannis Bar at the end of the alley he stopped, pointed to the right, and began to tell her, "My flat is just down there, that alley between Yannis here and Bar 404, and around the corner. So, I guess-"

But before he could finish she interrupted, not letting go of his hand but gripping it tighter as she surprised him with a question, "What? You're not going to walk me back to our villa then?"

His response was instantaneous. "Of course, of course, yes, sorry, of course. I think I know where it is, the general direction anyway, but I'm sure you can direct me when we get nearer to it. It's behind the church I think one of you said?"

"Yes, Martin, it is," she replied, with a mischievous smile starting to spread across her lips before she added, "and yes, I'm sure I can direct you when we get nearer."

She knew exactly what she meant by her "direct you" comment, her double-entendre, but there was nothing in his reaction that suggested to her that he did. So, she took his hand again and they went off to the left and down the alley towards the church. As they reached one of the small deserted alleyways behind the church he stopped, turned towards and asked, "Which way?"

She didn't hesitate, reached up to put her hand behind his neck, and firmly pulled his face towards her's to plant a strong, long, lingering kiss on his lips. As she finished kissing him she said, "This way, Martin."

Now it was his turn not to hesitate and he instantly returned the kiss. As he did so she pushed him back against the white wall of the back of the exterior of the church, burying her tongue firmly deep into his open mouth and lifting her right leg up to wrap it around his left thigh. Within a minute, as they continued kissing passionately, his hand was up inside her t-shirt reaching towards her breasts, while she grappled with trying to get her right hand down the front of the

75

quite tight waistband of his shorts. Just as she was about to succeed and reach her destination though he grabbed her right arm, telling her, "Wait, wait, listen, someone's coming."

"Shit!" she exclaimed as the flip-footed footsteps sounded louder as they got closer.

"Down here, quick," he told her as he took her hand and headed down another alley a few yards away and opposite the church back wall that they had been up against. They waited a minute or so as they heard the footsteps get much louder and then fade as whoever they belonged to passed where they had been embracing and went on down that alleyway.

"Phew! That could have been a bit embarrassing I guess," he told her.

She just laughed though, and replied, "Exciting, Martin, bloody exciting. I love it, a bit of excitement and danger of being seen, discovered, doing what I guess we were about to do. It gets me going."

"Really?" He looked a little shocked as he explained, "Can't say it does it for me, not here. I know too many people in this village."

"Oh, I see, yes, I hadn't thought of that. Of course you do. I've seen that in all the bars we've been in tonight, and Arches. You're hardly a one off holidaymaker here I suppose. Could be embarrassing."

They were both leaning side by side against another white wall, breathing quite deeply still. He did manage to let out a small chuckle though as he told her, "And against the back wall of the village Greek Orthodox Church. Blimey! That could have been a lot more than embarrassing here for both of us, but particularly me. That wouldn't be a good thing at all. They take these things, religion and religious grounds, bloody seriously here."

"Hmm … you'd have been damned to hell, or your soul would anyway, if you had one." Now it was her turn to smile and chuckle, before she added, "Okay, look I definitely don't want you to be condemned to hell, and inviting as what we were about to do I guess is, I have still got that early start in just over six hours' time. Bloody Sandra will be up with the lark, or whatever the early morning bird is in these parts, full of the joys no doubt and wanting to get to Rhodes Town, so-"

"Sure, of course, you need to get some sleep," he agreed.

"The villa is only just down the end of this alley actually, so I can find it okay on my own from here, Martin."

"You sure?"

"Yep, don't worry."

She kissed him again, this time on the cheek, telling him, "Thanks for this evening. I'll see you tomorrow night somewhere in the village. I'll text you when we get back from Rhodes Town, late afternoon I guess."

"Okay, sure," he replied and turned away to walk back up the slight alley slope.

He'd only gone a few paces though when he heard her call, "Martin, don't worry, to be continued."

He turned his head to look back at her with a broad smile that stayed fixed across his lips for most of his walk back to his flat through the almost deserted village.

9

Rhodes Town, Friday 24th June, 2016

"Here's your coffee. So, were you good, like I told you to be, or …?"

Sandra was quizzing her partly hungover, partly just tired from lack of sleep, friend as she handed her a drink to revive her as she sat at the table in the small kitchenette of their villa at eight-thirty the next morning.

"Of course I was good. I'm always good, Sandra, you know that. A good girl, that's me."

In fact, from the text from her husband she'd seen yesterday in Aileen's phone Sandra knew full well that was not true. However, she still hadn't decided how and when to confront her over their affair. So, she just left it, and decided to simply ask Aileen about the rest of the previous evening after she left her and Martin.

"Yep, it was good. He showed me some nice places. A bar called Lindos By Night with amazing views of the village and the Acropolis at night all lit up. We have to go there. You'll love it. Then we went to a club called Arches in the centre of the village. They've got this sort of sound vacuum door system as you go in so that the music doesn't blast out into the village after the one o'clock limit on the bars. It works really well. There's a courtyard in front of the club, but you can't hear anything there. When you get inside though the music is full volume. It was quite crowded. We only had one drink though. We should go later in the week perhaps."

"Sure," Sandra agreed, "and that other place, Lindos By Night too. Sounds useful meeting someone in Martin who knows Lindos."

"Yep, sure is. He seems to know lots of people here. Everywhere we went he introduced me to people, although they mostly seemed to be bar workers." She managed a small smile through her hangover as she finished that last sentence.

"Okay, we should go. There's a pastry there I got from the small shop at the top of the alley if you want to grab it. There's a bus to Rhodes Town from the square at the top of the village apparently at ten, so-"

"Taxi"

"What?" Sandra asked.

"Sorry, I can't face an hour on a bloody bus this morning. Let's just go and get a taxi from the Main Square. I don't mind paying, and it'll be much quicker."

"And by the way, I guess you haven't heard, but we're leaving," Sandra told her.

"Okay, okay, I know, but if we're getting a taxi we don't have to rush for the bus."

"No, Aileen, not the bus and Rhodes Town, the bloody referendum, 'Leave' won."

"Shit! Really? How? Why?"

"By about a million votes I think, seventeen something million to sixteen odd, according to what I saw online. It's gonna be a complete balls up, believe me. No one expected or predicted 'Leave' to win. Apparently, according to what I saw online, even that tosser Farage was saying last night before the result that he thought 'Leave' had lost, but that they'd keep fighting. Of course, no one has got a fucking clue what's going to happen now, no sort of plan apparently, least of all that dickhead Cameron. I tell you it's going to be a bloody nightmare for me business-wise as far as photo-shoots in the EU are concerned once we leave. Much more bureaucracy I guess, work permits and the rest, plus getting models from EU countries isn't going to be as easy as now, that's for sure."

Aileen put down her coffee, leaned forward to rest her elbows on the wooden table in front of her and bury her head in her hands as she mumbled, "Sod the bus, bloody taxi definitely now then."

By half-past-eleven the two women were sat at a nice tree-shaded café in Great Alexander Square in Rhodes Town drinking their mid-morning cappuccinos. Aileen was feeling a bit better. Her hangover had subsided, overwhelmed by copious amounts of bottled water during the taxi journey from Lindos, and even her tiredness from lack of sleep seemed to have declined.

Her recovery was such that she was even reading from her small guide book, suggesting that they "Should go and see the Street of the Knights and the Palace of the Grand Masters. It says it was all constructed and inhabited by the Knights of St. John between the fourteenth and sixteenth century, after the Crusaders were defeated and driven out of Jerusalem and the Holy Land. Sounds interesting don't you think?"

"Sure, we can go and have a look and then get a nice lunch somewhere after," Sandra agreed, although not with any noticeable apparent overwhelming enthusiasm.

"It says it was all constructed and inhabited by the Knights of St. John between the fourteenth and sixteenth century. Apparently, the knights were divided into seven languages, according to their birthplace – England, France, Germany, Italy, Aragon, Auvergne and Provence. Each of them was responsible for a specific section of the fortifications. The street has a palace or inn for each language," Aileen added, her face buried deep in the guide book.

Her tourist like enthusiasm for the history of Rhodes Town was clearly not matched by her companion. Sandra's mind was elsewhere. She thought that when she'd suggested it the day before that the trip would take her mind of what she'd discovered about Aileen and her husband. In fact, the more time she spent with Aileen the more it stayed firmly at the front of her mind. Also, she knew that she had to spend almost another two weeks with her, but she had decided that she wasn't going to confront her with it while they were on holiday together. She'd wait until they got back to London. Sandra wasn't someone to rush to address issues with a knee jerk reaction. She was definitely someone who believed revenge was best taken cold, when the person concerned was least expecting it, and when she could be calm and measured in taking that revenge. She'd learned that well in her training.

Nevertheless, that didn't preclude her probing whenever should could, in what she thought was a subtle way, trying to gain as much as she could about Aileen and her husband's affair without giving away that she knew about it. She'd been well trained to do that too.

So, three-quarters of the way up the Street of the Knights they found a small courtyard under an archway that lead to another nice café. Sandra suggested that they stop for a glass of cool white wine. "It'll liven you up, hair of the dog, just one," she suggested to Aileen, who agreed.

As they sat in the shady café courtyard out of the hot midday sun surrounded on three sides by the old medieval stone high walls Aileen once again read some stuff about the history of the place from her guide book. As she did so Sandra saw her chance and took it.

"Yes, it's fascinating. I bet Richard would love this place too. He likes all this medieval history stuff." She knew full well that he didn't at all, but she saw it as a good lead in to mentioning his name and trying to gauge Aileen's reaction, if any.

She watched carefully for Aileen's facial reaction as she finished speaking, but there was none. She kept her head down, peering at the guide book, and merely responded with, "Really, well if he does, then I guess he would love it here, there's so much historical stuff."

There was nothing. Not even a flicker of anything that would suggest her guilt, or even any sign of embarrassment, at the mention of his name. Sandra tried once more later over lunch and another glass of wine after they'd been to the Palace of the Grand Masters.

"He wanted to come you know."

"Who?" Aileen asked, frowning, but knowing precisely who Sandra was referring to.

"Richard, he wanted to come. We had quite an argument about it more than once when I told him I was coming away with you. It seemed like he was determined to come. As I told you before, when you and I first talked about a holiday together, things haven't been that great recently between Richard and me. It's not one of those things you talk about easily though, but at one point I even thought he might be having an affair."

Now Sandra was going as far as she wanted to do at that point, fishing once more to see Aileen's reaction. But again her face was blank, showing no sign of any emotion whatsoever as he responded.

"No, why? Why did you think that? Surely not?"

"Just little things, but sometimes they make you think when they all add up. He's been working away a lot more than he used to for one thing, and working late at the office a lot more."

"Right, but-" Aileen started to say, but Sandra cut her off. She wasn't prepared to go into it too much then, although she did have a bombshell comment, the equivalent of a missile launch, which she was eventually going to throw into their conversation to gauge her friend's reaction.

First though Sandra simply said, "Yep, I guess you're right, surely he's not having an affair. He said work has gone up a notch recently and he's been really busy. It's probably me just over analysing things. You know what I'm like."

"Well, could be, I suppose. You do like to analyse things to death, Sandra."

"Yep, of course, that'd be it, just me being stupid."

Aileen was leaning forward to pick up her glass of white wine and take a sip, thinking that the awkward moment had passed, that she had successfully and skilfully negotiated it, when Sandra unleashed her Exocet missile comment. She did so in a calculated fashion in order to exact the greatest possible revelation in terms of Aileen's reaction.

"Although the sex has all but dried up, he used to be rampant, but now he often doesn't seem interested at all, and I have to initiate it every time. Sometimes he even turns me down, saying he's too tired."

There wasn't even a flicker of a reaction across Aileen's face. Nothing. All she did was raise her eyebrows slightly, trying to look a little embarrassed at what she'd just heard. She tilted her head to one side a bit in some minimal acknowledgement, but then simply responded by somewhat clumsily changing the subject completely, "Let's have one more glass of wine and then I want to go back to that nice silver jewellery shop we saw. I might treat myself."

Sandra wasn't about to let her off that easily and tried one more provocative comment.

"Did you ever think of having an affair when you were married? I did once or twice."

Still there was no great discernible reaction from Aileen. She remained outwardly pretty relaxed and laid back about the whole conversation as she replied by ignoring the part of the question about herself, "You've had plenty of opportunities, all those young guys chasing after you in London on our nights out, and even here in Lindos last night."

At that point Sandra decided that was enough for now. It was as far as she wanted to go with it, for now anyway, although Aileen's reactions and comments hadn't really told her anything more.

10

The seeds of Aileen's Cassandra dilemma

In Greek Mythology Cassandra, a Princess, daughter of King Priam, was provided with the gift of prophecy, but was cursed by Apollo after she refused his romantic advances. The curse was that nobody would believe her warnings and prophecies. She was left with the knowledge of possible future events, but could neither alter them nor convince others of the validity of her predictions.

Aileen's 'Cassandra dilemma' was that she was fully aware of the possible future event of her affair with Richard being discovered by Sandra. Like Cassandra, she knew that event would happen. Eventually it would all come out and she couldn't alter that, or the dreadful consequences that might arise because of it. However, unlike Cassandra she wasn't particularly concerned or perturbed about that happening. On the contrary, that was the way she'd planned it. So, again like Cassandra, she could confidently predict it would occur at some point, because she would make very sure that it did, although she obviously wasn't about to try to convince anyone in her immediate vicinity of that. The only people she'd done that with already – predicted that circumstance – were those who had helped devise the whole exercise and plan with her. Most of all, when it did occur she needed to ensure that she was the one fully in control of how it did so, of the time and place that it did so, and of the dreadful consequences that might follow.

Richard's increasingly reckless actions after they ended the affair added a range of possibilities, a range of choices available to her in terms of how it could be revealed, and where and when. She fully anticipated he would eventually react in the reckless way that he did, and in some ways she encouraged it. It was what she aimed for, what she wanted. He seemed to have less and less concern about Sandra discovering it. In endless constant repetitive angry phone conversations Aileen was subjected to with him it became increasingly obvious that he had become besotted, and not in any way cautious that Sandra might find out what the two of them had been up to. Although, from what she had seen of his character close up during their affair she wondered if besotted was really the right word. From what she knew from her background information on him, obsessive was probably a better way of describing his actions and his needs. He was obviously totally used to getting his own way, getting what he wanted when he wanted it, and cared nothing about anyone else getting hurt in the process.

Just as Cassandra was with Apollo, Aileen was cursed by his obsession, and she was fully aware of the possible danger of future events spiralling out of her control when she read his text to her on that Saturday morning saying he was coming to Lindos to join them for the second week. Being in Lindos at that time on holiday with Sandra was not exactly one of the first or best places and times she would have chosen for her and Richard's affair to be revealed. It wasn't a time or place at all in which she felt sure she could retain control over how and when that happened or over the consequences afterwards.

When she had time to consider it a little more over the next few hours she resigned herself to the fact that she'd simply have to adjust to this different, unforeseen situation and deal with it. It wasn't quite the way she'd planned it to be, but she convinced herself that it really just opened up another possible opportune scenario to do what she aimed to do, and had wanted to do for so long. Adjusting to different unforeseen circumstances and taking advantage of them in the best possible way in order to achieve the overall objective was what she had always been taught to do. Flexibility to accommodate changed circumstances and situations was key; so that was what she decided she had to do. After all, in reality she had very little choice.

In Lindos there was now also, of course, the possible additional complication of her recent meeting with Martin and his obvious attraction to her to take into account in the equation of what she intended to do, and how to achieve it. She'd figure that out later though. Firstly, there was the question of her reaction to Richard's Saturday morning text, and what she knew would be a developing situation with Sandra once she was aware that he was coming to join them. Not that Aileen had any intention of conveying that particular piece of information to her, of course.

"Booked a flight. Arrive Wednesday early evening. Desperate to see you. Need to talk. xx," That was what his text said.

As she read it over her late Saturday morning coffee and scrambled eggs on toast outside Giorgos café her face initially betrayed her anxiety over what she saw on the screen. It rapidly turned to anger as she muttered to herself, "Bollocks! That's not what I planned, not here, not now you wanker," and began to quickly tap out a reply.

"Don't be an idiot, Richard. The three of us here together for a whole week, and in the same villa, are you crazy? From what she's told me here I reckon she already suspects you're up to something, although luckily I don't think she has any idea it was with me. But a week here? She's bound to pick up some things. Don't bloody come!"

A minute after she'd pressed the arrow icon to send it her phone beeped and his reply appeared. He wasn't going to be put off.

"I don't care. I'm coming. It's booked now. I'll text her on Tuesday to let her know. I guess she won't be pleased, but sod it I'm coming. Make sure you look suitably surprised when she tells you. xx"

As she looked up from the screen and reached for her coffee she saw Sandra approaching from thirty yards away down the alleyway opposite. She quickly tapped in a sharp reply to him of, "Fuck you. You're crazy!" and sent it.

She'd have to wait to see his response later now that Sandra had turned up. She knew it would get him angry, and that was exactly what she intended. If he couldn't be put off from coming, then she figured it was best to try and get him turning up angry. She knew that would mean he wouldn't be thinking rationally, making it easier for her to try and manipulate him in what was obviously going to be a tense situation between him, Sandra and her.

"Coffee?" she asked Sandra as she took a seat opposite her at the small table.

"Sure, and is that the remnants of scrambled eggs?

"Yep, it's good."

With that the waitress appeared and Sandra ordered the same as Aileen had.

"More texts?" Sandra asked, trying to appear only mildly curious. As she'd approached Giorgos she'd seen Aileen tapping away at her phone.

"What? Oh yes, bloody work, you know how it is. Did you find what you wanted at the Pharmacy?" she added, trying to change the subject. However, Sandra wasn't about to let her do that, not completely.

"Yes, they had loads of After Sun, but the supermarket had some anyway, so I bought it there. Really, on a Saturday?"

"What? On a Saturday what, Sandra?"

"Work? Calling you on a Saturday, and when you're on holiday? Blimey, that boss of yours likes to get his money's worth doesn't he."

"No, it was only a text, but yes he does like to get his money's worth. He's useless, I'm his P.A. but sometimes I reckon he thinks I'm his bloody wife, or even his nanny. Can't do anything for himself. He's in the office. Some big meeting scheduled for Monday morning and he's working on a presentation and a report he's got to give. He was stressing because he couldn't find a file he wanted on his computer, so he wanted to know if I had a copy on mine."

"And you let him root around on your computer? That's brave and very trusting of you. Hope there's nothing incriminating or embarrassing on there." Sandra was fishing to gauge Aileen's reaction once again.

As the waitress brought Sandra's coffee and Aileen ordered another for herself, her response was cool and measured, giving away nothing. To Sandra it seemed quite clear that her friend had not recognised at all what she was up to.

"No, of course not, it's my computer at work, why would there be anything embarrassing on there?" She even tried to make a joke about it, adding, "And anyway, Sandra, all the incriminating and embarrassing stuff is on my personal computer at home." She let a weak - ultimately false - smile creep across her lips as she made that last remark.

Returning the smile Sandra said, "Yes, of course it is. All that porn you like, I presume you mean."

"Yep, that's it. You know me too well from Uni."

At that point, much to Aileen's unease, her phone beeped again. She quickly picked it up, read the message on the screen, and was relieved as she told Sandra, "It's Martin. He texted me last night wanting to know if we wanted to meet up, but I replied I was too knackered after all day in the sun in Rhodes Town. So, he wants to know now if we want to meet for dinner tonight. He's suggesting Symposio restaurant at eight-thirty. He says it's on the main alley. I think I saw it on the way back to the villa after I left that club with him on Thursday night. It was closed up, but looked nice, an old stone building, but I guess they have a roof terrace. He says the food is excellent."

"Sure, why not. He seems keen on you. A real Greek holiday romance?"

As she tapped a short reply into her phone of, "Ok, see you there at 8.30," she just casually told Sandra, "Not so sure about that, about him, seems a bit too clingy for me."

"He seems keen though, and I can see you well suited to a Professor of Greek Mythology. Just think of all those interesting Greek holidays." Sandra was being ironic as the waitress brought her scrambled eggs.

After a lazy afternoon on Pallas Beach soaking up the rays from the hot sun, interspersed from time to time with cooling off in the clear calm waters of the sea in Lindos Bay, just on eight-thirty that night the two women made their way through the growing darkness of the narrow alleyways to the Symposio restaurant, right in the centre of the village. The evening air was still very warm and the village was filling up with tourists having a pre-dinner drink in some of the bars before going off to the many restaurants.

Already sporting the beginnings of a good dark suntan Sandra had plumped for a plain, sleeveless, short, sheer white dress, which matched perfectly the daytime shimmering white of the Lindos walls.

88

It set off her tan nicely. Aileen wore a similar plain dress, only in deep black, equally complementing her already good dark tan. Given the tricky uneven terrain of the Lindos alleys in places both women had sensibly decided on smart, expensive looking, flat leather strapped sandals.

Symposio was housed in a very imposing old Lindian style stone building. The entrance was through a raised terrace that had three dining tables on one side of it, at which customers could watch people pass by while they eat. Inside there were four more tables and a wrought iron staircase that led up to the roof terrace, where most of the restaurant's dining tables were located. High on the wall outside to the left of the terraced entrance was a digital display that as Aileen and Sandra arrived was displaying the time of eight thirty-five, followed by the temperature of a quite humid, even at that time, twenty-eight degrees.

As two women approached the stone steps to the terrace they spotted Martin chatting at the top of them with a tall, attractive middle-aged woman with long black hair. She was wearing a very striking red and black patterned long dress. He'd decided on another smart looking pair of white shorts for this particular warm Lindos evening, this time with a pale blue polo shirt. He immediately introduced the woman to them as Janis, explaining that she was the 'front of house' person for the restaurant. Just like a number of other people he'd introduced them to over the past couple of days, he pointed out that he'd know Janis for a number of years through his many Lindos visits. She'd left England twenty years before to live and work in Lindos.

Introductions over, Janis guided them inside, suggesting they go up to a table on the roof terrace, to which all three of them readily agreed. At the top of the narrow winding wrought iron stairs there was another round of introductions as they were greeted by the restaurant owner, Filip – another of Martin's Lindos friends of many years.

After the waitress approached their table, and while they scanned the impressive choices on the menu, Martin checked if they were all happy with white wine and ordered a bottle of a good Retsina. It was to be the first, but not the last, bottle they shared over dinner, as another followed later. Much to Martin's pleasure Aileen had seated herself next to him on the same side of the table, with Sandra opposite her. When they were halfway through their respective first courses and making general conversation between the three of them about how lovely Lindos was, his pleasure was increased considerably as he felt Aileen's lower right leg being deliberately rubbed against the calf of his left leg. He turned his head slightly towards her and tried as discreetly as possible to share a slight smile with her without Sandra noticing. Luckily she had her head down focusing on finishing the last part of her Calamari starter from her plate and so never noticed the gentle interaction between her other two dining companions.

The discreet touching beneath the table between Martin and Aileen continued, and actually became more and more frequent throughout the remainder of the meal, so much so that at one point as they were finishing their second bottle of Retsina Martin felt confident enough to place his left hand briefly on Aileen's bare lower thigh beneath the table. His confidence was well founded, as it was now her turn to fleetingly display a discreet accompanying smile to him as she briefly moved her right hand to beneath the table, placed it on his, which was still resting on her lower thigh, and gave his hand a comforting squeeze.

After they'd finished their main courses and declined a desert Martin asked the waitress for the bill. The owner, Filip, brought it, along with a small glass of cold lemoncello for each of them, and then asked, "Where are you three off to now?"

"Antika to start with, I think, and then we'll see, Filip," Martin told him.

As the two women looked at him a little bemused, not sure where it was exactly in relation to where they were at present, Martin informed them, "It's the bar next door. It's nice. An old stone building, similar to this one, but modernised inside, and with a roof garden and a small seated garden area at the back. It's completely different to Pal's and the Courtyard Bar that we were in on Thursday night. It's where those young guys who seemed so impressed with you outside Pal's were off to on Thursday night, Sandra, and invited you to join them, remember?"

"Yes, of course I do, Martin. I never forget young men who try to chat me up." For some reason she winked at him as she replied.

So, they had one drink in Antika after being greeted as they approached the bar by another one of Martin's barman friends, Ledi, followed by the owner, Paniotis. Then, in response to Aileen's, "Where to next?" as they finished their drinks Martin suggested the Atmosphere Bar, explaining that it was right at the top of the village near Lindos Reception, where the coaches dropped off the many holidaymakers transferring from Rhodes Airport.

"It means a few minutes' walk up the slightly inclined alley, but it's a nice bar, and we can sit outside if there's a table free. It's another bar where the view of the Acropolis lit up, and over the village, is spectacular," he told the two women.

"You're the tour guide, Martin, so we'll be guided by you and your choices," Sandra responded, with what Martin thought he detected was a slight sarcastic edge to her voice.

Five minutes later they were sitting down at a free table outside the Atmosphere Bar, all three of them puffing a little at the climb up the slight hill from the centre of the village in the still warm evening Lindos air. Once again, Aileen made immediately for the chair next to Martin on his side of the table. However, on this occasion Martin glanced briefly across at Sandra as they all sat down and thought he detected the slightest of frowns on her face. He began to wonder just what it was that appeared to be contributing to her growing irritation. He certainly wasn't about to ask though, thinking that surely it couldn't be simple jealousy. After all, she hadn't shown any inclination whatsoever to be even the slightest bit friendly with him, let alone anything more. He quickly dismissed it as perhaps just being down to the fact that she didn't want to be playing 'gooseberry' throughout her holiday. Whatever it was, he certainly wasn't going to let it put him off his growing attraction to Aileen, particularly as she seemed to be constantly reacting to that. She was never slow to react and laugh at his funny comments as the evening wore on, and a few times as she looked him straight in the face as they spoke she did that act of tucking her black hair back behind her ear or running her hand through it and tossing it back. He'd once been told – he couldn't remember by who, but knew it was a woman – that those were always good encouraging signs.

This time the initial greeting and introductions in the Atmosphere Bar was with a young blonde English waitress, Sophie, and her older fellow waitress, Jackie This time it was them who both explained, that they knew Martin well from his many Lindos visits.

A few minutes after Sophie took their order of a bottle of Mythos beer for Martin and a Gin and Tonic for Sandra and Aileen it was time for another greeting and introductions as the jovial Greek owner, Stavros, arrived at their table. Stavros was a convivial owner, well known to the many British couples, families, and groups of individuals who returned regularly year after year to his bar.

As Sophie appeared with their drinks and Stavros made his way back inside the bar to serve some customers Sandra appeared a bit more relaxed at least as she complimented their tour guide, "You were certainly right about the view, Martin. It's stunning. Even well worth the climb up the short hill."

He smiled, deciding that his concerns about her frown and comment earlier were just down to his usual slight paranoia.

"Glad you think so. It's a lot worse during the day and in the hot sun, especially around midday, although they do a good breakfast and lunch here. Much cooler at this time of the evening though, or should I say approaching middle of the night as it's already nearly twelve-thirty."

As he told the two women that Sophie was passing their table on her way back into the bar having just served another table their drinks. Overhearing Martin's comment about the time she couldn't resist saying through a grin, "That's early here, Martin, you know that. Glow later?"

"Glow?" Sandra asked.

"A club, I mentioned it the other night in Jack's Courtyard Bar, along with the other club, Arches that Aileen and I went to that night," Martin explained.

As he told Sandra that it was his turn to now feel Aileen's right hand reach down beneath the table and squeeze his left thigh, much to his delight. He presumed she was signalling to him that she remembered fondly what they'd got up to, or nearly got up to before they were interrupted by the sound of footsteps, in the alley late that night as he was walking her back to their villa after Arches.

Leaving her hand there squeezing his thigh she mischievously turned her head to face him, and looking him straight in the eyes, said, "Oh yes, I remember Glow. You pointed it out to me as we went up to that bar, Lindos By Night, after Sandra went home to bed, didn't you?"

Trying, with great difficulty, to remain as calm as possible he replied, "Yes, that's it, opposite Jack's bar."

Fortunately, Sophie helped him out of his predicament, although the look she gave him as she spoke suggested that she had noticed, figured out quite well and quickly, what was going on.

"So, no doubt see the three of you in there later, Martin?" Sophie asked.

Before he could answer though, Sandra intervened, "Not me, not tonight. Going to be a kill joy again. This drink and bed for me. Too tired I'm afraid. Another night, thanks, Sophie."

As Sandra gave her apologies Martin felt the pressure from Aileen's continuing squeezing right hand increase.

The waitress must have once again noticed something in his facial reaction, however slight, as she simply said, "Okay, Martin, just the two of you then. See you there later," followed by a slight tilt of the head and a knowing sardonic smile to herself as she walked away and back inside the bar.

Just after one o'clock the music stopped inside the Atmosphere Bar, as the local by-law required. They finished their drinks, paid the bill, and said goodbye to Stavros, Jackie, and Sophie, who told Martin again, "See you and Aileen later in Glow."

Martin and Aileen walked back down the hill into the village with Sandra, saying, "Goodnight" to her as they left her by Pal's Bar. They offered to walk her the rest of the way back to the villa, but she declined their offer, saying she would be fine.

Pal's was still pretty packed with late drinkers, including some of the Brit and Greek bar and restaurant workers. A couple of them who Martin knew tried to persuade him and Aileen to come in for one drink as they spied them passing. He almost gave in, but much to what seemed once more to be Aileen's obvious pleasure as she held and squeezed his hand firmly, he eventually declined, and they headed off towards the steps by the Courtyard Bar and along the alley to the entrance to Glow.

Behind the club entrance archway with open wooden doors was a small courtyard with a couple of cushioned benches in alcoves. On one of them just to the left was a heavily entwined young couple, obviously enjoying each other's late night company. As they spotted them Aileen, who had continued holding Martin's hand from outside Pal's, gave it another firm squeeze, accompanied by a nod in the direction of the couple and a broad smile to Martin whose hand she was now gripping very firmly. Before he could react she said softly, "When in Rome," released his hand, reached up behind his head to pull his face firmly towards hers, and planted a long lingering kiss eagerly on his lips.

As they finished he told her, "Well, technically, it should be 'when in Greece here', shouldn't it?"

She allowed a slight smile to spread across her lips and then placed the index finger of her right hand on his lips, telling him, "Well you didn't seem that worried just now which country we were in, Martin, but let's see this club you promised me now, before I decide it's time for bed."

"Okay, although if you're that tired, we could always give this a miss and come back another night. It's open every-"

He never got to finish. Once again she placed her finger on his lips and interrupted with, "Who said I was tired?" This time her comment was followed by a very mischievous looking smile and raised eyebrows as she took hold of his hand once more, headed towards the entrance and added, "Come on, let's get one more drink and check out this club of yours."

11

After Glow, and Martin's afterglow

Glow was fairly crowded already, although the clientele was mainly tourists at that time. "It will get much busier after about two, when the many bar and restaurant workers in the village turn up once they've finished their shifts and cleared up," Martin told her as they emerged through the club entrance. "There's a few young Brits who come to work in the village for the summer, but they'll also be some of the Greek workers who will turn up."

Now it was his turn to take her hand as he made his way through a couple of groups of three and four tourists towards the right-hand end of the bar that stretched along the back wall of the rectangular club. This time the introduction, hugs and handshakes were with the owner, Michalis, sat at that end of the bar, and then his son, Giannis, working behind the bar.

After half-an-hour, as they finished their drink, Martin asked her, "Are you still not tired? Do you want another?"

She reached up to pull his head down slightly to whisper in his ear above the loud music. He was shocked by her blunt, forthright answer, "No, not another drink, thanks, but yes I am still not tired, so I want us to go to bed now."

She moved her mouth away from his ear and stared straight into his eyes with her wide open piercing dark brown eyes. He gulped visibly, nodded his head slightly, and eventually could only manage a solitary word, an obviously slightly embarrassed, "Okay."

She let out a small mischievous laugh, revelling in his evident embarrassment. She enjoyed that, not just with him, but with other men that she'd been involved with or who had tried to chat her up in various bars in the past. She enjoyed disorientating them, taking them out of their comfort zone of being in charge. She preferred to be the one in charge, at least as much as possible. That was one of the parts of the relationship game that she enjoyed the most.

At first it felt awkward on the way to his flat after they left the club. At least he was awkward, felt awkward. She most certainly didn't though, far from it. She knew precisely what she wanted, and she wanted it now. She was determined. Driven, it seemed. In effect, he was left with very little choice. He was overwhelmed by her. A couple of times in the alleys on the way to his flat she stopped walking, grabbed a fistful of his polo shirt, and forcibly pulled him towards her to kiss him passionately, although only for a few seconds. Then she just pulled away from him, grabbed his hand and told him firmly, "Come on!"

His feeling of awkwardness, unease even, continued as she grabbed a handful of his polo shirt and again kissed him passionately in the inner courtyard in front of the door to his flat. She repeated it once more when they were inside, in what passed as a lounge in the flat, barely furnished as it was with a couch, a small table and one chair.

She pointed at an open door off the lounge and asked, or rather said, looking for confirmation from him, "That's the bedroom." Without waiting for his reply she grabbed his hand and led him through the open door.

He went to turn on the ceiling light, but she told him firmly, "No, leave it." So, he switched on the small bedside light as she said, "Good, a large double bed, plenty of room for us. I like plenty of room."

He guessed she wasn't talking about plenty of room in relation to sleeping.

"Yes, it's a decent size, unlike most beds in tourist accommodation in Lindos. Although, it's a bit firm, bordering on hard, and the mattress is thin, and a bit-"

He was waffling nervously, although he couldn't figure out why. Maybe it was merely her aggression, taking him by surprise and unsettling him. She didn't let him finish his description of the bed. She put her hand on his shoulder and gently turned him around to face her. Initially he thought she was going to kiss him again, but instead she reached behind his back with both her hands and pulled his polo shirt up over his head to remove it completely. Momentarily she planted two soft kisses on his chest and then looked up into his eyes with those stunning dark brown do-eyes of hers. While she remained staring up at him her eyes appeared to be darting and exploring every part of his face. Without moving her head or her eyes from that she simultaneously unfastened his shorts and allowed them to drop to the floor.

She'd discovered from a seemingly frivolous conversation between him, Sandra and her earlier in the evening that he never wore boxer shorts, or indeed anything beneath shorts. She pulled him close so she could immediately feel him aroused against her.

After a few seconds she whispered an invitation now for him to undress her, "You already appear to like what you see, Martin. Don't be nervous. Your turn now, why don't you reveal a little more of me, see if you like that even more. I'm sure you will."

This was a very confident woman, and he certainly did like what he saw. Although it was not something that he would ever consider telling a woman of a certain age for fear of annoying them, or even getting a slap, she did have a very finely toned body and figure for a woman of her age. That was what was racing through his brain at that particular moment anyhow, even if he wasn't about to allow those words to come out of his mouth. It was a body perhaps on the final edge of being described as lithe, but still more than eligible for such a description. Her perfectly proportioned breasts were firm and nicely protruding. She exhibited no sign of any deteriorating growing stomach. It was flat. It was obvious she was a regular gym visitor, or at least cared about her fitness. Even without heels and shoes her legs were nicely shaped and already sported a good attractive shade of tan.

He moved his right hand to one of the thin straps of her dress and briefly planted a soft kiss on her bare suntanned shoulder. Then with his index finger he pulled the strap off her left shoulder, then the one on her right shoulder, and then slowly slid her short low cut black dress down over her breasts, her slim hips, and her bare thighs to the floor. As the dress landed beneath her and she stepped out of the crumpled heap of it at her feet to kick off her sandals she took hold

97

of his right hand in hers and guided his fingers firmly to the top of her skimpy black lace panties.

"And?" she told him as she once again fixed a stare up at him with her dark brown do-eyes.

He didn't need any further explanation or encouragement and he gently smoothly pulled the panties down over her thighs with his right hand. Now she stepped out of those as they hit the floor, moving immediately to place both hands on his chest and push him back down onto the bed. As his back hit the bed she lowered her finely formed bare body down on top of him and pressed her lips firmly to his in a long, lingering, passionate kiss. For a brief swift moment he thought she was going to take him inside her instantly, but she had other ideas.

She told him in no uncertain manner, in a clearly decisive tone that suggested this was a woman who liked to be in control and knew precisely what she wanted, "Not yet, wait."

She rolled off him to lie on her back close alongside him. In turn, he rolled over to this time lay on top of her, all the while exchanging passionate kisses between the pair of them. Eventually, as he stroked her thick dark black hair with his right hand while remaining lying on top of her she placed her right hand on his left shoulder and then proceeded to gently, but firmly, push him down towards the lower part of her body. Simultaneously she whispered softly telling him, instructing him almost, exactly what she wanted him to do, expected him to do to her, or rather, from the way she said it, for her.

He slid down her expectant tanned body, pausing to kiss her breasts, the smooth pit of her slight stomach, and the small mound beyond it. Eventually his face reached the smooth bare place at the top of her legs. He stopped for a brief moment of satisfying anticipation, for both of them. Within seconds she reached down with her right hand, grabbed a clump of his hair and pulled his face fully into her sensitive spot between her upper thighs. As the end of his tongue slowly protruded from his already moist mouth and finally delicately reached its treasured destination she let out a small gasp, followed by a short low moan of anticipated pleasure. She didn't intend to wait long for that, her pleasure. Within a minute the circulatory movement of his tongue brought her to a crashing climax, accompanied by a tightening of her thighs around his head, rhythmic convulsions of her whole body, and a much louder scream of pleasure. She had quickly covered his face with the smell and taste of her.

As he went to remove his face from between her thighs she again grabbed a clump of his hair with one hand while placing two fingers of her other hand inside herself briefly. Then she removed them and wiped them slowly and deliberately over his lips and chin. Finally, she placed the two fingers in her own mouth and licked them slowly and deliberately.

"Now you taste and smell of me, but I want to taste of me too," she told him softly.

He made to roll off of her, but as he did so she rolled with him to sit astride his lower body, telling him as she did so, "I want more, again, more, and I want you inside me again, but not your tongue."

He was still hard as she guided him inside her, manipulated and then slowly sat down firmly on him.

"Control yourself," she started to tell him, "Wait until I tell you when."

Although it was undoubtedly a pleasurable experience for him, he was a little discomforted at how forceful, even demanding, she was. His concern was only added to when he tried to sit up a little while still inside her and she reacted by reaching down and placing the palm of her left hand firmly on his chest, pushing him back down flat on the bed, while continuing to slowly rock back and forth and up and down on what he had inside her. Almost as disconcerting for him was the slight grin on her face throughout, which only widened into a broad smile as the palm of her hand pushed him back down flat on the bed. She followed that by grabbing his right wrist and lifting his hand up to place it on her left breast, forcing him to make a circular motion with it as she did so.

Intermittently as she rocked back and forth her face would contort, even as if in pain, and then she would tell him, again firmly, almost shouting "Wait! Don't you … wait … you just wait …. wait till I tell you!"

Gradually her rocking movement got faster and more frantic.

When the winter storms sometimes came roaring into Lindos Bay in November, whipping up large, crashing, incessant waves rolling into the bay, it could feel like the sea and the elements were completely out of control. A total contrast to the calm, clear sea in Lindos Bay in midsummer. She was now just like one of those winter storms, building up to an uncontrollable crescendo, which in some cases of the winter storms could only have consequences of damage and destruction. She was completely out of control, out of control of herself at least, yet managing, indeed seemingly determined to be, in absolute control of him. It was a total contrast to the earlier midsummer evening calm, almost reserved, cool character she had exuded.

Eventually, after what was around five minutes, but to him appeared a lot longer as it seemed the air got even hotter and more steamy, her moans got louder and longer, the rocking got even more frantic, and the contortions on her face became more frequent, until finally she exclaimed, almost ordered him, "Yes, yes, yes, now, now!"

Her thighs tightened once again as she threw her head back in obvious ecstasy. After more convulsions of her whole body she slumped forward on top of his upper body and then immediately rolled off him to lay flat on her back next to him on the bed.

After a minute of silence between them she half turned towards him while brushing some damp strands of her hair from across her face. Even with the air conditioning rattling at full throttle their exertions, particularly hers, had produced a glistening layer of sticky sweat covering parts of their upper bodies and within her trailing long hair. As she turned on to her side while still laying there alongside him he was transfixed, almost in a trance, partly over what had just happened, but also focusing on the individual lines of sweat that trickled and shimmered down her tanned body like the rays from the hot sun in the clear Lindos sky hitting the calm, crystal blue sea in the bay. He lay there on his back, motionless with his own beads of sweat trickling down his still heaving, breathless chest.

Between continuing deep breaths, the consequence of what they had just done, she eventually asked, "What … what happened … you didn't-"

"No, no ... no, I didn't. It's not usual. I usually do. Don't know why. I'm sure it'll be alright next time. As long as you did though? I'm sure you did. It certainly seemed like you did, and more than once."

He did know why, or at least he thought he did. Her whole attitude, aggression, and actions had somehow discomforted him, disconcerted him. Not something he had expected, but then he hadn't quite expected her to be like that, although he still couldn't really completely fathom out why he had been so discomforted. Why should he be? She obviously enjoyed sex a lot and so did he, so why should there be a problem? Whatever the answer to that particular conundrum, from what they'd just done, or to be more accurate what she'd just done, he was certain of one thing. This was one determined woman, who clearly liked to be in control at all times; control of herself and whoever she happened to be with.

While he was quickly running that through his brain she answered his question about her obvious enjoyment.

"Oh, yep, of course, I always do. So, you think there will be a next time then, Martin, do you, me and you? Bit presumptuous?"

She had thrown him off balance once again, deliberately so it seemed. Once again the thought that this was obviously a woman who liked to be in charge was running through his brain. Perhaps it was the result of what had happened to her with her ex-husband and the Czech twenty-two year old, he wondered.

"Well, I ...err ... I just thought we're going to be here in Lindos for another week or so and well ... err-"

But he never got a reply straightaway. Instead, she quickly got up from the bed in total silence, dressed, and then leaned down to kiss him briefly while he remained laying on the bed. Finally, she simply told him in a quite 'matter of fact' way, "Yes, we'll see. I better go. It's late and Sandra will be wondering where I am if she wakes up and finds I'm not in the villa."

Before he could even get up from the bed she was gone, out the door of the flat, across the courtyard and through the door into the alleyway outside.

He lay there for a full five minutes or more, unsure about what had just happened, bemused and confused. Yet, somehow, and for some reason he couldn't fathom or comprehend, he had actually enjoyed it, more than enjoyed it, and knew instantly he wanted more, wanted it all over again.

She'd had an overwhelming effect on him, in more ways than one. He hadn't felt like that in a long time. In fact, the only other time he'd been so disorientated by a woman - his feelings knocked sideways, out of kilter - had been just over five years before in Havana. He'd gone there for a week for a break in February, and some sunshine relief from the British winter. Havana was an infectious city anyway, and she was the total embodiment of that – vibrant and full of life. Banesa was how she introduced herself to him in a bar late one night in the part of the city known as Old Havana. She followed that quickly by explaining that in English her name would be Vanessa. But she definitely wasn't English. Her Cuban character shone through immediately. Initially he thought she might be a prostitute about to proposition him in a bar. But, as later events between them proved, very soon he was sure she wasn't. She was too innocent to be that, and at no point did she ever ask him for money. She sparkled, and that wasn't just her smile. Like Aileen's, her eyes were bright and wide, with deep brown pupils, and full of movement as she seemed to be studying intently every part of his face, every growing crease. The most striking part of her appearance though was her jet black, dark as the night, big hair. It wasn't so much curly as unruly. Yet it was an obviously well managed unruly effect, if there was such a thing. She played with it constantly, running her fingers through it and occasionally pushing it back or up on to the top of her head as they spoke. Her English wasn't great, but then nor was his Spanish. Somehow though, they communicated for almost two hours. Her smooth as silk tanned skin glowed, just like her character. She told him she was twenty-six, at least that was what he could make out, thought she was telling him, in Spanish.

Her body was complete, in her prime, or at least approaching it. Deep down he knew that ultimately he couldn't be with her, not forever anyway. He knew he could be with her temporarily, but that was not what he really wanted. What he really wanted just wasn't possible. Realistically he knew that. It was a beautiful agony that nevertheless was never going to put him off from trying to find a way for them to be together. Even with his ex-wife at the start he had never felt like this, and when that ended in divorce he never thought, even fleetingly, that the opportunity of such deep feelings as these would ever arise. But with Banesa it had, and it consumed him in crashing, soul destroying waves of emotion in vibrant Havana. He felt that now something similar was happening to him in Lindos with Aileen.

Ironically, considering his comparison with Aileen's eyes now, the bar he met Banesa in was in a Havana street in the Old Town called O'Reilly. She had an instantaneous mesmerising effect on him. He was totally consumed by her striking looks, her charm, and her innocent effervescence. She explained to him that she didn't have much to her life. Materialism wasn't an option in her life in Cuba, even though she had what she termed a good job as a receptionist in one of the large central Havana hotels. Confirming her comment that that she didn't have much to her life, and that materialism wasn't an option for her, the night they met she wasn't exactly dressed in expensive clothes. Beneath her big dark striking hair she wore a simple black and white patterned t-shirt and cut off denim shorts. Her grey canvas shoes were flat. She had a single thin gold chain around her neck and medium sized gold coloured circular earrings. Despite her comments about her Cuban life's lack of materialism her dress exuded a simplistic perfect charm, well suited to her character.

After she'd told him what her job was she asked what he did. She looked a bit surprised, intimidated perhaps, when he informed her he was a Professor of Greek Mythology at a university in London. So, he quickly added that his hobby was writing, and that he was trying to finish a first novel and get it published.

"Like Hemingway," she asked with a wonderful cheeky smile that completely melted him.

"Not quite, Hemingway," he eventually told her after a deep breath and a small laugh.

"He spent a lot of time here, you know that?" she asked.

"Yes, of course, I've seen he's everywhere here in Havana. He spent over ten years here I think. A national icon, or should that be a national treasure, perhaps?"

"Both, he's both, like Fidel and Che," she agreed. "Hemmingway loved Cuba, especially Havana. There are lots of photos of him with Fidel. They liked each other a lot. Similar rebels, is the way I think you'd say it in English, but yes, he loved Havana."

"Not surprised," Martin agreed, although his admiration for Havana had much more to do with the vision in front of him that he was conversing with than any thoughts of rebellion or revolution.

By the time they had stumbled through their mixed conversation of broken English and Spanish for two hours he'd totally succumbed. He was infatuated, instantly in love with her. He knew that was crazy, but couldn't help himself. Finally, on the penultimate night of his holiday they slept together in his hotel room, and again the following night. He left to return to London, but flew back to Havana to see her a week later. This time he stayed for three weeks, the Easter holiday break at his university in London. But instead of spending the whole time in Havana, they went to the coast, to the resort of Varadero with its beautiful long stretch of sandy beach and clear blue sea. They spent two wonderful weeks there. She had never been. As a Cuban she never had the chance. They stayed in the Hotel Blau, a large international chain hotel, and at the end of the first week she told him she'd never been happier. Deep down he knew that it couldn't last though, and in reality so did she. He couldn't stay forever, and she would never get to leave Cuba, be allowed to. He went back to Havana once more at the end of June when the semester and exam period ended at his university. But it wasn't the same. The sadness of the obstacles of their different lives and different countries overwhelmed them both. Finally, after much agonising and talking endlessly, at the end of that week they both agreed to reluctantly end it.

He knew it was the worst decision to make, to finish with Banesa, or rather him and Banesa agreeing to end it. For a few years after that he'd resigned himself to being alone, that nothing could be as good as it had been with Banesa. Now though, there was Aileen.

12

Sunday 26th June, 2016

As Martin finally woke and raised himself from his bed the next day, immediately flinging open the shutters to his bedroom, the burning midday sun in the clear Lindos sky was bouncing brightly off the white walls of the alley outside. It was hot, blisteringly hot, unusually hot, even for late June.

The exceptional heat had begun to build up the evening before, instead of cooling off a little in the June evenings as it usually did. Even the shirts of the local Greek waiters had become soaked with sweat, drenched, as they climbed the stairs to the restaurant rooftops carrying their large trays full of plates with the evening meals of the tourist diners. The hot evening air was still, with no wind at all, causing the humidity to build up. In most of the bars it was okay. The full blast air conditioning units saw to that. In some of the holiday relationships, however, no doubt the sticky temperature had been reproduced in a steamy, sweaty night, or at least part of the night, even with the air conditioning in the apartments.

Martin's had been one of those, even if only briefly. Now, over a quickly made coffee in the small kitchen of his flat he was reflecting on what had happened between him and Aileen, and considering what his next move should be. He was obviously very pleased over what had happened, but in his usual indecisive way he couldn't decide immediately what he should do next, how to play it with her. Instead of pondering endlessly over that, he decided that an afternoon on Pallas Beach and a cooling swim or two would help him determine that. And anyway, he may see her there on the beach with Sandra, and, if he did, he could determine his next move depending on Aileen's reaction. Play it by ear, he told himself. But, if he didn't come across them on the beach he'd text her later to see if she wanted to meet up again that night.

So, he grabbed his swim shorts, pulled on a t-shirt and his flip flops, picked up his towel and stuffed it into his rucksack to head to the beach, stopping only at Giorgos on the way for a quick cooked breakfast, fresh orange juice and a cappuccino.

When he finally made it down to the quite crowded, beautifully white sanded small Pallas Beach early in the afternoon and quickly scanned along it the two women were nowhere to be seen. To some degree he was relieved. At least there was no option for him to go marching up to them on their sunbeds and risk an embarrassingly awkward moment with Aileen. The way she had somewhat abruptly left his bed and his flat last night left him totally unsure of what her reaction to him was likely to be now, the next day. He briefly thought about texting her at that point informing her he was on Pallas, but decided that would appear a little too keen. So, he settled for getting a bottle of very cold, chilled water from Jack's supermarket at the back of the beach, finding a vacant sunbed and parasol, and, after a quick swig of the water, going straightaway for a cooling swim in the calm, clear sea in Lindos Bay.

Fifteen minutes later as he collapsed onto the towel draped on the sunbed, his body still wet from the swim, he reached into his rucksack to check his phone. Still nothing. No message from her. This was growing more and more difficult. It was completely against his nature to continue to desist and not send her a text there and then. It was approaching two-thirty in the afternoon now, but perhaps she was just catching up on her sleep. And she did have quite a few Gin and Tonics last night, so maybe even a slight hangover was bothering her.

Not that he knew, but that wasn't the case at all. It had, indeed, been approaching three-thirty when she tumbled into her bed in her room in the villa. Sandra had made it to her bed quite a few hours earlier, so she was ready by ten that morning to hit the beach and work on her tan. She knocked and then appeared in Aileen's room clutching a large mug of coffee for her just after ten, telling her, "I knocked because I wasn't sure if you'd be alone."

Aileen brushed her hair back off her face and tossed her head back a little as she sat up in bed and let out a small chuckle, before taking the mug of coffee from Sandra as she sat down on the side of Aileen's bed.

"Thanks, why wouldn't I be?"

"Well, when I left you two last night I'd have bet money that you were going to end up in bed together. Don't forget I know you, Aileen, known you a long time. You've never been slow to-"

"You'd have won your bet. We did, of course we did," she interrupted and confirmed, pausing to take a much needed sip of the coffee before continuing. "But this isn't the only bed in Lindos you know, so why would we come here. Martin does have a flat, and a bed, of his own."

She shifted her lower body at little uneasily as she added, "Even if it is a little hard and uncomfortable, big though, big enough anyway." As she finished she smiled a knowing smile at Sandra.

"I'm guessing a hard bed wasn't really a problem, Aileen. I don't suppose you actually did much sleeping in it. What time did you get back here? Any idea? I never heard you come in."

Aileen took a deep breath, another sip of coffee, and then grinned as she told her friend, "No, no sleeping. I left soon after we'd … you know. Got back here sometime after three, I guess."

"And?" Sandra asked.

"And what, Sandra?"

"You know precisely what. Did you have a good time? Was it good? Was he good?"

"I always make sure I have a good time. Can't speak for Martin, of course. You'll have to ask him that yourself." She smiled once again as she made that remark. "He seemed happy enough though. Bit quiet when I left, probably because that was a bit abrupt, the way I left. I didn't say much. Just a quick kiss, a 'see you', and then I left. I like to do that. Leave them guessing. Nice walk through the empty village in the darkness, though. It really is a beautiful place."

"Wanting more?"

"More what, Sandra?"

"Leave them wanting more. Keep them keen. That's what you do, isn't it? Anyway, just be careful what you're doing with him. I'm sure you won't, but be careful what you say to him. Don't be careless with even the smallest thing you say to him. You know the score,

107

and you don't really know him at all, or even if he's what he says he is. Just remember your past, Aileen."

"I know, I know, I'm not that stupid, but what makes you say that about me, wanting more, keep them keen?"

Through the continuing haze of her slight hangover Aileen was a little taken aback, wondering again in the back of her mind if Sandra had gathered some sort of inkling about her and Richard, and their affair.

Sandra was, indeed, taking the opportunity to play just a little bit of a probing psychological game with her friend's guilty secret. In her own mind though, she was hardly displeased that Aileen had found someone new to climb into bed with. However, Sandra's intended mind games in relation to Aileen and her new man, Martin, could wait. They would be put on ice and stored away for future use at a time she would choose to be the best to inflict the most damage, exact the most revenge on Aileen..

Instead, rather than respond to Aileen's "keep them keen" question she decided to change the subject. "So, are you ready to hit the beach, or do you need more sleep?"

Aileen took a final gulp of her coffee and then replied, "No, I'm fine, can sleep on the beach, and a swim will help. Need to grab some food though. I presume they'll be somewhere to get some on the beach, and I suppose it's pointless asking if it's hot and sunny."

"It's bloody hot. Temperature app on my phone says thirty four degrees already, and it's only just gone ten. Forecast says it's going to be around forty. You'd better put plenty of that P20 sun lotion of yours on. Shall we try the Main Beach? It probably won't be as crowded as that other one we went to on Thursday, Pallas."

"Sure, give me fifteen minutes to jump in the shower and get sorted."

"Okay, no rush," Sandra told her as Aileen reached for her phone on charge on the bedside table and turned it on. Just as Sandra reached the bedroom door Aileen's phone beeped.

"See, he's keen, leaving him abruptly and wanting more obviously worked," Sandra commented.

Aileen looked up from the screen of her phone and replied, with a slight hesitation in her voice, "Err ... oh yes ... see what you mean. It obviously did."

As Sandra closed the bedroom door behind her Aileen swung her legs out from under the solitary sheet and sat on the side of the bed naked staring at the phone screen intently once more. But the text message wasn't from Martin. It was from Richard.

"I need you. I want you. I want us, want there to be an us. I've decided, and I know you want it to. Xx"

"Shit!" she muttered quietly to herself, followed by, "What now? I need to do some serious thinking today about what to do now about all this shit and this wanker."

"You haven't gone back to bed have you?" Sandra shouted through the door.

"Fuck it! He can wait," Aileen muttered quietly to herself once more. "No, just coming for the shower. Just a text from Martin, as you guessed. I'll reply when we get to the beach. Make him wait. That'll keep him keen still."

She heard Sandra laugh the other side of the door, turned off her phone, pulled on a t-shirt and headed out of the bedroom to the shower.

13

Sunday afternoon and evening: text bombardment

The village was already beginning to fill up with day-tripper tourists from the coach trips from Rhodes Town and around the island by the time the two women made their way through the white-washed alleyways to the Main Square. Consequently, by the time they reached the donkey station for the donkey 'Lindos taxis', just before the square, negotiating a way through the crowds of curious tourists was frustrating. So, although it only took them a couple of minutes to get to that point from their villa, it took a little longer to negotiate the tourist hordes there, get across the square, and onto the dusty dirt track gentle hill down to the Main Beach.

Lindos Main Beach was a long strip of pale yellow sand stretching right along one side of the beautiful bay. At the back of the beach were a selection of restaurants, cafes, and bars that survived largely from the beach tourist daytime lunch trade. The beach sloped gently down into the clear, calm sea, enabling the tourist bathers to glide easily into the shimmering shallow water, warmed nicely by the hot sun above. There were already a good number doing so all along the busy beach at that time in mid-morning. Because of its length though, the beach never felt crowded within its rows of sunbeds and parasols, or in the warm sea with the bathers intermingled with the white pedalos.

By the time the two women got to the bottom of the slight hill, found a couple of free sunbeds and a parasol, and paid the Greek guy at the small stall at the back of the beach for them, they were both suffering from the incessant heat of the bright sun now high in the clear blue sky. Sweat was dripping off them and soaked patches were clearly visible on their t-shirts.

After Sandra pulled hers over her head she suggested to Aileen, "Swim?"

"Definitely, I need to cool down," she agreed.

Sandra couldn't help noticing though as she glanced behind her on her way towards the water's edge over the hot sand that Aileen had firstly taken her phone from her beach bag and purposefully turned it off.

They swam for twenty minutes. The sea was warm, but it still cooled their hot bodies after the walk. As they both collapsed onto the shaded sunbeds Aileen reached into her bag and turned on her phone. Immediately it beeped, signifying another text. It was from Richard, although when Sandra asked if it was Martin again she lied, telling her, "Yep, I guess it's because I hadn't replied to his earlier one."

At that point Aileen decided she needed to put her phone on silent, which proved to be a good move as she got nine more texts from Richard over the next half-an-hour. All of them were on the same theme of, "I need you, want you, want us to be together. I've decided. xx"

She ignored them all, not least because she didn't feel exactly very comfortable sat on a sunbed next to Sandra texting her husband. Even she couldn't deal with that sort of awkwardness. There was eventually one other text later though that was not from Richard, but actually was from Martin. He simply wrote, "Meet tonight?"

Around half-an-hour later she took her phone out of her beach bag, told Sandra she was going to one of the cafes at the back of the beach to get some food, and asked if she wanted anything. Sandra replied, "Just a bottle of water, thanks. I'll get some food later. You can check out what they've got first."

After she got to one of the cafes and ordered a tuna baguette, a cappuccino and a couple of bottles of water, she replied to Martin's text, while continuing to ignore Richard's by now multitude. However, with all the hassle from Richard, and trying to decide within her overall plan what to do about that and his impending visit, she didn't feel she could cope with meeting up with Martin so quickly, and more than likely ending up in bed with him again so soon. So, she replied, "Not tonight, should spend some time with Sandra, said I'd show her Lindos By Night."

He wasn't put off that easily, however, and replied immediately, "Shall I join the two of you?"

She knew she had to prioritise. She needed time and space to try and think about, revise, her intended approach to the rapidly developing Richard situation. So, she really couldn't be bothered for the moment with Martin's obvious eager, seemingly needy, advances. She replied curtly, "No, I said, not tonight."

The abruptness of her last text threw him a bit. Now he was confused. She was definitely blowing hot and cold, and the hot was certainly last night. But perhaps he'd totally misread the situation. Maybe for her it was just a one night holiday bit of fun. However, all through the previous evening she certainly hadn't given that impression. On the contrary, she'd been keen, and it was her who bluntly told him in Glow, "I want us to go to bed now".

He tried to put it out of his mind as he spent a lazy afternoon sunbathing and swimming on Pallas Beach, grabbing a couple of cans of thirst quenching Mythos beer and a bottle of water. By the time he'd got back to his flat from the beach at just after seven, showered, shaved and pulled on a clean polo shirt and white shorts he still hadn't heard anything more from her. He decided to go and grab a pizza at Nikos by Bar 404, and once more try to put her out of his mind. After the pizza he went to Pal's for a couple of beers and then to Jack's Courtyard Bar for a couple more. He was trying to ignore the lack of communication from Aileen as much as he could, although that was hardly helped by Jack asking him as soon as he entered the Courtyard where his women friends were, "From the other night".

He shrugged his shoulders and replied, "Not sure, LBN I think."

In the end, after another beer, his anxiety got the better of him, and at around midnight he decided he'd just go to LBN anyway. Why shouldn't he? It was a bar he knew well, and the staff there knew him well. So, wasn't it only natural that he might turn up there at some point in the evening?

As he climbed the first flight of stairs from the entrance to LBN he saw his friend, Angelos, who he'd introduced Aileen to on Thursday evening, standing at the top of the second flight of stairs up to the top bar. He stopped to talk to him while carefully scanning behind him to see if he could spot Aileen and Sandra. In fact, they were both sat at the small bar, obviously being entertained in conversation by Panos, the barman. As they had their backs to where Martin was chatting to Angelos they hadn't seen him arrive.

When Angelos finally got round to pointing out to him, "The woman you came up here with on Thursday night is over there," he decided to take the plunge and go over to them. Any initial awkwardness he may have felt was alleviated a little by Panos, who he also knew well, who spotted him a few yards away from the bar and called out, "Martin," as a welcome. The two women turned around slightly on their bar stools, but while Sandra said, with a smile, "Hi, Martin," Aileen merely offered a very brief nod of acknowledgement and turned back immediately to face the bar. Although, he only got to see it for the briefest of seconds Martin was perfectly able to see from the look on her face that Aileen was not best pleased.

Panos gave him his bottle of Mythos, and at least the short conversation Martin had with him while he went about his work preparing cocktail orders from the waitresses provided the Englishman with some relief from the obvious annoyance and unhappy vibes he was getting from Aileen. Despite the continuing heat of the Lindos evening, the atmosphere emanating from her towards Martin was decidedly frosty. Now he was really confused.

She wasn't happy at all that despite what she'd written in her reply to his text he'd still ignored it and turned up there. Basically, she was far too preoccupied with the thought of bloody Richard turning up in a few days and how she was going to handle that new, unforeseen situation. Martin ignoring her text reply wasn't her being in control of all aspects of the developing situation at all. She didn't like that at all.

After an awkward half-an-hour spent chatting with Panos, and a few brief conversations with Sandra about how beautiful the view of the lit up Acropolis was from there, Martin took the hint and decided to retire back to Jack's and then Arches. Needless to say, there was no chance of another passionate episode with Aileen that night for him.

14

The second time

Despite Aileen's obvious coolness and apparent anger with him at Lindos By Night on Sunday night it wasn't actually by any means the end of Martin's passionate encounters with her. Much to his growing confusion it happened again the very next night, Monday. That afternoon he did see both her and Sandra, this time on St. Paul's Beach, the small beach in the stunning bay on the edge of the village. St. Paul's was always popular with certain groups of tourists, especially some of the younger ones or those in their thirties and forties who returned to Lindos year after year, sometimes a couple of times each summer. It really was a beautiful setting, the entrance to the bay being between two high rock cliffs, and the shallow, calm sea water was a transparent pale blue. It was a favourite spot for weddings, a key part of the Lindos wedding industry. There was a charming traditional small Greek Orthodox Chapel at one end of the beach. As with all three Lindos beaches, St. Paul's was approached down a quite steep slope at one end of the bay. The chapel was on an area of slightly raised ground at the bottom.

Martin didn't go to St. Paul's until mid-afternoon. He actually chose to go to that beach that afternoon because he didn't think Aileen and Sandra knew of it. Consequently, being wary after Aileen's obvious coolness at LBN the night before, he decided it was best to leave her and not bother her for a day or two. He thought he was very unlikely to bump into the two women if he went to St. Paul's instead of Pallas or the Main Beach. However, he was wrong. As he reached the bottom of the slope leading to the beach he spotted Aileen and Sandra sitting on the clear blue water's edge as it lapped gently over their legs. This time Aileen seemed like a completely different person from the one the night before who had given him the cold shoulder. As soon as she saw him she waved him over to them, telling him they had a couple of sunbeds and a parasol a row back from the water's edge and pointing them out, then adding that she thought one bed next to theirs was free, so he should grab it.

He was pleasantly surprised, found the sunbed, pulled off his t-shirt and went back to join them sitting on the water's edge. Within minutes Sandra left them to it and went back to her sunbed.

"I didn't think you knew about this beach," he told Aileen.

"So, you came down here thinking to avoid us then? Sandra's friend Gill told her about it, you know the one who recommended Lindos to us for the holiday."

His initial reaction to the first part of that comment from her was to think she was continuing to play games with him. Not that he noticed it, but it was actually said with a very slight sarcastic grin across her lips. He was just a bit too nervous to recognise it at all, as his response indicated.

"No ... err ... no, I didn't mean it like that. It was just that you seemed preoccupied with something at LBN last night. It had me wondering if it was something I'd done the night before, or even that you might just have regretted what we did, because I thought it was-"

"Great, yep, so did I," she interrupted, finishing his sentence for him. She was actually bubbling at the thought of what they'd done, but explained, "I had something on my mind that needed sorting, that's all. That's why I was preoccupied last night."

"And is it?"

"Sorted? Not sure, but it can wait," she explained, adding immediately, in what he could already now perceive was a much more encouraging to him frame of mind, "So, what about tonight? I should eat with Sandra. I am supposed to be here on holiday with her after all, but you could join us if you like. I'm sure she won't mind, and I guess you can recommend yet another decent restaurant?"

"Of course, yes that'd be good. We can try another good one I know, although actually they are all good here really. I've never found a bad one."

Her invitation had brought a smile back to his face, which got significantly broader when she responded bluntly once again with, "And I'll need to try that bed of yours again. See if it's got any softer."

115

After she told him that the prospect of his afternoon in the blazing Lindos sunshine with the two women in the beautiful idyllic surroundings of St. Paul's Bay suddenly improved a hundred per cent. As it turned out it could hardly have gone any better as far as he was concerned. His expectation levels had completely rocketed once more.

After another good dinner at Dionysos, and a few drinks in Pal's Bar, plus this time a different new bar for the two women, the Lindian House, Aileen began blatantly urging Sandra to leave her and Martin to finish the evening alone. Sandra did actually yawn a couple of times after their second drink in the Lindian House, which prompted Aileen to ask if she was tired, and if so she should perhaps have a relatively early night. "Don't feel obliged to stay out just because of me. I'm sure Martin can take care of me again," Aileen told her with a cheeky grin.

Sandra wasn't obliging that easily though, which prompted something of a scowl of annoyance towards her from Aileen. In fact, Sandra insisted that she wasn't all that tired and anyway she wanted to try one of those clubs that Martin had been on about before, that he had taken Aileen to. "What about the one you guys went to on Thursday night?" she asked.

"Arches," Martin informed her.

"Yep, that's the one. That's where you two ended up on Thursday night isn't it, Aileen? Where you got your lovely hangover for when we went to Rhodes Town the next day?"

Sandra knew that was precisely the place. She was just taking the opportunity to have a not so sly dig at her friend. Aileen wasn't reacting, however. She wasn't playing those sort of games. She was simply more focused on getting Martin alone again, just her and him, and into his bed once more. That, at least, was the one thing that she had been able to decide upon within her deliberations about in what ways to adjust her plans over the unforeseen circumstance of Richard turning up. She was determined to get into Martin's bed as much as possible, and enjoy herself, before the added complication of the unpredictable Richard arrived. When that time arrived she knew she would need to focus back on that in terms of what she planned to do.

116

So, rather than rising to what she perceived as Sandra's sly dig, she merely confirmed, "Yes, that's the one. Let's go. I'm sure you'll enjoy it, Sandra."

In fact, this time it was Martin and Aileen who left Sandra in Arches about an hour after they arrived. Once more she was surrounded by young guys; three young Greek guys this time, in their early twenties. Martin recognised them as all working in various restaurants in the village. While she was preoccupied with their attention at one of the club's two bars Aileen whispered in Martin's ear, "Let's go now, while she's being distracted."

He nodded, and she immediately grabbed his hand and led him quickly through the crowded club to the exit.

So, they did try Martin's bed again. Just like the first time she was aggressive, apparently once again knowing precisely what she wanted, and was not slow in telling him while they writhed around on his hard bed. This time though, much to his bewilderment and some psychological self-discomfort, he was growing to like it, and her, more and more.

She, on the other hand, was not discomforted by her actions in any way at all. On the contrary, she enjoyed it, loved it. It all seemed natural to her. Again, as was the case the first time she'd ended up in Martin's bed with him, she liked to be in control. That was always the clash she had sexually with Richard, despite what she always told him was great sex between them. She meant it though, it was still great sex. However, they both wanted to be in control, and clearly competed to be. Perhaps, after all that was what actually made the sex great between them? Anyway, that's how she rationalised it; it was all down to the competition. Of course, at different times throughout their affair each of them found themselves not to be in control at all. That was true not only of the sex, but also their relationship in general, with all the accompanying dangers of it being discovered by Sandra.

Sandra, however, was someone who believed she could out-control most people, not least because of what had been her type of training in her other secret life. Sandra's control though, was much more subtle than Aileen's or Richard's. She had perfected it - the subtlety of control and revenge, cold, calculating revenge - as she was now determined they were both to find out and experience soon.

Although even Sandra was struggling with her own personal dilemma. Her training in her secret other life had taught her to analyse and make judgements as much as possible devoid of emotion. In her professional secret life that meant not letting personal emotions cut across or cloud her decisions and judgement; never to let emotions conflict with rationality professionally she had been taught. Yet here, right now, she was on the verge of doing just that. Tussling with professional feelings about Aileen and all they'd been through together in the Service against, and in conflict with, the personal emotions she was experiencing; the anger over her friend's betrayal through her affair with her husband. No matter how much she tried to think rationally about it in line with her Service training, the emotion and anger was slowly gradually consuming her.

15

Aileen's dilemma: changed circumstances not part of the plan

If emotion and anger was gradually consuming Sandra as they approached the end of the first week of their holiday, it was an agonising dilemma that was consuming Aileen at that time, and the crunch point was rapidly approaching with her ex-lover Richard's imminent arrival. As far as she was concerned the husband of her best friend was her ex-lover. From the text messages he had been bombarding her with every day since she arrived in Lindos it appeared that he was not ready to recognise the 'ex' part at all. It seemed he had experienced some sort of spiritual conversion, perhaps even some sort of visitation to show him his true feelings about how he felt about her. But then she also knew him quite well from their affair, and certainly very well from the background information she'd been supplied with about him.

Consequently, she seriously doubted that he could really have changed that much. She knew he wouldn't have. He was a selfish realist prat, and always would be. So, just how much of the content of the texts he'd sent was really about his now recently discovered unrelenting feelings for her, and wanting them to be together, and how much were they simply a reaction to a growing fear on his part about her being away on holiday with his wife, Sandra? She was totally certain she knew the answer to that question. He was merely fearful that she would let something slip about their affair one night when she'd had too much to drink. She was a hundred per cent sure that his texts were simply him being concerned about his self-preservation.

She'd always planned to get him to that irrational state of mind throughout their affair, and certainly as a consequence of her apparent easy acquiescence in agreeing to end it. She knew he wouldn't be able to leave it at that though. His ego wouldn't let him, together with the fact that she knew he'd eventually miss the great sex with her. He'd come running back to her, displaying all the pent up anger and aggression that was always within him just below the surface. The more she rejected him, and refused to respond positively to his renewed fervent advances, the more angry and irrational, reckless and careless he'd become. She knew full well that would be the case, and now it was happening, just as she planned. The only snag in her plan, however, was that she didn't expect it to come to a head in Lindos. Him turning up there wasn't the scenario she expected or planned. She knew he'd be even bloody angrier over her going on holiday with Sandra, but she assumed that he would eventually accept it, and therefore everything would come to a head once the two women returned to London from their holiday. Nevertheless, she knew she'd have to adjust and deal with the changed circumstances and situation accordingly, as was necessary. She just had to figure out how.

She understood completely, however, that key to doing that was figuring out just what he was actually playing at? He wasn't an entirely stupid man. Aileen had learned that quite quickly during their affair. Everything Richard Weston did was for a reason. Usually the reason was his self-interest. He was a calculating game player, and the games he played were always played to achieve the best outcome first and foremost for one person, himself. She'd seen him do that, experienced it herself, a few times during the period of their relationship, not least in the games he'd played to avoid Sandra discovering it. So, what was he trying to achieve, hoping to achieve, by turning up in Lindos for the second week of their holiday? What game was he playing this time? She was certain he wasn't actually turning up there because he'd miraculously suddenly discovered his undying love for her.

Then there was her own dilemma. What to do about Martin when Richard turns up? Even though it had only been a week, she liked what they had. She definitely wasn't about to tell Martin about her affair with Richard, however. She didn't know him that well, and she knew Richard too well. If he got any inkling at all that her and Martin were sleeping together he would undoubtedly be his obnoxious self, as he could be, and as she'd seen him be on a couple of occasions with guys when Aileen was out with him. What if, having told him, Martin reacted to Richard's goading by blurting out something about his affair with Aileen? That'd be a complete disaster, not part of her plan at all, especially with Sandra likely to be there too. Aileen knew that would mean she definitely wouldn't be in control of the whole situation then. So, she certainly couldn't tell Martin about her and Richard for now. Nevertheless, her dilemma over Martin and Richard certainly wasn't going to get any easier when Richard turns up, especially if he starts playing his mind games with the three of them – her, Sandra and Martin.

When it came down to it she was a rational, calculating, individual. Martin was a nice, unexpected diversion that she was simply enjoying, plus she already recognised that her liaison with him on their holiday was pissing Sandra off, even though she appeared to be trying her best to hide that. When it came to pissing off Sandra, Richard was the key element of Aileen's plan though; a key part of her operational task. However, him turning up in Lindos for the second week of their holiday wasn't part of that. She hadn't accounted for that, calculated for it. The timing was all wrong for her and it could make the whole thing a lot more messy and difficult. But she couldn't control that, his irrational actions and decisions. It was difficult to plan her overall strategy now in Lindos in advance precisely because of that, his unpredictable irrationality, much of which she'd recently provoked and heightened deliberately. Consequently, she came to the conclusion that she'd have to rethink things and think on her feet once Richard arrived, in terms of both her overall strategy and plan, as well as in relation to her new acquaintance with Martin.

Then there was Sandra. She couldn't believe that Richard hadn't told her about his imminent arrival, but by the day before, Tuesday morning, Sandra still hadn't said anything about it to her. Aileen was somewhat confused over that. Why would Sandra not tell her? She surely couldn't think Richard had told Aileen? Why would she think that? That would indicate that Sandra knew about their affair, and Aileen was pretty sure that wasn't the case or Sandra would surely have confronted her over it, especially after she'd told Sandra she'd slept with Martin on the Saturday night. That would have been the perfect opportunity for Sandra to confront Aileen over Richard, but she basically showed almost no reaction, nothing negative anyway. To Aileen that confirmed that Sandra didn't know about it.

In fact, Sandra was bloody angry when Aileen told her that, but was determined to remain cool about it and in her reaction. Inside she was boiling with anger still over what she'd discovered from Richard's text to Aileen on Pallas Beach on the first day of their holiday. Now, not content with having an affair with Sandra's husband, Aileen was 'putting it about' with another guy, Martin. That made Sandra even more determined, if that was possible, to get her revenge on Aileen, but she was also determined to do it at a time of her choosing, a time best suitable for her and at the most uncomfortable for Aileen. That was the way she'd taken her revenge – cold - on the woman that Richard had an affair with years before, turning up calmly at her office and humiliating her in front of her work colleagues. This time she also had an extra weapon to employ in her revenge on Aileen, Martin. He was obviously keen on Aileen, and she seemed to like him, so she would use that when the time was right. She would turn her attention on Martin when the time and opportunity was right, and in doing so she would completely undermine any apparent growing trust between Aileen and him. Two could play at that game, she thought.

First though, she would pick her moment that evening, the night before Richard arrives, to tell Aileen he is coming the next day, and she would do it purposefully in front of Martin to gauge Aileen's reaction. Just the two of them had dinner. Martin had declined Aileen's invitation, explaining that he had already promised to meet some friends for dinner, but would join them later for a drink at the Courtyard Bar around ten. So, Sandra waited until then before announcing to the both of them that her husband was arriving the next day.

Aileen's response was well disguised. She knew Sandra's announcement of Richard's impending arrival would have to come at some point in that evening. After all he was arriving the next day. Over dinner she hadn't done it, so Aileen had already anticipated that Sandra would do it later, deliberately in front of Martin.

Aileen was prepared. She had calculated precisely what her response should be. She feigned surprise. It was all over her face as she responded to Sandra's announcement with, "But how do you feel about that? I thought you wanted some space and time apart?"

"Not great, but he's determined to come it seems. Are you really surprised though, Aileen? You know what he's like."

That was a double-edged comment if ever she'd heard one. For the briefest of moments in her brain Aileen again wondered if Sandra knew something about the affair. Although that was going on in her head, her facial expression was a picture of calm surprise at his impending arrival, with not the slightest indication at all of a reaction to Sandra's 'You know what he's like' comment. Instead, she just opted for a shrug of her shoulders.

Sandra's plan, and trap for Aileen, hadn't really worked as far as any embarrassing moment from it arising in front of Martin. He stayed out of it completely. He'd decided that was the best approach. Instead he engaged in a conversation with Jack Constantino while ordering the three of them some more drinks and suggesting to Jack that the two women, him and the bar owner have some shots. He thought that would lighten the atmosphere. To some extent it did. Richard Weston's impending arrival in Lindos never entered the conversation between the two women again that evening, at least not while they were in Martin's company.

However, that evening didn't all work out the way Martin would have liked, or at least, the end of it didn't. Just after twelve-thirty, as the now packed Courtyard Bar was buzzing with customers, mostly tourists, knowing that the music would stop in a half-an-hour at one, Martin discreetly whispered in Aileen's ear about his bed getting softer. She knew exactly what he was suggesting, but he wasn't expecting her abrupt, curt reply of, "Not tonight."

Once again, confusion was invading Martin's brain, but he decided that from his recent, albeit limited, experiences with Aileen it was best to merely leave it at that. He definitely didn't understand her blowing hot and cold on him and she never even made the

123

slightest attempt to explain why. She hardly could, of course. It was basically just the fact that she had plenty of other things to think about in preparation for Richard Weston turning up tomorrow. She didn't want any distraction at all from that, as pleasant as what Martin was obviously suggesting would be.

16

More secrets: Tuesday 28th June, 2016

There was more to Sandra Weston than met the eye, more than it seemed; more to her past and even more in her present. Aileen Regan knew about her past. She'd shared it with her, shared their secret life. It was Sandra who had recruited her for the Service when they became friends in their first year at university in Bristol together. Sandra had already completed her training by then, and was being urged by her handler to look for suitable recruits from amongst the student population. Aileen seemed open to some of Sandra's comments as she carefully sussed her out before formally putting the suggestion to her. Aileen didn't appear to need much persuading. If anything she was eager, keen.

Aileen knew far more about that part of Sandra's past than even her husband, Richard, who knew absolutely nothing of it. When it came to Sandra's present secret life though, she believed that Aileen knew, and was aware of, just as little as Richard, which was precisely nothing. Sandra was convinced that Aileen thought, understood, that like her, Sandra had left behind her secret life in the Service over a decade before, when they both left it. In fact, Sandra didn't, despite what she led her friend to believe. It was still very much part of Sandra, her life, and her ruthless, calculating character, even if not perhaps to some extent as intense as it had been before. She'd had her ups and downs, made her mistakes in the past when she was more fully engaged in the Service, one of which had been particularly calamitous and nearly broke her will. However, as far as Sandra was concerned now there was absolutely no need for Aileen to know that she was still actually actively part of the Service. That was required of her, of course, under the Official Secrets Act. That requirement was brought home to her again in the early evening of

Tuesday. While Aileen was in the shower Sandra got a call on her second mobile, one that Aileen was no longer aware she still had.

She stepped quickly into her bedroom with her handbag and closed the door as she reached into the bag and answered the call. "Gill? You must have some sort of psychic powers. I was going to call you today. I wanted-"

"Well, you know it's the training we did, Sandra, we're supposed to think one step ahead and all that remember? That's why I called you."

"Yes, but I wanted to ask-"

"How is it?"

"How's what, Gill?"

"How's Lindos?"

"Oh, yes, of course, the place is beautiful, just like you said."

"Good, and I hope you manage to relax for the next week or so because we've got a job for you as soon as you get back."

"Where?"

"Paris, you'll be perfect, your cover will be perfect I mean. It's during the Paris Fashion Show. An elimination, a termination."

"But I stopped doing that. You know I have. I don't do that anymore. I'm done killing people." Sandra's tone of voice changed as she added, "Well, I had, maybe with the exception of two people right now."

"What?" Gill asked.

"Nothing, forget it, just thinking aloud. Anyway, I had an agreement with the Service that I was all done with that. Getting information for them, yes, fine, no problem, but termination, no, no more. After ten years in the Service we agreed, they agreed, I was all done with that. That was the deal."

"But you aren't going to be the operative on this one. They want you to be the facilitator, organise and brief the team, positively identify the target, check out the best location for the termination, that's all. Look, I didn't want to have to say this, but you don't have much choice do you, not if you want the rest of your cosy life at your photo agency to continue smoothly without any hitches"

"That sounds like a threat."

"Get real, Sandra, that's because it is, and it's come from the very top. So, if I were you I'd take it seriously, very seriously."

"Do I have any time to think about it?"

"No, it's in the week after you get back from there, and as I said, you don't really have a choice. So, they are hardly going to give you time to think about it are they? I need an answer now."

"Fuck them! They never let go do they?

"You knew that when you joined the Service, Sandra. Once you're a member of the club you're always a member, for life. There's no getting out, not until you die, or they have you terminated. To them you're always an asset, the product of all that costly training, and they don't give those up easily, if ever."

"Fuck!"

"Come on, Sandra, calm down, just do it. It's only being the facilitator, and River House reckons that being a fashion photographer gives you the perfect cover for it. You'll easily get access to all areas at the show."

"Bloody River House, bloody MI6, why couldn't that bloody Bond film be real and the place get blown to smithereens, and all the prats on the top floor with it."

"Careful, Sandra, watch what you're saying. I know this is a protected line, but that doesn't mean people aren't listening, some who are connected to the people you're talking about perhaps."

Sandra hesitated, took a deep breath, and then said, "Okay, okay, they win, as usual. How many, and Paris, for how long?"

"Two operatives, a man and a woman. They're good, so it shouldn't be too much trouble. One target, an American fashion journalist, or at least that's her cover."

"American?"

"Yep, freelance, and I'm not talking about her fashion journalism. She's worked for our rouble paying friends, amongst others, but she's also got some decidedly shady links to some groups in the Middle East and parts of Africa, if you get my drift. Her own little side-line in sex trafficking, mixed up with her cover and links in the fashion industry. She even did a couple of jobs for River House at one time, but that's all become a bit too murky now and she's all over the place, if you get my meaning, can't be trusted. That's why it has been decided it's time to dispose of her. I don't want to say any more on here though. You'll get all the details, background and including flights, accommodation, contacts and fashion show credentials through the usual channels when you get back to London. It's only three days. Get in, reconnoitre, brief the team and then out and back to London while they do the job. Then you'll be done. There's a Paris contact who will assist you on the ground. The French are cooperating, but it's our operation."

"Okay, okay, will do. Having someone from the French on the ground should help and speed things up."

Yep, although Christ knows how something like this is going to work after bloody Brexit, Sandra. It appears that no one has got a clue at this end at the moment. Cameron and his bunch of clowns just assumed the result would be to remain. The suits at MI5 and at River House are furious. How's MI6 supposed to function properly without EU security cooperation? Cameron and the bloody idiots in the government never gave that a thought when they called the sodding referendum!"

Sandra remained silent while her MI6 handler let off steam over the referendum result. Eventually, she just simply agreed, "Obviously, Gill, everyone could see that before the vote, except the smug bloody politicians in the government like Cameron."

Finally, once she had vented her anger and frustration fully, Gill asked, "So, what is it you wanted? You said you were going to call me. Problems?"

"Oh, no, no problems, I just wanted a favour from you, and I think after what you've just asked me, told me, to do, you owe me one now anyway."

"Sure, if I can, what is it?"

"A Martin Cleverley, can you run a background check on him for me. I know it's not strictly protocol, but I just want to be sure about some things. Probably just a bit over suspicious these days, but, you know how it is. He says he's a Professor of Greek Mythology. I Googled him and he seems genuine, but I'm sure you can dig a bit deeper for me and see if there's anything. Maybe it's that training kicking in again, but can't help to check. We met him on the plane, well Aileen did mainly. She was sat next to him. He's here on holiday too. Says he comes here a lot and does seem to know a lot of people here. He seems interested in Aileen, well more than interested actually. They've already made a connection, if you know what I mean. He just seems a bit too keen in asking things about me through her for my liking. Probably nothing, but as I said I just wanted to be sure."

"Okay, I'll run a check asap, discreetly of course, because as you said, it's not anywhere near proper protocol. I'll let you know on this line if I turn up anything dodgy. This wouldn't have anything to do with killing two people that you mentioned before would it though?"

"No, just being flippant, Gill. You know me."

The two people Sandra was referring to were Richard, and Aileen, of course, but she wasn't going to get into that with her handler. She knew from experience, and once again from her training, that the least conveyed to people in and around MI6 about your personal life the better. Those things, casual comments, could come back to haunt you later, be used against you.

"Okay, I'll get back to you soon as," Gill told her. "Enjoy the rest of your holiday, and beautiful Lindos. Bye"

Sandra wasn't being completely honest with her handler though about why she wanted a background check run on Martin. It wasn't just about his obvious interest in Aileen. It was also because of what she'd decided to do, was planning to do, soon. Before she did she wanted to ensure her MI6 connection wouldn't be compromised if, by any chance, he wasn't actually who and what he claimed to be.

17

Wednesday 29th June, 2016: interrogation or conversation?

The two women were on the beach the next day, on Pallas this time, when Sandra got her return call from her MI6 handler, or in fact, she initially got a text message from her saying simply, "Call when you can." Sandra's MI6 phone was in her beach bag on silent, so it was only when she checked it at just gone eleven while Aileen was swimming in Lindos Bay that she saw the message. Crowded Pallas Beach wasn't exactly the best place to take a call of what would be a sensitive nature in terms of security. She placed the phone back in her bag, checked to see where Aileen was in her swim, and looked around for a good secure place to make the call. Aileen was a long way out in the bay, so she wasn't going to be returning to her sunbed any time soon. She spotted some rocks at the far end of the beach, just beyond the Skala restaurant and before the long jetty that the Glass Bottom Boat and the boats from Rhodes Town tied up at. She judged that looked a deserted enough place, with no people close by. Even if Aileen returned to her sun bed from her swim while she was at that far end of the beach she reckoned that she wouldn't spot her immediately as she wouldn't think to look towards that end of the beach for her. Anyway, on the off chance that she did, Sandra would simply tell her it was Richard calling from Gatwick before he boarded. So, she grabbed her beach bag, with the phone in it, slipped on her t-shirt and flip-flops and quickly made her way towards the spot to make her call.

Before Sandra could even say anything Gill told her straightaway as she answered, "Check didn't turn up anything concrete, nothing concrete or incriminating on the record. He does have a bit of a murky past though, and in the past associated with some shady individuals we were watching, who we had under surveillance at the time. He was in the Soviet Union three times in the eighties before it collapsed. Not sure what that means or indicates though. From checking his social media background stuff he appears to be very sympathetic to the Irish Republican cause, and some of our more dubious Irish 'friends'. Could all be innocent political involvement and persuasions, of course? What makes you so concerned about him though, Sandra? Something in particular that you've picked up?"

"Nothing clear or certain then, Gill? I'm just concerned that Aileen could have been compromised by what she told me she's been up to with him. Perhaps targeted by him, even though she's no longer 'active'? She told me she slept with him the fourth night we were here and I'm sure she's slept with him at least once more since then. He seems keen, too keen for my liking, and she seems completely reckless over it all, like she's forgotten all about her life in the Service and the caution we had drummed into us. That would have definitely been emphasised to her even more in the debrief she had before she left."

"So, what do you think, Sandra? You recruited her. You know her best, better than we do now since she left the service. Try and gauge it over the rest of your holiday. You obviously shouldn't do anything there anyway. Perhaps we should eliminate him just in case, but obviously wait until he gets back to London. How long is he there for?"

"Not sure, three or four weeks, I think he told Aileen, but I didn't really get involved in the conversation between them about that on the plane. I'm sure she'll know though. I could find out for sure casually from her. You're right though, nothing can be done here. That would be crazy. I'm sure Aileen doesn't suspect anything, about me still being in the Service or about him. She seems to have let her guard down completely and, as I said, totally forgotten everything we learned and everything she would have been told in her debrief when she left. Anyway, it'll give me more time to try and check out what he's up to here and see what I can get out of Aileen about him."

"You're sure she's got no idea you're still in the Service, unlike her?"

"No, I'm certain she thinks I'm done with all that. I'm hundred per cent sure about that."

"Okay, keep me up to speed, anything at all that you pick up about him let me know immediately, or anything more you want checked out. At the moment, without any more information, this sounds as though it can wait until he gets back to London, and we'll deal with him, or both of them if necessary, then.

"Both?"

"As I said, if necessary, yes Sandra, both. You know the rules. Even though she's no longer in the Service, no longer active, if she's been compromised in any way because he isn't all he's made out to be we can't risk her having been turned and him trying to reactivate her for the other side. She knows too much from the past. We'll deal with it. You just pick up what you can from her and keep me informed on this line, and just start thinking about the Paris operation after you get back."

With that Gill rang off and the line went dead.

Sandra wasted no time in trying to garner more about Martin's political persuasions. She took the first opportunity that arose. As they cut through the shimmering white Lindos alleyways on their way back from Pallas Beach later, just after six, they spotted Martin relaxing with a beer in the Rainbird Bar, with its wonderful panoramic scenic views over stunning Lindos Bay below. Richard wasn't due to arrive until nine, so Sandra suggested that they join Martin in the bar, or rather in the beautiful courtyard outside the bar, for a refreshing cold beer. Aileen was somewhat surprised at Sandra's apparent change of attitude towards seeing Martin, but readily agreed. She was even more surprised at the direction in which Sandra seemed to want to take their late afternoon, early evening, relaxing over a beer, conversation after they joined his table and ordered a small beer each.

"So, what do you make of the referendum result then, Martin, and Brexit?" Sandra ignored any pleasantries and chit chat and jumped straight in with a forthright question.

Aileen looked sideways at her, even more bemused by her start to their conversation with Martin. She let out a small chuckle, followed by, "Bit of a heavy subject to begin a conversation with in a place with such a beautiful view, Sandra."

Martin joined her bewilderment and agreed with, "I'd say an ugly subject, given what it's surely going to produce. Surrounded by all this peace and beautiful scenery here it does seem a complete contrast."

"Maybe, but I just wondered what you thought about it, what with you being involved with all that Greek stuff, the mythology I mean, Sandra explained. "I would have thought you'd be very European inclined, voted remain I guess?"

"It was a secret ballot, remember, but, yes, I do like to think of myself as European." He evaded the vote part of her question.

"So, what do you think will happen now then," Sandra pressed him.

Aileen tried to lighten the mood with, "Well, this is certainly not the sort of conversation I thought I'd be listening to when we left the beach fifteen minutes ago."

Now it was Sandra's turn to throw a stern sideways glance at her friend. It was clear to Aileen that something had happened to put her in what seemed a quite aggressive, bordering on dark, mood.

"If I knew that, what was going to happen next with Brexit, I probably wouldn't be sitting here with the two of you and looking at this wonderful view and the scenery. Very enjoyable though your company obviously is, of course," Martin started to reply to Sandra's question. "I guess I'd be making quite a lot more money somewhere, in the government or maybe the Civil Service, or-."

Sandra interrupted with a different tack on her questions before he could finish. "So, that's important to you then, is it, money?"

He looked more than a bit bemused and startled by Sandra's complete change of tack with her questions. "Err ... Bit difficult to live without it, don't you think, but no, it's not all consuming to me."

Aileen couldn't figure out what was happening at all, what Sandra was up to. She thought that she wasn't too keen on Martin, and his liaison with her, but Sandra's aggressive questions seemed to go quite a way beyond not being keen on him. She hadn't seen her get this aggressive in her questioning and attitude since they worked together in MI6. This obviously couldn't be anything to do with that though, Aileen assumed. She put it down to simple jealousy, not amorous jealousy, but purely jealousy of him coming between the two women on their holiday together.

Sandra was like a Jack Russell terrier with its teeth in a rabbit's throat as she ploughed on with her incisive questions, while Aileen tried once again lighten the mood by saying she wanted some nibbles with her beer, "Some crisps perhaps?" she asked the waiter after she called him over.

"It's not all about materialism for you then, Martin?" Sandra jumped in.

"No, not all about that, other things are important."

"Like what?" she pressed him again.

"Like health, happiness, caring about other people, I guess, Sandra."

If Sandra's previous questions and comments were a bit confusing to Aileen what she said next, asked next, definitely cleared the fog in her mind. Aileen was shocked, but suddenly it was as clear as the bright, hot, Lindos sky to her just what Sandra was up to. She was, indeed, reverting to her old ways in MI6, and increasingly aggressively it seemed.

"Socialism then, Martin? That's what you're talking about then isn't it? That's what's important to you?"

Now it was Martin's turn to be confused. He certainly hadn't expected to get into such a heavy political discussion as this on his holiday, especially after what had happened between him and Aileen on two nights of it.

Before he could answer though, Sandra threw another curve ball at him. "Not a fan of Margaret Thatcher then, I suppose?"

This one he found much easier to bat away. "Is anybody now, Sandra?"

Aileen decided to keep well out of it. She'd ask Sandra what it was all about, what she was playing at, once they were alone back in their villa. For now she settled for waving the waiter over again and ordering three more small beers. She never even bothered to ask the other two if they wanted one or not, and they were too heavily engaged in their conversation to be concerned with more beer or not.

Although, Aileen was increasingly feeling that the conversation was more of, or growing into at least, an interrogation.

"She changed the country in the eighties don't you think, Martin?" Sandra suggested to him, deliberately probing.

From Sandra's last few questions, Aileen was now convinced there was more to this than met the eye, and for some reason she couldn't quite fathom Sandra was definitely reverting to her MI6 techniques of probe, let the suspect talk and eventually give something away.

"Yep, I couldn't disagree with that, but whether it was for the better or not is dubious, as far as I'm concerned. As I said, looking back at it now I don't think many people think it was for the better really. Didn't she once say that 'Economics is the method, but the object is to change the soul', or something like that? She certainly did that. Although personally I reckon she totally destroyed the country's soul, ripped it out."

Now, it was obvious to Aileen that Sandra's technique was working and he had, indeed, given something away. Sandra was moving in to dig away at that opening. "Important for you then, soul, is it, Martin? You ever considered doing anything to change people's soul?"

Before he could answer this time, Aileen realised she needed to put a stop to the interrogation. Martin clearly didn't have much of a clue about what Sandra was up to. He clearly thought it was merely some innocent political discussion. Aileen certainly did though by now. She was beginning to think that if she let it go on much longer Sandra would have got her thumb screws out to use on him. She took a final swig of her second beer and interrupted with, "Enough of this heavy politics talk you two. I need a shower now, and if we're going to meet Richard at the taxi rank in the Main Square at nine we should head back to the villa now, Sandra."

Martin told them, "Okay, don't worry, I'll pay for the beers. You two get off. Maybe catch you later in the Courtyard Bar or somewhere in the village no doubt, after your husband arrives, Sandra?"

At least his relief was helped by Aileen's, "Definitely," plus a parting pleasant smile and a kiss on his cheek.

135

Sandra's interrogation of Martin did nothing to allay her worries about what or who he might really be, who he might be working for. In effect, his answers only added to her concerns. Not that she was in the least bit worried about Aileen's feelings now after what she'd recently discovered about her affair with Richard, but her questions to Martin had also not helped her growing antagonistic relationship with her Irish holiday companion.

They'd only gone a few paces up the slope away from the Rainbird Bar towards their villa when Aileen stopped walking, turned to face Sandra, and demanded, "What the hell was all that about? It was like some sort of interrogation worthy of our past."

Sandra brushed away her question though with a casual laugh, "What? That? Interrogation? Oh come on, you've seen my interrogation techniques years ago, remember. That was nothing like an interrogation. It was just an honest political discussion. Maybe a bit brutal in places, but you know me, blunt. And bloody socialists, do-gooders, can't bloody stand them and their high ideals. Fuck them!"

She wasn't pulling any punches about what she had just done with Martin, and she ended by making sure she landed a low blow on Aileen. "Anyway, just because you're getting into his pants when you want that's no reason to be so defensive on his behalf. You actually don't know much about him at all really you know. Well, at least thanks to me, you know a bit more about him now. Given both our pasts you should be more careful, Aileen, especially when it comes to who you fuck!"

"Phew!" was the word that was racing through Aileen's mind at that last comment. Was that another barbed remark aimed at letting her know that Sandra was aware of her and Richard's affair? She wasn't about to check though, deciding at that time to just agree and not react at all.

"Okay, I guess you may be right there, Sandra. I don't really know that much about him and it's only a holiday fling after all."

Sandra wasn't really looking for a confrontation there and then anyway over Aileen's affair with Richard. She'd decided that she had plenty of time to pick her moment on that. At that time she'd decided that it was best left until the final day of the holiday, when she'd confront both of them. That would also give her the best part of the next week to carry out her little plan in respect of Martin in order to take her revenge on Aileen in more ways than one.

But Sandra wasn't letting it drop completely. Aileen was shocked as she told her, "Well, you better get your facts straight about you fucking Martin, and about what you might have let slip to him, because you're going to be pulled in by the Service after you get back to London. They'll want to know about you and Martin in particular. I asked them to do some checking on your lover boy, and he's got some pretty dodgy associates all in all. He may not be quite what he seems."

"What? What the fuck!" Now Aileen's conciliatory, passive mood had completely instantly disappeared. She was clearly very angry. "How could you do that? Why would you? I don't believe you. Why should I believe you? It's bullshit! We both left all that shit behind us years ago. Why would you have access to all that now, after all these years?"

Sandra knew she should be more careful, but perhaps what she had recently discovered about Aileen's affair with her husband had made her less so on this; had destabilised her normal calm, rational self. She couldn't resist blurting out the truth as the two women stood in the narrow alleyway facing each other, both getting increasingly angry. Luckily they knew from their past not to raise their voices for fear of being overheard. However, that didn't have the effect of quelling their anger.

"You may have, but I never did. When you're in the Service, working for the Agency, you know full well, Aileen, that you're not allowed to have any anchorage in your life, you have nowhere to go in your private life, nowhere to run to except inside yourself. Even Richard doesn't know about all that and me. And you can never really leave, despite all that crap they tell you when you actually think you do leave. You know too much and they are always, constantly worried, that you might go over to the other side, or one of the bloody multitude of other sides these days, and spill your guts to them about what you know. So, yep, when you get back be prepared to be picked up one day and subjected to a full debrief, and once that happens, depending on what you tell them, and anything else they dig up on your new bed friend, they'll probably pull him in too. I guess that'll well and truly fuck up any possibility of any relationship you may have been dreaming of having with him. Could never really actually see you as the bloody wife of a Professor anyway, dear."

Sandra finished with a nasty smirk across her face. Aileen simply told her, "Fuck you and your bloody Service buddies, or the Agency, or whatever you want to label them these days," and turned and walked off up the slope towards their villa. Aileen knew that when she finished by saying "Fuck you" to Sandra it was about more than just the argument they'd just had over her checking up on Martin. It was about a lot more, and Aileen was indeed more determined than ever to 'fuck over' her so-called ex-MI6 colleague in as many ways as possible.

Part Four:
Lindos, the second week

18

Richard Weston; oil on troubled waters

While Aileen waited with Sandra just before nine on that Wednesday night as the both of them sat on the small wall surrounding the tree in the centre of Lindos Main Square, opposite the taxi rank, she was summoning up all she had learned from her previous MI6 training about remaining calm under stress and pressure. She was under no illusion. It was going to be a difficult and awkward second week. She assumed that straightaway when she got Richard's text saying he was coming, and he subsequently couldn't be persuaded otherwise. The three of them together - her, Sandra, and him – not only in the same small village, but also even in the same not very large villa, was going to be tricky.

The atmosphere between her and Sandra was already somewhat frosty after their argument earlier on their way back to the villa from the Rainbird Bar. They had barely spoken since, just the simple necessary question about who was going to use the shower first after they got back, but little else passed between them.

Of course their argument had related to what had happened in their first week in Lindos; an added ingredient to the relationship mixture, Martin and her. Aileen realised she would have to somehow deal with just how Richard reacted to Martin, and even vice-versa? And she was still trying to work out precisely what the bloody hell Richard actually hoped to achieve by coming to Lindos for the second week anyway? What was he really aiming to do, hoping to do? She needed to find out what it was exactly, and be sure about it as quickly as possible after he arrived, so that she could figure out her own adjusted best plan of action. If his texts to her were to be believed he was coming to tell her in person he wanted them to be together, no doubt declare his undying love. But, as she decided earlier, that wasn't likely to be true at all, even if she wanted it to be, which she most certainly didn't. This was Richard Weston, one of the most unreliable and untrustworthy men she'd ever come across. Everything she'd seen and read about him, to some extent experienced with him at certain times in their affair, confirmed that. And he definitely didn't do undying love, or even any meaningful commitment.

What was equally as bizarre was that even if he was sincere in what he wrote in the texts to her this was the most unreal and inopportune time and place to do that surely, while she was actually on holiday with his wife. Someone, incidentally, that Aileen knew well, and had seen in action. She knew that Sandra could be pretty bloody ruthless. She certainly wasn't going to take anything Richard told her, explained to her, about him and Aileen without kicking up the biggest ruckus she could. The worst part of all this mess now, as far as Aileen was concerned, was that she felt she increasingly had very little, or even no, control over looming events and the people who were going to be part of them. That wasn't what she was supposed to be about at all. She was well aware that if her plan and operation was to work she needed to make sure that she was the one in total control of the events of the next week, and beyond. She was determined to do that. Although no doubt Sandra and Richard Weston would also be determined to do so for their own particular reasons and ends, she reminded herself.

Sat on the low wall alongside her as the taxis and tourists came and went down the slope into the square Sandra was coolness personified, and it wasn't because of her now immaculate tan, highlighted by her pristine white t-shirt and white tight-fitting jeans. She knew precisely what her game plan was, and how she was going to play the next week between not only her and Aileen, but also the two women and Richard, as well as Martin. She had it all worked

140

out. She knew she wouldn't be able to resist the odd barbed, possibly double-meaning, comment, but generally she'd wait until the last day of their holiday before she exploded her nuclear option and confronted Aileen and Richard. Also, at some point, she wasn't exactly sure precisely when, but definitely in the second half of that second week, she'd exact her maximum revenge on Aileen through Martin. It was all in place. All she had to do was wait for her perfect time. In the meantime, however, she knew it was necessary to firstly quickly thaw the frosty atmosphere that was lingering between her and Aileen after their argument. She reckoned that the more she could put Aileen at her ease in terms of the relationship between them, the easier it would be to do what she intended to do without her becoming more and more suspicious. She started that process as they sat waiting for her husband to arrive.

"Now he's almost here I'm actually beginning to look forward to seeing Richard you know. Strange, I never thought I'd be saying that a few weeks ago. What about you?" she asked Aileen, still unable to resist fishing slightly.

"Err … yes … it'll be nice for you, of course it will. It'll be good to see him I suppose, but more so for you obviously."

"Yes, I suppose it will. I thought it might be a bit awkward him turning up here, awkward for you, I mean, when it was supposed to be a holiday for just the two of us girls together." Sandra was continuing to fish when she added, "But now you've met Martin I guess it'll be all okay, not awkward at all really, will it?"

As Sandra asked that last thing she turned her head and body slightly towards Aileen sat alongside her on the wall and stared straight into her face. Although she once again briefly wondered whether Sandra knew about her and Richard, Aileen was prepared and ready now for those sorts of remarks. She realised she might have to face a week of them.

"Yes, I'm sure it'll all be okay, sure Martin and Richard will get on fine too," she replied with as cool and reassuring a tone in her voice as she could summon up.

"You think so? Hmm … hope you're right. It'd be a bit of an awkward second week if they didn't, I suppose."

There was a deliberate hint of childish wonder and innocence in Sandra's voice as she said that. As she did so, she equally deliberately twirled a couple strands of her hand around the index finger of her right hand and stared up into the dark starlit Lindos sky, giving off the impression that she was contemplating deeply what she'd just said.

Sandra couldn't help herself in the game that she was obviously now playing to its full. She waited half-a-minute or so as the two women sat in silence while she continued to peer up into the sky aimlessly and twirl the ends of the strands of her hair. Then, much to her own sole amusement, added a real killer of a calculated double-edged comment, "But I think you're right, it'll be okay. I reckon they have quite a bit in common, from what I've seen of Martin so far, of course. Guess you've seen more of him though, if you know what I mean. In fact, when you take the two of them together I'm sure you're even better qualified than I am at judging if they'll get on."

Aileen knew exactly what Sandra meant in every part of those comments of hers, but she wasn't taking the bait, especially her final, "you're even better qualified than I am at judging if they'll get on," one. However, that comment did now completely convince her that Sandra had somehow got an inkling about her affair with Richard. Nevertheless, she merely opted for trying to change the subject slightly. "I'm sure they'll get on, as long as they don't get on to politics, like you did with Martin this afternoon."

"That's true. Richard can be a real bloody fascist sometimes, on some things particularly, like immigration. He said he voted Leave, obviously."

"Obviously," Aileen agreed.

At that point, ten past nine, yet another black Mercedes Rhodes taxi pulled into the square and Richard Weston emerged from the front seat alongside the driver, wearing a pair of light beige chinos and a white open neck linen shirt, that was by now quite creased as the result of his journey, In his left hand he held his laptop bag. While the driver went to the boot to get Richard's bag before he paid him the fare Aileen decided to hang back and remain by the tree in the centre of the square. At that time her first moment of uncertainty entered her head. His first action would be to greet and kiss Sandra wouldn't it? Surely even he wouldn't be so stupid as to kiss Aileen first. She wasn't taking any chances. He was unpredictable at the best of times, and this certainly wasn't one of them, the best of times. So, she stayed back by the tree as Sandra headed straight over to greet him and plant a slight kiss on his cheek.

Despite firmly telling herself to stay calm and cool when Richard turned up, Aileen's first moment of slight panic gripped her as he and Sandra turned to walk over towards her from the taxi. She instantly decided to drop into her fall back mode. After she said a quick, "Hello, Richard, good to see you," she told Sandra, "I'll head to Jack's now. Leave you to show Richard the villa. You'll obviously want to catch up and don't need me around. I'll meet you at Jack's later. If not I'll be outside Pal's, with Martin if I bump into him." She deliberately dropped Martin's name in to what she said before she left them.

With that she immediately turned away from them, without even waiting for Sandra's agreement, and walked off across the square towards the alleyway and up the slope by the donkey station towards Lindos By Night bar and the Courtyard Bar.

As soon as she left Richard asked, "Who is Martin?"

Sandra couldn't wait to tell him. She clearly delighted in doing so, of course, and was determined to embellish it as much as she could, turning on her best very bouncy, jolly, happy sounding tone in her voice as she did so. Happy for Aileen was the effect she was trying to convey to him.

"We met him on the plane. Well, Aileen did really. She was sat next to him, so I barely spoke to him. We've been to dinner and for some drinks with him a few times in the past week. He's a Professor of Greek Mythology, he says, comes here regularly apparently. He certainly seems to know quite a few people here. Oh, and he's written a novel based on Lindos, had it published apparently, and is working on another one at the moment he told us. Seems like a nice guy, and clever. Aileen looks to be getting on well with him."

"Yep, he sounds like a clever, busy guy. Where-"

Richard was about to go on and ask where Martin was from, partly just to make polite conversation to get around any immediate awkwardness with Sandra. But also because his jealous trait was already growing inside him, and he was considering whether this latest liaison of Aileen's was likely to continue once she got back to London if this guy Martin didn't live too far away from her. Sandra knew precisely what she was doing, however, and she wasn't about to let Richard finish what he was saying. She interrupted, plunging her metaphorical knife deep into his back.

"Yep, very busy, if you know what I mean, Richard. Aileen and him have been shagging here, a couple of times at least as far as I know, as far as she's told me."

Inside Sandra was beaming over what she had just conveyed to him – the manure-like information she had dropped on him from a great height. He was stunned, but tried desperately hide his expression giving it away. Sandra had just casually dropped it into their 'welcome to Lindos' conversation in order to deliberately make it sound as nonchalant as possible to him.

Before he could respond she quickly added, "Good for her, don't you think? Good that's she's met someone and having some fun after all she's been through over the past few years and recently?" Now she was baiting Richard in connection with his affair with Aileen.

"Recently?" he asked.

Sandra stopped and turned her head towards him as they were now outside the door to their villa. She explained, "Her divorce and all that shit she found out about after, about her ex and that young Czech woman he was cheating on her with for ages. When I said recently, I just meant what happened at that time and how she's tried to get over it, the way she's tried to deal with it, recently."

Another loaded comment, but he wasn't taking any of that sort of bait. He just let her continue without interrupting, except for a very quiet, mumbled, "I see."

Sandra wasn't stopping anyway. She had the knife plunged deep between his shoulder blades metaphorically, and now she was determined to twist it as much as possible to see just how uncomfortable she could make his arrival. She was good at this sort of tortuous mind games stuff. She'd had plenty of practice at it before in that part of her other secret life.

As they stepped through the doorway into the courtyard of the villa she continued.

"She didn't have a clue about all that. Personally, I don't know how some people can do that, hide stuff like that for so long from their partners and cheat all the time. Apart from anything else it must be very wearisome, hard work being such a bastard, don't you think?"

Sandra knew exactly what she was doing, coldly and calmly planting a seed of doubt in his mind. Now it was Richard's turn to begin to wonder if she knew about his affair with Aileen.

As that thought passed through his head Sandra told him, "This is it. It's quite a nice villa."

She put the key in the lock and opened the front door to the villa. As they entered, straight into what passed for a lounge area, she informed him, "Our bedroom is just off the lounge, to the right. Aileen has the one to the left off the lounge, opposite."

Sandra couldn't resist one final turn of the knife though as she continued, "Not that she's used it that much this past week though, at least, not that I know of. I haven't heard her, if you know what I mean, Richard. If she's come back here with Martin I mean, of course. But if they have been back here shagging I haven't heard them, and he must have left before I got up in the morning."

Now he really was fuming inside, struggling to contain his anger, jealousy and rage, and any possibility of Sandra noticing. All he had done throughout her somewhat graphic dialogue in respect of what Aileen had been up to that past week was simply exhibit a weak smile across his lips and nod his head a couple of times in agreement and acknowledgement of what Sandra was gleefully throwing at him. She, of course, had managed to keep a completely expressionless, stony faced look throughout, that at times bordered on one of even disapproval.

What he was really thinking about was all those bloody pleading texts he'd sent to Aileen over the past week. How stupid had he been? No wonder she'd tried to put him off coming. As was usual with Richard Weston, however, his anger soon turned to a thirst for revenge, and a quick form of it. Revenge on Aileen of course, but although he hadn't actually met him yet, also on this guy Martin. He wasn't about to wait very long to begin to get his revenge on Aileen, however. He wanted it rapidly, and now was as good a time as any to start.

As they entered the bedroom with his bag Sandra suggested he unpack later and that instead they go and meet Aileen for a drink straightaway. However, he had other ideas, something else in mind now after what she'd told him Aileen had been up to over that past week. From behind he grabbed her by the shoulders, turned her round, and staring straight into her face told her, "I know you said you wanted space, wanted last week away for that, but I've missed you so much."

As he finished speaking he leaned forward to kiss her full on the lips passionately. Much to her own surprise she didn't exhibit any sign of resistance, but on the contrary engaged her mouth firmly with his.

As he pulled back from the kiss he told her determinedly, "I want you now, right now. Let's make love now, right now. I want to. I need to, with you, right now, right here. I've missed that so much. And I bet you want to as well, don't you?"

She hadn't heard him use those words to her for a while, "Let's make love." He was usually a much more coarse man when it came to sex between them, a much more coarse man in most things, particularly relationships between men and women though. She had no clear idea why she responded as she did. Perhaps she merely didn't want to give him any reason to be suspicious if she declined; suspicious that she declined because she knew what he'd been up to with Aileen. Knowing him as well as she did, she did suspect that what she'd purposefully told him about Aileen and Martin shagging had raised once again the jealousy in him. It was always there just under the surface of his personality. She knew that. Consequently, perhaps now this was just his way of getting back at Aileen quickly.

Sandra decided to have one brief, ultimately feeble, attempt to put him off though as she told him, "But Aileen will be waiting for us."

Ultimately, however, it only took the briefest of a few more seconds for her to come to the conclusion that what could possibly be better to annoy Aileen with than her having sex with Richard within half-an-hour of his arrival. So, that's what she, they, did, and she made perfectly sure she threw herself into it completely. In fact, she

146

became totally aware part of the way through it that she was actually getting possibly more excited and fulfilled by the fact that she knew she was not only fucking Richard, but also screwing over Aileen in the process. That must have added quite a bit to her performance as even Richard couldn't resist commenting how good it was when they finished.

Sandra knew, however, that the climax she had just had with him was going to be well and truly complemented - maybe even exceeded - by how she would feel soon when they met up with Aileen. She was more than delighted, and revelled in blurting it out to Aileen, even in an innuendo, as soon as she had the opportunity after her and Richard finally met up with her in the Courtyard Bar an hour later.

"Sorry we were so long. Had something we had to do," she took great pleasure in telling Aileen when they arrived, accompanied by a wink.

Although Aileen clearly got her drift, she showed no sign of any obvious anger, or even disappointment. Sandra knew, however, that she must have been seething inside. She threw another potential volatile ingredient into the mix by asking, "No sign of Martin then? Richard said he was so looking forward to meeting him didn't you dear?"

As she finished Sandra deliberately slowly placed her arm around Richard's waist and gave him a squeeze as he responded with, "Yes, of course. Can't wait to meet him, Aileen," staring intently straight at her.

The tension between the three of them could be cut with a knife. It was only slightly eased by Aileen introducing Richard to Jack, who had come along to their end of the bar to take their drinks order.

"Jack said he expected Martin will be in later," Aileen told the two of them.

19

Thursday 30th June, 2016

Martin never made it to the Courtyard bar on that Wednesday night that Richard arrived. He got side-tracked drinking with some Greeks he knew in the Lindian House. He finally got round to sending Aileen a text just after midnight letting her know where he was, and telling her he didn't think he was going to get to join them at Jack's until one at the earliest.

Aileen wasn't really angry at all at Martin's 'no show' at that time. She sensed from Sandra and Richard's attitudes that it probably wasn't a good idea to involve Martin immediately in their games. Leaving his meeting with Richard for another night would at least also give her more time to figure out just how to deal with it, given Richard and Sandra's apparent revived fondness for each other and more.

So, Aileen just texted a short reply, "No worries. I'm tired anyway and going off to bed soon. See you tomorrow."

So, that is what she did soon after, leaving Sandra and Richard drinking in the Courtyard Bar after she explained that Martin wasn't going to make it there that evening.

Sandra was disappointed that she wouldn't get to play out all her schemes that night, particularly introducing Richard to Martin. However, it would happen eventually, and then she could merely sit back and watch the anticipated sparks fly between them. She knew Richard well, particularly about his jealous streak. Even though he'd actually just had sex with her, he wouldn't easily cast aside that he and Aileen had been lovers recently and that now she was soon sleeping with another guy. So, Sandra wasn't overly concerned when Martin didn't show up. Her time would come, plus there were a few more elements of her plan to play out yet.

She didn't have to actually wait long for that time to begin, just under twenty-four hours in fact. The three of them - the two women and Richard - spent the next day on Pallas Beach, complete with the ongoing tension between them. In the early afternoon she asked Aileen, "So, when is Richard actually going to meet this Martin of yours? He might be thinking that he doesn't really exist after all."

"Oh, I'm sure he does exist," Richard intervened before Aileen could answer, adding pointedly, "Aileen wouldn't make up something like that, would you? She doesn't make up things, do you Aileen? Anyway, you've obviously met him, Sandra, so he must exist."

Aileen decided to stop being so defensive and instead chose to attack, and face the issue of Richard and Martin head on. It would have to be dealt with at some point that week, so might as well get it over with as soon as possible.

"I'll text him and suggest we all go for dinner tonight, if that's okay with you, Richard?"

"Sure, you do that, can't wait," he told her.

Martin responded straightaway, agreeing that was fine by him, and suggesting they meet outside Pal's at eight, and then maybe go to Symposio again for dinner.

Aileen relayed his suggestion to Sandra and Richard as they relaxed side by side on their sunbeds. They both readily agreed. However, Richard couldn't resist adding a sarcastic, "Can't wait."

Martin got to Pal's early, at quarter to eight. There were hardly any customers in the little bar at that time. It never filled up until later in the evening. As he asked for a bottle of Mythos the two barmen, Lou and Stelios, looked surprised to see him there so early. He never usually turned up until around ten or even later, but he explained he was meeting some people there to go to dinner. Stelios immediately asked, "The two women you were in here with last week, I bet, véry nice."

Martin nodded in agreement as he paid for his beer and told him, "And the husband of one of them. He arrived last night."

"Still leaves one," Stelios commented sharply, with a grin.

Martin didn't respond. He just took his beer and walked outside to sit on the low block of concrete that passed for a bench seat against one of the outside walls. While he sat there in the early evening watching the passing tourists, mostly ones making their way to one of the restaurants for dinner, he began to wonder what Sandra's husband would be like. He realised that she had hardly mentioned him or spoken about him during the times they met the previous week. As for Aileen, who obviously knew the husband of her best friend he assumed, he couldn't recall her mentioning him at all.

He didn't have long to wonder about Richard. Just after eight the three of them turned up. He was pleasantly surprised when Aileen straightaway gave him a kiss on the cheek and grabbed his hand as he stood up. The previous times they'd met she'd never greeted him like that. While he was enjoying his pleasant surprise Aileen did the introductions, or at least introduced him to Richard. Martin extended his hand and Richard shook it, with what to Martin seemed an unusually firm grip, one that was almost painful for the recipient.

Introduction over, Aileen asked, "Shall we have a drink here first or go straight to the restaurant to eat?"

Martin had almost finished his small beer and was about to suggest that they just go to Symposio, only a few yards away along the alley, when Richard chimed in abruptly with, "This place looks pretty dead. Let's just go and eat. Hope the bars liven up later or it could be a long evening."

"It will, they will, the bars I mean. They always get busier later, after nine-ish. People, the tourists, are eating in the restaurants at the moment," Martin explained. But Richard wasn't entirely convinced. He seemed to be in a bit of a mood, as far as Martin could sense.

Janis, the 'front of house' person at Symposio was the next person Martin introduced Richard to, and then once they had climbed the wrought iron staircase to the roof terrace he introduced Richard to Filip, the owner. Filip showed them to a table for four. Once again as he did so Aileen took one of Martin's hands and guided him to the seat next to her, on the opposite side of the table to Richard and Sandra. There probably wasn't much likelihood of Richard stupidly attempting to sit next to her anyway, but Aileen wasn't taking any chances by giving him the option.

For a few moments, as the four of them engaged in small talk while they perused the menu, Martin began to think Richard's mood was changing, and he was becoming more relaxed and friendly. But then Martin suggested they have a bottle of Retsina, the same as he'd had with Aileen and Sandra over dinner there last time. Richard refused, saying instantly, rather rudely, and a little loudly "No, I'm not drinking that Greek muck. Have they got any good Italian red?"

Not wanting to make a scene, and knowing how awkward he could get over the slightest things – like a spoilt child – Sandra tried to take the heat out of the situation by telling him, "I expect so. I'm sure they do, of course."

Aileen tried to help by adding, "But the Retsina we had here last week was very good. I can recommend it."

"Not for me, whether it's very good or not in your opinion," Richard told her forcibly.

It was Martin who suggested the compromise that actually calmed Richard down, or he thought it did. "Why don't we get a bottle of each? Then we can drink what we want," was what he suggested.

Richard agreed, but then couldn't resist muttering so that only Sandra could hear, or so he thought, "Oh good, a compromiser."

Martin did pick it up though and the remark prompted him to turn his head towards Aileen with a confused look across his face. She just shook her head ever so slightly, accompanied by a barely noticeable roll of her eyes at him, which he took as a suggestion that he shouldn't respond. Richard never noticed any of that as he was too busy with his face buried in the wine list searching for his bottle of Italian red as he muttered his comment. He found one to his liking, ordered it, and then consumed it completely himself throughout the meal.

Generally, the rest of the meal went off without any further disagreements and awkward moments. Richard wasn't exactly jovial company, it seemed to Martin. Even when he progressed to have almost consumed the whole bottle of red, his mood didn't appear to lighten. If anything, it darkened with the more he drank. He definitely appeared to have a chip on his shoulder about something, although Martin hadn't a clue what it was. He decided he'd leave it, make the best of the evening and Richard's difficult company, and ask Aileen about it later, when hopefully they would be alone.

Sandra, meanwhile, was just enjoying the sport. She'd seen Richard do this quite a few times before. He was bubbling up to boiling point, and she guessed it would be Martin, not Aileen, who would get the brunt of his anger and intimidation. He was a bully and enjoyed it, particularly when he was angry about something, and was drinking. She'd seen him take his anger out on someone, anyone, just to get it out of his system. Although it wasn't always the person who had caused him to get angry that he focused on. She knew all that process would be fuelled by the more alcohol he consumed as the evening progressed. In fact, she was quite smug in priding herself that she was actually the only person out of the four of them who knew what was going on, what all Richard's anger was really all about. To that extent, she believed she was the only person out of the four who was really in control of events about to unfold, or so she thought. Aileen had other ideas, however.

The next flashpoint came when the bill arrived. Martin went to pick it up, but Richard grabbed it off him, telling him abruptly, "Give it here."

Again Martin looked sideways at Aileen, and again she shook her head briefly to discourage him from saying anything. In fact, he put his rudeness down to the fact that perhaps Richard had already had too much to drink. Richard Weston was only just getting started in that respect, however. His alcohol capacity was far greater than merely a bottle of red wine.

For that erroneous reason he decided to remain quiet while Richard proclaimed, "Okay, let's split it in half. That'll be half for Sandra and I that I'll pay, and I presume Martin will be paying for you, Aileen, won't he? So, he can pay the other half."

There was a sharp edge to his tone of voice. It was sprinkled with a heavy portion of sarcasm. Aileen knew precisely what the meaning behind his, "I presume Martin will be paying for you, Aileen," comment was, and it was by no means innocent or pleasant. Besides which, Martin wasn't actually enamoured by being referred to as though he wasn't there, when Richard could have asked him directly.

However, now Aileen decided enough was enough. She'd learned that the best way to deal with a bully like Richard Weston was to confront him, and put a stop there and then to his games. In Richard's case she'd learned that from experience, of course. Before Martin could agree that of course he would pay for Aileen's dinner, she responded sharply with, "Not sure quite what you mean by that, Richard, but I'll pay for myself, thank you." She couldn't resist adding a barbed, "You know I always prefer to do that." She was sure that would, at least briefly, put a stop to his little games, as well as having the effect of alerting Sandra's suspicions over how he would know that, or so she thought.

It certainly quietened Richard down for a while. Once the bill had been paid, and Filip gave them all their complimentary lemoncello, Sandra asked, "Where to next, Martin?"

Before he could answer Richard piped in with, "What about that bar we were in last night?"

"Jack's, sure, why not, let's start there," Sandra agreed.

As they got up to leave the table Aileen tucked her arm into Martin's and told him, "Just for support in case I fall down those bendy wrought iron stairs, Martin."

Richard was once again looking daggers at her, as well as Martin. Sandra, meanwhile, was trying to conceal a small, smug smile of satisfaction.

When they got to the Courtyard Bar a few minutes later it was already very busy, mainly with tourist couples. Jack spotted them immediately through the crowd of customers and greeted them with a smile in his usual convivial way. Richard insisted they sit at the bar, rather than at one of the free tables outside in the courtyard. Although it was pretty full they managed to find four free stools at the far end of the bar. The stools were in a row against the shortest part of the bar towards the back wall, opposite the doorway and stairs down to the toilets. Aileen headed straight for the one furthest away from them, next to the wall. As she did so, she grabbed Martin's hand once again and guided him, actually almost tugged him, to sit on the stool next to her. Richard was alive to her little game now, however, and quickly plonked himself down on the stool next to Martin, on his left. Sandra was actually happy to take the end one of the four. She knew what Richard was up to, and within a matter of minutes after they'd ordered their drink, she was proved right as he began to try to engage Martin in conversation. That left Aileen stuck in the corner, with Martin constantly having to turn away from her, almost turn his back on her and towards Richard to answer his questions.

"So, Sandra tells me you're a Professor of Greek Mythology, Martin," Richard began.

"That's right, and I do a bit of novel writing, fiction. That's my first novel up there on the shelf." He pointed to the paperback that Jack had displayed by his drink optics.

"One of those liberal do-gooders in universities who've never had a real job then, in the real world, I mean?" Richard was not hanging about in trying to put the boot into Martin and try and antagonise him.

Martin didn't rise to it, however. Instead, he simply responded with, "What is it you do, Richard?"

"A real job, for a multinational company based in London." There was a trace of a sneer across Richard's lips as he spat that out and added, "If you want the full job title it's Senior Global Digital Project Executive."

"Sounds important," Martin replied. Although Richard never picked it up, Aileen identified the slightest hint of sarcasm in his voice, which caused her to allow a smirk to spread across her face, hidden from Richard's view by Martin between them. It seemed that Martin was giving Richard as good as he got.

Richard wasn't giving up that easily though. "Aileen works for the same company, don't you," he threw into the conversation.

"So, I expect you see quite a lot of each other at work then?" Martin asked.

Now it was Sandra's turn to smile to herself discreetly, at what to her was obviously a statement that had a double meaning, not that Martin had any idea of that, of course.

However, Aileen wasn't going to let the conversation go down what for her was a particularly dangerous avenue. She jumped in with, "No, we work in different sections and in difference offices in London of the company. We did bump into each other at the company Christmas party this year, or I suppose that should be last year really, anyway last Christmas."

Now it was Aileen's turn to deliberately push Richard to the limit, living dangerously and enjoying his growing discomfort.

154

That was only enhanced when Sandra commented pointedly, "Oh, you never said, dear. Funny that you never mentioned it, you two bumping into each other at that Christmas party." In no time at all she had obviously pieced together the conclusion that must have been when their affair started. She was determined to make him even more uncomfortable when she continued with, "That was the night you stayed over in the hotel the Christmas party was in, wasn't it? Booked a room because you said you'd be drinking, didn't want to risk driving or be bothered with trying to get a taxi. That's what you said, wasn't it?"

Aileen thought she was merely causing Richard some uncomfortable moments with their conversation, and was determined to push the fact that Sandra might be suspicious of what Richard got up to that night to the very edge. What she didn't know, of course, was that Sandra had instantly worked that out, prompted by the text she saw on Aileen's phone on Pallas Beach on the first day of their holiday. By now she was well aware that they'd had an affair.

Martin merely took it to be small talk between the two women and Richard. If nothing else, it appeared to have moved the conversation on from some of Richard's more aggressive comments, and away from him as the target of them.

After one drink in the Courtyard bar Martin suggested they move on to Pal's, saying, "It will be a lot busier there now. Packed inside I expect and probably groups of people standing outside. Just like here, the music is very good there too."

When they got to Pal's it was, indeed, packed inside, with some couples and group of three or four younger men and women standing outside in the alley drinking. One of the groups of young men were four of the guys that Sandra had been talking to outside on the second night of the two women's holiday, the Thursday of the previous week. Richard insisted he would get the drinks, even though Martin explained that with such a crowd inside the bar he could probably get served quicker as the two barmen knew him well. Richard was determined though, saying firmly, "I said I'd get them."

Martin retreated and told him he'd have a bottle of Mythos, while the two women asked for their usual Gin and tonics. Two of the young guys who had been the most determined in chatting up Sandra the week before spotted her, Aileen and Martin as soon as Richard disappeared into Pal's. One of them lifted his hand in a brief wave of acknowledgment, and then him and another wandered over to say hello. The one who had been most ardent in chatting up Sandra the week before was clearly just as keen, if not more so. Now he quickly positioned himself leaning against the white wall opposite one of the entrances to Pal's so that he was directly next to her and half turned to face her. He was a good looking young guy and she was enjoying the flattery and attention once more.

Richard didn't appreciate that at all though. He emerged from the bar with the women's two Gin and Tonics just at the point where the young guy had placed his hand on the right side of Sandra's waist. Richard calmly handed the drinks to Aileen first and then Sandra, but when the young guy didn't remove his hand Richard grabbed his wrist, pulled his hand away and held it firmly in his clenched fist.

"Don't touch, son! Go and play with your own toys," he told the guy as he spat the words firmly into his face. His three mates surrounded Richard, who was clearly still fired up about everything that he'd seen so far between Aileen and Martin that evening.

"Stop it, Richard!" Sandra screamed at him, and he let go of the guy's wrist. But one of his mates was obviously feeling brave, no doubt from his alcohol consumption already that evening.

"You want some then mate?" He shouted at Richard.

But much to Aileen's surprise it was Martin who stepped in and stopped the situation escalating, as he told them all, "Just bloody calm down. It's just a misunderstanding, that's all. We're all on holiday. We don't need this, and I'm sure you guys don't."

Not bad for a Professor of Greek Mythology Aileen thought, and one without a "real job", as Richard claimed earlier.

Anyway, Martin's peace-making intervention worked and the young guys backed off, then left a few minutes later. Richard was still seething. It was clear that he wanted to fight someone. Something inside him was making him want to do that, although Martin was the only one of the four of them that didn't really have a clue what it was.

He tried to calm Richard down some more by telling him, "That sort of thing doesn't happen here, Richard, fights, violence, not in Lindos, not between the tourists. It's not that sort of place."

Richard never responded. He just gave him a withering look and shook his head. He did seem to calm down a bit though for the next hour or so while they had a couple more drinks.

Just after twelve Aileen suggested that they all go to Arches. Sandra had other ideas, however, mainly because she didn't think a probably crowded club full of people drinking and bumping into each other, however accidentally, was such a good suggestion in Richard's present volatile frame of mind. She never voiced that opinion however, preferring instead to just decline, and then suggest with yet more deliberate provocation towards Aileen, "I'm sure we can have an early night, if you know what I mean, Richard. We can always go to Arches another night."

Sandra presumed what she said would add to Aileen's anger over what she and Richard had been up to back in the villa just after he arrived. On the contrary, however, Aileen merely saw Sandra's suggestion as an opportunity to wind up Richard even more. She told him, obviously sarcastically, with a slight tilt of her head, "And I'm sure you want to spend some time alone with your wife don't you, things to work out between you and all that."

That produced a scowl at her from him, but he obviously had to reluctantly agree. Both women had united and succeeded in confusing and disorientating him in different ways. Ironically, both of them were pleased with the outcome of their individual scheming.

The other person who was pleased with the outcome of that little conversation was Martin. He was now going to get Aileen to himself alone again. She did want to go to Arches however, and so they went just after Sandra and Richard left them outside Pal's to head back to the villa. Aileen couldn't resist a parting shot for Richard's sake as she told Sandra, "I've got my key, so don't wait up. I'll let myself in quietly, whenever I get back."

Just before two-thirty, after a couple of hours in Arches, Martin and Aileen were once more rolling around having sex in his bed. This time it seemed much more relaxed between them, with no sign of any tension. She appeared perfectly at ease, with herself and him, at one point even joking, "It isn't getting any softer, and thankfully I'm talking about the bed, Martin."

Aileen was enjoying herself and had managed to put everything about her and Richard, and Sandra, out of her mind. She was too preoccupied exploring Martin and his body, every part. Martin, of course, couldn't help but be preoccupied with every part of her body, and was definitely enjoying himself, this time completely.

Something else was happening to him though. He was starting to enjoy being with her, and not just in his bed. Was he beginning to fall in love with her? Could that be it? He'd only known her just over a week, but certainly wanted all the time to see more and more of her, and he didn't mean her body. He'd seen all of that, and liked it a lot, every piece of it.

As they finished and lay side by side on their back in his bed this time he was not only thinking of her, however, but Sandra and Richard pushed their way into his brain for some reason. He asked her, "Do you think they are happy, Sandra and Richard? He seems a very angry man about something."

She was surprised, not only by his question, but it seemed a strange thing to ask about those two while they were laying their side by side naked.

"Err … I know Sandra more than Richard. As I told you on the plane, we go back a long way, to Uni, but she hasn't said anything to me about their marriage, or about her not being happy."

She lied in her reply. It was a very cold, matter of fact lie. She was good at that, and at moving things on and away from awkward subjects. She knew the perfect way to do that in this situation as she told him, "Now, are you going to make me leave you soon, or are we going to try to soften this mattress up a bit more?"

She didn't wait for his answer, but just rolled over, raised her body up above him and climbed on top of him. As she lowered herself slowly down onto him, him simultaneously grabbing a clump of her beautiful jet black hair in his left hand produced a gratifying moan of expectation from her. Continuing to hold her hair he pulled her face down to his. The kiss he planted on her full red lips conveyed all the passion he felt, sending it screaming through her body.

158

20

Friday 1st July, 2016: Martin's perfect day

Aileen never made it back to their villa at all on that Thursday night. Instead, she saw the sun come up through the slats in the shutters of Martin's bedroom. Just after four in the morning she'd said she should go, but he told her, "Stay, stay here tonight." He even joked, "Three words I never thought I'd say to a woman again, stay for breakfast."

She looked a little concerned when he said that about "Three words," wondering what he was about to tell her, but when he actually said them she laughed. Although she couldn't resist telling him, "When you look at me the way you do sometimes I can see more than just lust in your eyes, and I don't only mean when we are having sex."

Now he felt warm and happy, and not just from the Lindos air. He pulled her body in to him and she curled herself around him as they drifted off into a deep contented sleep.

It was nine-thirty when they both woke, smiles etching broadly across their faces at each other. She poked him with her finger saying, "Didn't you promise me breakfast?"

He laughed, but then told her, "I can do coffee, and one of those chocolate filled croissants that come in a packet from the supermarket here, if you can call that breakfast, but that's about all I have."

"A feast!" she said, "But already a broken promise. I hope you're not going to break your promises to me all the time," she added with a small laugh.

"There's going to be an 'all the time' then?" he commented, smiling.

"Maybe," she told him. "We'll see."

So, they had breakfast, such as it was, in the sun in the courtyard outside his flat. Then at ten-thirty she told him, "I'd better go. Sandra will be wondering where I've got to."

"Oh, I doubt that," he said. "I'm sure she'll guess, but of course. Text me if you want to go to the beach later, around twelve maybe? I know a nice beach at a hotel just outside the village, with a nice tavern with a lovely view and good swimming. We could have lunch there. It's a taxi ride, but only five minutes."

"Sounds good," she agreed. "But I'm paying for lunch. You got breakfast after all."

Her broad charming smile was engulfing him completely as she finished telling him that and she got up from the small plastic courtyard table. She bent down to kiss him full on the lips and told him, "See you later, around twelve."

"In the Main Square, for the taxi, at twelve," he told her as she headed for the courtyard door, followed by, "Aileen."

"What," she asked as she turned around to look back at him.

"Nothing, I just wanted to look at you one more time this morning," he told her.

She laughed and left him there sitting in the sunshine.

At five to twelve he was in the square waiting for her, sat on the small wall in the shade under the tree in the centre. Dead on twelve she turned up from out of the alleyway that led alongside the donkey station. She was glowing, her dark black hair flowing behind her in the slight breeze. He hoped it was from the night they'd just spent together. A smile covered her lips as she spotted him. This time she greeted him with a kiss on the lips. Her fine body was accentuated by a tight fitting white vest type t-shirt and light pink smart designer shorts, with dark brown leather flat sandals. The white vest and the pink shorts highlighted the beautiful tan of her shoulders and legs perfectly.

He told her she looked great, but that he felt a bit underdressed in his swimming shorts and t-shirt, asking, "Do you have your beachwear?"

She pointed to her beach bag over her tanned shoulder and told him, "In here, of course. There's somewhere there I can get changed surely?"

"Yep, of course, let's go," he confirmed.

Five minutes later he was paying the taxi driver and the pair of them walked hand in hand into the Lindos Memories Hotel. The hotel was a low rise, only two storey, light sandstone block complex, with an impressive vista out over the swimming pool to Navarone bay, as it had become known having been used for a scene in the movie 'The Guns of Navarone'. The whole setting was very picturesque, very quiet, and exuded a very relaxing atmosphere. They strolled through the intermittently stepped open central plaza of the hotel with the guest rooms on each side.

As they arrived at the end of the plaza he pointed to the right hand side of the swimming pool and the small taverna type covered area, suggesting, "Lunch first, before the beach, it's just down there in front of the hotel?"

"Definitely, I'm starving, even after that big breakfast you made me," she told him sarcastically, with a contented smile.

"Well, you're paying," he reminded her.

"Of course, Martin, this place is lovely, by the way. Thanks for bringing me, but now I'm wondering why Sandra and I aren't staying here?"

"Yep, it's great. I've stayed here a couple of times, and the rooms are good too. Only slight disadvantage is that you're out of the village, so it means a taxi in and out if you want to go to the village each night, and could be four taxis if you want to go in during the day as well. That can work out expensive, I guess."

"Not sure why you would want to go into the village and leave this place during the day though. It's so quiet and peaceful here compared to the beaches in Lindos," she suggested.

"The beach down there is like that too, quiet and peaceful I mean." He pointed to some steps that led down from one side of the tavern as he continued, "The swimming isn't quite as good as on Pallas Beach or the Main Beach, however. It can be a bit rocky and full of coral covered rocks before you get a bit further out. The sea is crystal clear once you're out there though."

It was probably just a little too early for lunch for most of the hotel guests as it was only twelve-fifteen. So, there were only two other couples at the tables in the tavern. Still holding her hand Martin

161

guided her to a free table right at the front with a great view out over the bay.

As soon as they sat down a Greek curly dark haired attractive female waitress approached smiling. "Martin, lovely to see you, and looking so well, in Lindos once again. I heard you were back" She kissed him on both cheeks and he introduced her to Aileen as Crisa. She gave them a couple of menus, and then said she'd be back to take their order shortly.

As she opened the menu and started to look at what to have Aileen asked him, "Is there anyone you don't know in Lindos?"

"I've known Crisa for years, starting from that time I stayed here with my friend, Mark. You wouldn't believe it, but she's a grandmother, twice over. But you forget Lindos is a village. Everyone knows everyone, just like in every other village, I guess, and word soon gets around here, gossip you know."

"So, tomorrow will we be the subject of this village gossip, Martin? The English writer Professor and the Irish woman?"

"The good looking, very attractive Irish woman," he corrected her. "Of course, probably already are in the village, especially if you choose to sample my lovely prepared breakfast in the courtyard of my flat, and then do, what is it they call it, oh yes, the walk of shame through the village the next morning."

"So, I should be ashamed, should I? You didn't seem to be thinking that last night, or in the early hours of this morning, I seem to remember. And anyway, you know there's a lot of this walk of shame, as you called it, which goes on in the village, do you?"

"Err ... no ... no, of course I don't, although when I was staying at an apartment towards the top of the village a few years back I came back in the early hours of the morning to find a bra and pants on the steps up to the row of flats mine was in. Someone obviously couldn't wait to get them off."

"So, did you pick them up then?" she asked with a grin all over her face.

"Of course not, I..." He stopped, realising she was teasing him, and enjoying it. At least, she was until he changed the subject, "Talking of returning to your villa this morning, what did Sandra have to say when you appeared?"

162

"Nothing, I never saw her, or Richard. I assume they must have gone to the beach early. I'll text her later. Tell her we'll meet up later, this evening, for a drink."

Hmmm ... I bet that's a fun day, all day on the beach with the lovely Richard, he thought to himself as he studied the menu. And all that hot sun, I bet that'll do wonders for his short temper. He told her, "Okay, yes for a drink later, but I'd already arranged to meet a couple of Brit guys I've known for a few years for a drink tonight. Met them here on holiday a couple of years ago and they are here now for a week. You could come if you want. It'll only be in Bar 404 in the village."

"That's fine, no problem. I'll have dinner with Sandra and Richard and we can meet up later. I'll suggest to them that after dinner we show Richard Lindos By Night. The view of the Acropolis might calm his temper a bit, well maybe. You can come and meet us up there later."

"Sure, sorry, but I arranged that with those guys before I came, when we knew we were going to be here at the same time. Guess it could be a bit awkward for you, you not knowing them."

"It's no problem, really. It would have been nice for just us two to have dinner together. We haven't done that yet have we, but I'm sure there will be plenty of other times, and not just this week."

Encouraging, he thought, as he replied, "Definitely." As he told her that Crisa reappeared and took their order of calamari and salad for both of them. Martin asked if Aileen wanted wine and she told him, "Just a small glass of white, and a bottle of water." So, he ordered the same.

They had a very pleasant lunch looking out over Navarone Bay, and as they spoke and laughed she occasionally reached across the table and squeezed his hand for no reason. After they'd finished they went down to the beach, found some very comfortable sunbeds and a parasol, and had a couple of very refreshing swims. Martin was right, it was a bit rocky and covered in coral near the beach, but he took her hand and they navigated the worst of it into the clearer sea. As they walked down to the sea for their first swim she curled her hair up and fastened it on the top of her head, exposing more of her bronzed shoulders above her sparkling white bikini. This was one stunning, beautiful woman were the words that were silently running through his mind.

As the sun was going down behind the hotel at just after six-thirty she leaned across to the sunbed next to hers, kissed him, and then said, "I hate to say this, but we should be going. I should be getting back. I'd prefer to stay here forever, but I texted Sandra earlier and said I'd catch up with her and Richard at eight for dinner."

"Another time, we can do this again another time," he told her. "No problem, let's go. Reception here will call us a taxi."

Fifteen minutes later they were getting out of a taxi back in the Main Square. It was buzzing, already humming with busy tourists crossing it to go into the village for a drink before dinner, and then on to one of the restaurants. As he paid the driver and turned around she grabbed a handful of his t-shirt off his chest, reached up with her other hand to place it behind his neck and kissed him strongly.

"Thank you," she started to tell him as she finished the kiss. "Thank you for a lovely afternoon, and a lovely night last night."

"And thank you for lunch," he told her with a smile.

She took his hand and they weaved their way across the square through the tourists. When they got to the fork between the two alleys just past the donkey station he stopped. Pointing to the one on the left he told her, "You're down there. Just follow that alley round past that bar, The Sunburnt Arms, and it'll bring you to the back of the church and eventually your villa."

She reached up behind his neck and kissed him again, then said, "See you later. I'll text you if we go anywhere other than Lindos By Night."

He wandered through the alley to the right and back through the village to his flat. He felt like he was walking on air, even though it was actually the uneven Lindos cobbles.

21

Richard and Aileen: the second element of Sandra's revenge?

Aileen, Richard and Sandra had dinner in the Village House restaurant that Martin had recommended before, and the two women had gone to on the first night of their holiday. The owner, Aris, remembered them, as he did most of his customers of whichever nationality. He could speak at least five languages, so that always impressed customers of various nationalities. Even arrogant Richard was impressed, by that and with the good food. What he wasn't so impressed with was Aileen telling the two of them over dinner what a great day she'd had with Martin, and what a lovely place he'd taken her to.

Aileen knew perfectly well what she was doing. Her bubbling exuberance over the enjoyment of her day was designed to deliberately annoy Richard, and raise his jealous demons once again. It was only heightened further when she said, "You two should go there for the day, or even just the afternoon. It's called Lindos Memories Hotel and it's only a five minute taxi ride from the Main Square. Martin can tell you all about it when he joins us later. I told him we'd probably go to Lindos By Night after dinner, if that's okay with you two. It's a great view of the Acropolis all lit up from up there, Richard. I'm sure you'll love it." She couldn't resist finally adding, "I'm sure Sandra would love to show you. It's very romantic." She was winding him up nicely.

There was an awkward silence for a few seconds until Richard couldn't contain himself any longer. "So, where is he tonight then, this new romantic interest in your life, Aileen? If you had such a great day why isn't he here having dinner with you now?"

"He arranged to meet a couple of guys for a drink in Bar 404 that he knows from the U.K. who are on holiday here this week. He arranged it weeks ago apparently, before he came. Not a problem though. He said he'd join us for a drink later."

Richard didn't look happy at all over Aileen's obvious new attraction. Sandra tried to lighten the mood by saying, "That sounds good, Lindos By Night later. Shall we get another bottle of wine now though?"

"Red, a bottle of a decent red this time, not this Greek Retsina muck." Richard's mood had not responded at all to Sandra's attempts. They ordered another bottle of wine, red, as Richard insisted, and he drank most of the bottle anyway while they finished their meal. Then they paid the bill, and as they left and complimented him on the meal, Aris wished them a good evening, and told them, "Say hi to Martin for me." It wasn't a remark that produced any sort of positive reaction on Richard's face.

It was still warm, more than warm, hot and humid, as they made their way through the now busy alleyways with the evening drinkers heading between the various Lindos bars. Eventually they climbed the first flight of steps from the entrance to Lindos By Night, to once again be greeted by Angelos, who remembered Aileen from when she was there with Martin and asked, "Where's Martin tonight? Not with you this time?"

As Richard muttered to himself incoherently, "Jesus, is everyone here bloody Martin's friend?" Aileen told the young Greek, "Not yet, he'll be here later." She introduced Sandra and Richard to Angelos and then told him, "So, a table for four upstairs if you've got one please, with a nice view of the Acropolis."

"Sure," he told her and led them up the second flight of stairs to a low table with comfortable chairs at the front of the upstairs bar area, and with a great view of the Acropolis all lit up.

After he took their drinks order Aileen couldn't resist saying, "See Richard, I told you it was romantic." He simply nodded in begrudging agreement, and then added a caustic, "If you say so."

Aileen had once again prevented any chance of him sitting next to her by immediately sitting on one of the chairs on one side of the table furthest away from the edge of the upstairs bar area. She ensured that he wouldn't be able to squeeze past her to take the empty chair alongside her as there wasn't enough room between her chair and the one at the next table behind her for him to do that. But he had managed to usher Sandra into the inside chair on their side of the table and therefore take the seat opposite Aileen.

Angelos brought their drinks. Richard had declined the Greek's suggestion of a beer, but instead ordered a Gin and tonic, like the two women. They were only halfway through their drinks though as he finished his and ordered another, this time from the young Greek waitress. He asked Sandra and Aileen if they wanted another, but they declined. Both the women could sense that he was clearly on a mission to get very drunk, very quickly. The more he drank, the more aggressive he became. Sandra was well aware of what was happening. She'd seen it quite a few times before. As the object of his aggression was once again the absent Martin she wasn't about to stop it just yet, however. Let Aileen deal with it, squirm over it a bit, she thought.

He was bombarding Aileen with questions about Martin; "Her new love," as he put it a few times, with an obvious large dose of sarcasm in his voice. She was batting his questions away quite easily. It wasn't difficult, not least because at that point she didn't actually know a great deal about the subject that was the increasingly embarrassing fixation of Richard's questions; except, of course, that she'd had some great times in Martin's bed with him. However, she certainly wasn't about to go down that road in answer to Richard's enquiries, even though she knew it would definitely irritate and wind him up even more. That was far too dangerous. The unpredictable, irrational Richard she knew well might veer off on all sorts of awkward embarrassing tangents in front of Sandra in relation to Aileen and her 'bedside manner'.

She needn't have worried, however, as Sandra was also becoming increasingly annoyed at Richard's fixation on the subject of Martin, and by connection Aileen. By the time her husband was finishing off his fourth Gin and tonic, while the two women were still halfway through their second, she'd really had enough of the talk of Martin for one evening. Although, thanks to her enquiries to her MI6 handler back in London, Sandra reckoned she definitely knew much

167

more about Martin Cleverley than Aileen anyway. She obviously wasn't about to share those things with Richard though. That would be far too dangerous. He definitely couldn't be trusted, was reckless, and often beyond any control, as he was presently demonstrating extremely well.

Sandra tried to change the topic of conversation by commenting about, "The stunning view of the Acropolis," followed immediately by an attempt to rattle off a potted history of Lindos. "I did some reading up on it before we came. Apparently Lindos has been successfully fortified over the centuries by the Greeks, Romans, Byzantines, and The Knights of St. John during the period when they were defeated and expelled from Jerusalem, as well as by the Ottomans. Parts of the Acropolis date from the fourth century BC, and-"

"Really, very interesting," Richard interrupted. It clearly wasn't very interesting to him at all judging by the tone of his voice.

"Well, I think so, even if you clearly don't, Richard," Sandra admonished him.

His total disregard for her, and her history comment, was just about the last straw for her that evening. By now she was totally pissed off by his constant obsession with trying to steer the conversation back to Martin and Aileen, and whatever had gone on between them. He hadn't actually got to any very blunt, unsubtle questions part of that interrogation as yet, but while he kept consuming alcohol the way he did she knew it wouldn't actually be too long before he basically didn't give a fuck and would ask some very embarrassing and awkward questions.

Sod this game, Sandra thought. Why should she even bother trying to stop him? Anyway, they bloody deserved each other, Aileen and him. Even if she wanted to, she knew she couldn't stop it if he wanted to continue to pursue her. And it'd only be for the sex, nothing more, she convinced herself. So, she decided she'd had enough of this for that evening, and of him and Aileen, as well as constant talk about Martin and her. She waived Angelos over and asked where the toilet was. Aileen looked a bit concerned that Sandra was going to leave her alone with Richard, even if only for a few minutes while she went to the toilet. As it turned out it was actually going to be a lot longer than that, the rest of the evening in fact.

Angelos told Sandra that she'd have to go down one flight of the stairs to the bottom bar, and that the toilets were down a spiral staircase in the right-hand corner of the bar.

Overhearing Angelos' directions to Sandra for the toilets Richard realised that Sandra was going to be away from them for a while. So, he tried to take his first chance at having Aileen alone to himself. He leaned across the table and attempted to get hold of her hand, but she pulled it away, telling him firmly, "Don't, Richard."

He wasn't backing off that easily, however. He knew he would only have a few minutes alone with her, or that is what he thought at the time.

"I miss you," he continued, again trying to get hold of her hand, but once more she pulled it away. "You saw all those texts I sent. They must have meant something to you. I love you, surely you know that now."

She looked across at him steely eyed and with a completely blank face, devoid of any positive emotion. She knew this would happen at some point, but it wasn't where, or what, she'd planned. So, she decided she needed to respond angrily; focus here and now on playing on his obviously fake, mistaken emotions by airing her own seemingly emotional anger, equally false as it was. That was the psychological weapon she would employ at this time. She'd gotten him precisely in the place she wanted him to be emotionally and psychologically, but in all her planning she just didn't account for it to be, or want it to be, here at this time in Lindos. It was all supposed to happen back in London, not here in Lindos on her and Sandra's holiday.

So, she feigned emotional anger in her response, although in a quiet tone of voice so it couldn't be overheard. "And where is this love, Richard? I can't see it. I never did, never could see it when we were together. And I definitely couldn't touch it or feel it from you. I can hear it now. I can hear some words, but I can't do anything with your easy words. It's all too late, much, much too late. We've even been here plenty of times before, Richard, you and your meaningless words. That's all they are to you, just words in your game, all about you, and what you want. You even know that really. You've shown that every time. It's just all about the sex with you isn't it? That's all, just that. You've even fucked Sandra since you've been here, and probably more than once, just for the sex, of course. Forget all that love crap. You don't love me, we both know that. You're just jealous of Martin. If you can't have me, then why should someone else. That's what you really think, isn't it? What you really mean when you say you love me. So, tell me, Richard, I want to know, I'm intrigued. Why is the sex so important? It's really about ownership with you, isn't it? That's it really, isn't it?"

She was good, bloody good. Even as the words were tumbling rapidly out of her mouth she was surprising herself at how good at this she was. Yep, emotional anger, she did that bloody well, faked it bloody well. What's more, she actually thought, "Christ, I'm enjoying this!"

Not that she would have let him interrupt her anyway, but he just sat there opposite her while she ripped into him. Meanwhile, he was now growing increasingly angry inside, over her obvious clinical psychoanalysis of him, as well as her rejection of what he thought was him baring his soul and telling her he loved her. Aileen was a lot tougher than he knew, however, and was one very cool, determined woman.

As she finished he responded to her question about the importance of sex in the only way he knew. Of course, being angry he started by immediately raising his voice, which provoked her to instantly raise her hand to indicate and tell him, "Keep it down, Richard. I'm sure you don't want an audience."

To an extent that only made him madder, but he did at least lower his voice. His face was full of rage as he leaned further forward across the table and told her, "Because I'm a fucking stone age caveman. That's why I love it, love the sex. That's why it's important to me. Does that answer your bloody question? And don't pretend with all that psychoanalysis crap that you don't love it too. I know you, remember, bloody biblically, and you love it anyway, loved it with me. Don't say you didn't. I know you did."

Before she could respond she spotted Sandra over his shoulder at the top of the stairs, returning from the toilet. "Bit of a jaunt is it,"

170

she asked her while she was still behind Richard, letting him know Sandra was within hearing range.

"Yep, it is a bit, but I think I've got a bit of a stomach upset. I think I may have to call it a night and head back to the villa, just to be on the safe side," Sandra explained.

Aileen asked, "Do you want one of us to come back to the villa with you, just to make sure you're okay. I've got some Imodium in the villa, if that would help."

"No, that's okay, I've got some as well, and Martin will be here soon, so he'll be wondering where you are if you're not here when he arrives."

"Well, if not me, I'm sure Richard will go with you," Aileen suggested.

"No, it's nothing serious, I'm sure I'll manage. I'll take some Imodium and plenty of water and I'm sure I'll be fine in the morning. No need for either of you to come with me and spoil your evening," Sandra insisted.

Richard never actually offered to go with her anyway. He just sat there in silence, still fuming inside at the psychoanalytical lecture Aileen had just given him. Sandra never even bothered to sit back down at the table. Instead, she just said, "Goodnight," to both of them and leaned down to give Richard a quick kiss on the cheek.

Aileen wasn't overjoyed at being left alone with Richard, but as she glanced at her watch she thought it would be okay as Martin would be turning up soon. Then they could ditch Richard and leave him to his own devices to get drunk somewhere in the village. But that scenario didn't exactly pan out the way she hoped. A few seconds after Sandra left her phone beeped. It was a text from Martin, and not one she was pleased to receive at all. "Can't put up with being in the company of that pompous arrogant shit tonight again. Gonna stay here with these guys for a bit. Meet you in Glow later, about one?"

Richard quickly continued in his angry sarcastic mode, "From lover boy?"

But Aileen ignored his comment. She certainly wasn't going to tell Richard that Martin wasn't going to turn up to meet them at Lindos By Night at all. She just sent Martin a short reply of, "Okay,

171

see you there," although she was actually wondering in her head just what the bloody hell she was going to do between now and one o'clock. She briefly thought of just up and leaving, going to Bar404 where Martin was drinking, but what if Richard insisted on going with her, or even followed her. That wouldn't be very pleasant at all in his present mood, and she was sure Martin wouldn't be best pleased if she turned up there with a very angry, and now very drunk, Richard.

While she was busy running that through her head and wondering just what to do, Richard got to those blunt and unsubtle questions that Sandra had anticipated earlier would eventually arise from him. Now there were just the two of them there was no holding back for him.

He launched into her aggressively. "You fucked him didn't you! Sandra told me you did, and I know you, it's all over your face every time he's around. I've seen that look remember, lots of times."

He continued without allowing Aileen any chance to respond, not that she was actually going to. She knew the best way to deal with those sort of aggressive questions was just to let the questioner get it all out of their system, and eventually just run out of steam. Her secret life training had taught her that. She'd learned the lesson well from experience in a lot of those sorts of situations, although none that were actually pointedly addressed to her personal life in the way this did. So, she let him ramble aimlessly on with his questions.

"Where was it? In the villa with Sandra in the other bedroom, was that it? You'd have loved that wouldn't you? That's just that sort of perverted kink you'd like, fucking another man in the room near to the wife whose husband you've been shagging! Was it? Was it there?"

He banged the table with his clenched fist. His voice was getting louder again, and she was looking around anxiously, worried that his raised voice and the slam of his fist on the table would be heard over the music by people sat near to them. Some people on the table behind him were looking over. So, she told him quietly to, "Calm down, lower your voice, Richard."

He did, but he wasn't stopping with his animated questions. They felt even more sinister and aggressive in a much lowered tone of

172

voice, almost a whisper. Before he continued he got up from his seat opposite her, walked around the table to her side, and attempted to squeeze behind her, asking the person sat in the seat directly behind her if he would move momentarily so he could get through. When he did Richard was able to sit down in the seat next to her. She assumed it was so he could lower his voice and still be heard over the music, but it felt very much like he was increasingly invading her personal space. Her concerns were confirmed as once again he tried to touch her, this time gripping her lower arm. She got hold of his hand firmly and quickly removed it, telling him once more forcibly, "Don't."

"Where? Just bloody tell me where for Christ's sake?" he continued.

"What does it matter to you where it was? It's not important is it?"

"What's not important? Shagging him? You mean that's not important?"

He was playing with her words, but she was well aware what he was doing, what he was trying to get her to say, to admit.

"You know what I mean, Richard, where, why is where important? How is that so bloody important to you? It's not sodding important at all."

"So, just bloody tell me then. I need to know! Did you moan and scream like you usually do, like you did with us? Did you, did you? We both know you're a screamer, Aileen, don't we. You like that, don't you! Did he like that? Did he? I bet he did, the useless piece of shit. I could have him; take him easily, a bloody liberal loving professor. Or, I bet he's a bloody socialist!"

His voice may have been lowered, but his anger wasn't subsiding. With every question he spat out of his mouth at her his face became more contorted with rage, and he again leaned closer to her, staring angrily directly into her face only inches away.

However, he wasn't the only one getting angry now, although Aileen's reaction was more one of calm annoyance rather than complete anger. She'd had enough now of his aggressive behaviour and decided it was time to fight back, rather than be defensive in any way and take any more of it. Now it was her turn to move her head close to his face and stare straight into it. She told him quietly, but

173

with a cool, determined, aggressive firm tone in her voice that even he couldn't misread. "Just fucking back off, Richard, stop this, stop this now! In his bed in his flat, if you must bloody know, although God knows why you think you need to, or even think you have any right to know. And no, your sodding wife wasn't in the next room, or even the same bloody building or the same part of the village. Now, calm down, for Christ's sake, people are looking. You're causing a scene."

People sat all around them were staring over at their confrontation, some even as far away as the bar. He did actually back off a bit, physically at least, and he moved to sit back in his chair next to hers. Although he couldn't resist telling her, "God, you always knew that it really turned me on when you got angry."

She told him determinedly, "Just bloody stop it, Richard, I said, just stop it. Whatever you're thinking, it's not going to happen."

As she did so, Angelos, who had heard some of Richard raised voice comments earlier and then watched the animated quieter discussion develop between the two of them, brought them over a shot each, with one for himself to have with them. It was his way of trying to take any heat out of the situation, for which Aileen was grateful. Although she wasn't too sure that more alcohol for Richard was going to help in the long run. Nevertheless, they accepted the shots, drunk them down with Angelos, and then Aileen thanked him.

For some reason the shot did appear to have an effect on Richard. Perhaps he was just getting too drunk by now to be as aggressive as before. Anyway, that's what Aileen concluded, and that as a result he was becoming morose. She was still left with the conundrum of how to get away from him in order to either go then, at eleven-thirty, to find Martin in Bar404 or later in Glow at one. The first option was her preferred one obviously, as she had no idea how to cope with Richard's company and continued drinking for another hour and a half. Of course, there was always the possibility that he would drink himself into such a stupor that he would simply pass out eventually. Perhaps she could just persuade Angelos to keep giving him shots, have a quiet word with the Greek. However, she'd seen Richard consume large amounts of alcohol before at times during their affair, and his capacity was pretty extensive in that regard.

She came to the conclusion that the best course of action would be to try to get him back to the villa and Sandra. She would go back there with him initially, and then slip back out to meet Martin once he was deposited there and she was free of him. So, just as he was trying to catch Angelos' eye to order another Gin and tonic she told him, "Actually, I'm feeling really tired, Richard. Must be all this heat here. I think I'm gonna head back to the villa and get some sleep. Are you staying here or are you going to walk back with me?"

As soon as that last sentence came out of her mouth she realised it wasn't exactly the best way she could have put it. Was he going to interpret that as an invitation to go back to the villa with her and into her bed, rather than Sandra's? She didn't put that past him taking it that way; even after all he'd just been accusing her off about sleeping with Martin in the room in the villa while the wife of the man she'd been shagging, Sandra, was in the other bedroom.

His response didn't really offer any clue as to the answer to that though, as he just easily agreed straightaway and called Angelos over, this time to pay the bill for all their drinks, which Aileen insisted on splitting with him.

She anticipated a much more Richard type response, reading into her suggestion much more than she initially intended, and then him making some suggestive comment about getting into her bed. It never came though, maybe he really was too drunk. It wasn't a comment from him that disorientated her, however, but in fact what happened as they made their way down the second flight of stairs on the way out of Lindos By Night. She was totally surprised and nonplussed by her own reaction.

As they reached halfway down the stairs he slipped slightly. She caught his arm to prevent him falling completely. As she held it and he recovered his balance she looked up at him, intending to ask if he was okay. Before she could do that he quickly leaned his head into her face and kissed her passionately on the lips. What surprised her was that she made no attempt to pull out of the kiss, pull away from him, or push him away. She had no idea whatsoever why, especially after the episode of anger and argument she had just experienced with him over the past hour or so.

As they finished kissing she spotted Angelos at the top of the stairs, who had been watching them. He shouted down the stairs, "You two okay?"

"Fine, we're fine, thanks. He just slipped a little on the steps, but he's fine. Really, he's okay," she shouted back. Then she turned back to Richard, telling him, "This way," and led him down the remaining steps. As they reached the bottom she told him once more, "This way," and added, "Let's go along here." With that she led him off towards the dimly lit deserted alley that went past, and behind, the Courtyard Bar.

22

Sandra and Martin: the final element of Sandra's revenge, not quite to plan

The storm clouds were gathering. The storm was about to break, but it wasn't going to be one of the dramatic Lindos weather ones. This was a quadruple impending storm; a volatile concoction of the four elements of jealousy, suspicion, infidelity and lies between four Lindos holidaymakers, the two men and the two women.

Sandra hadn't actually been feeling unwell at all. The upset stomach was just a pretence. She had decided she needed to get out of Aileen and Richard's company for a bit. Her anger in their company was bubbling over at what she knew they were hiding from her, had been hiding from her. Also, she wanted to leave them alone together to see where anything might lead between them. She knew they were both volatile characters, and guessed, hoped, they might end up having sex, even if only in one of the deserted back alleys in the village. Obviously they couldn't go back to the villa for that as they believed Sandra would be there. Sandra was sure that if he succeeded Richard wouldn't be able to contain himself and would certainly make sure Martin knew about it. That would destroy Aileen's new relationship with Martin for sure. It was perfect revenge as far as Sandra was concerned.

Instead of heading back to the villa Sandra headed off through the village. She had in her head precisely what she aimed to do. She headed for Bar404 in the centre of the village, where Aileen had mentioned earlier Martin was going to be drinking with some friends. So, as she turned into the small square in front of it she wasn't surprised to see Martin there, sat outside the bar. It was what she intended, to find him. Although she was surprised to see that he

177

was alone, and not drinking with the guys that he'd told Aileen he was meeting, and was the reason he couldn't join the three of them at Lindos By Night.

Bar404 was another small bar where its clientele also spilled out into the small square, in the centre of which was a large tree surrounded by a circular low white wall. Customers would sit on the two wooden benches and stools around the small tables either side of one of the entrances to the bar, or when the bar was really busy perch with their drinks on the circular wall. It was a popular bar with some of the Brit ex-pats who lived or worked in Lindos, or the surrounding area. It was also popular with the regular tourist returners to Lindos, mainly the slightly older regulars, and was usually busy for most of the summer nights.

Martin had managed to get himself a seat on one of the benches to the left of one of the entrances to the bar, facing across the square and one of the alleys off it from which Sandra appeared. "Thought you were off drinking with some of your friends?" she asked as she approached and immediately sat down next to him on the bench.

"I was, met them earlier. I know he's your husband, but I was just having a few drinks here, trying to build myself up for another evening in his company. Not easy man to like, I think, your husband. He's one angry man over something."

Sandra, "I know, I don't disagree. He can be real arse sometimes, especially when he's had a few, believe me. That's why I made an excuse about not feeling too good, a stomach upset, and left him and Aileen up at Lindos By Night. He's only been here a few days, but I needed a break from him as well. That's also the reason I initially decided to get away with Aileen for a couple of weeks, a break from him for a while. We've been having problems, obviously."

Martin was a little concerned that she has left Aileen to cope with him.

"Now I feel guilty about not coming up to LBN earlier. It's not really fair to leave Aileen to deal with him on her own. She won't be happy. Maybe I should get up there now," he suggested.

"I'm sure she'll be okay with him for a while longer. They seemed to be getting along okay when I left, getting on quite well, in fact," Sandra told him, deliberately emphasising the last part of what

178

she said, trying to plant initial seeds of doubt in his mind. She was preparing the ground for what she intended to tell him later in the evening, after she had got a few more drinks into him.

"Let's have a drink here first, before you go to join them though, plenty of time yet. Give Aileen a bit more time. She seems to be a good influence on him," she suggested, planting another seed of a snippet of information.

Without hesitating or waiting for his reply she got up, went into the bar, and returned a few minutes later with another bottle of Mythos for him and a Gin and tonic for herself. When they had finished those drinks he again said he should make his way up to LBN. But she said she wanted to talk to him about Aileen, something she wasn't sure he knew about her. He was intrigued and asked, "What, what sort of thing?"

"Just something I think you should know, have the right to know, I reckon. Then you can decide for yourself if you want to do anything about it." Dangling a little bit more of the bait in front of him she added, "And it's also related to precisely why Richard's so angry at the moment."

He frowned slightly and now was totally confused. He couldn't for one second fathom out how anything she was going to tell him about Aileen could relate to Richard's current anger. "Just tell me now then," he insisted.

But she held off a bit longer, deliberately changing the subject and telling him instead, "Look, I feel a bit awkward sat here with you, Martin, when you are supposed to be going to meet Aileen at LBN, and I'm supposed to be back in the villa with a stomach upset. This is a really exposed public place right in the centre of the village, and it would be really embarrassing for both of us if Aileen or Richard suddenly appeared from one of these alleys and saw us, don't you think?"

Now he was even more confused. His confusion caused him to hesitate slightly while he tried to quickly figure out what exactly was behind everything she'd just told him, or rather indicated she wanted to tell him - about Aileen, and about Richard's anger, and why she was so concerned that her and him might be seen by either one of them in a public place, as she put it.

While he was trying to find his way through the fog of all that seemingly unconnected raft of information in his mind he told her, "I … I guess so, but if you just tell me now whatever it is you think I should know about Aileen I can just go up to LBN then and see her. Then you can actually head off back to your villa, can't you?"

He was shocked and distinctly uneasy over her reply. "Somewhere more private, less public than this place would be better," she suggested. "What about your flat? It's near here isn't it? That's what you told us last week, I think."

There was no way he was going to his flat with her, even though it was only a few yards away down the alley and around the corner. How would he ever explain that to Aileen, especially if Sandra chose to tell her she'd actually seen his flat, been there, and seen the bed Aileen had slept with Martin in. "Err … no, no, I don't think that's such a good idea, Sandra, not at all."

She placed her right hand on the shorts covering the upper thigh of his left leg as she stared into his eyes and asked softly and invitingly, "Why not? Sounds like a very good idea to me, don't you?"

He knew precisely what she meant. He could certainly feel it from the way she squeezed his thigh as she spoke. But he was determined not to succumb.

"No, not at all, definitely not, Sandra, that's not a good idea at all. Let's go to Crazy Moon instead. It's only just along from here and in one of the alleys off the main one. It's not on the main street, so there won't be any chance of Richard or Aileen seeing us if they turn up in the centre of the village. It's a nice bar. I don't think you and Aileen have been there yet."

He was talking rapidly, a bit discomforted by her suggestion, rattling off his proposal about going to Crazy Moon, and determined to get her on the move there as quickly as possible.

He had no idea why he thought adding that Crazy Moon was a nice bar was necessary. It was, but it certainly wasn't the case that she was going to be persuaded by any suggestion from him to that effect. In the end she did agree, "Okay, let's go and try that. I can just as well tell you what I was going to say there."

"Then I'll get off to LBN after one drink there," he told her, although she clearly had other ideas.

Crazy Moon was only twenty yards or so along the alleyway to the right of Bar404, and then another ten yards up another narrower alley off at ninety degrees to the right. Through a stone arched entrance it had a pleasant garden courtyard outside the bar in which a dozen or so customers were sat drinking around ornate white metal tables in more comfortable padded chairs. Inside, the small bar was nicely decorated with some great photos of various music icons on the walls.

"This is rather nice, very pleasant. How come you haven't brought us here before?" Sandra asked as they crossed the courtyard and headed for the open-doored entrance to the bar.

"Just haven't got round to it, I guess, but I would have done eventually, don't worry. I'm sure Aileen would like it. It's relatively new, used to be a couple of different types of bars in its previous incarnations. It's mainly a cocktail bar now though, with the obligatory Lindos good music, of course," Martin explained as they sat down on a couple of empty high stools at one corner of the bar.

I'm sure Aileen would like it, Sandra thought to herself, and that she would love the opportunity to weave into a conversation with her at some point just how Martin had taken her to it and how nice it was. She realised, of course, that given she was supposed to be back in the villa with her upset stomach, the opportunity to tell Aileen that, and thereby put some doubt in her mind about Sandra and Martin, was limited at the moment, almost non-existent, in fact, unless she could find a way round it.

While she was pondering that conundrum a tall, dark curly haired young guy, obviously Greek, came over to say hello from behind the bar and shake Martin's hand. He introduced Sandra to Marcos, explaining that he was one of the two young guys who ran the bar, the other one being Nikos, who was busy at one corner of the bar sorting the music.

Martin ordered himself a bottle of Alfa Greek beer this time from Marcos, saying to Sandra, "Another G and T, I presume?"

However, she told him she wanted to have a look at the cocktail menu first before she decided. So, Martin reached over and picked one out of one of the wooden slotted drinks menu holders next to him on the bar and handed it to her. While she perused it, trying to decide, the other guy behind the bar brought Martin's beer, also said, "Hi," and then shook his hand too. He was also young, in his early twenties, but English. Martin introduced him as Callum.

Eventually she chose a cocktail, after first asking Callum to recommend one, and he went off to make it. Introductions over, and drinks ordered, Martin was determined to get back to whatever intriguing thing Sandra wanted to tell him about Aileen, whatever was so important that she felt he should know. Not least, he was anxious to get that over with, drink his beer, and get up to Lindos By Night to rescue Aileen from Richard's no doubt boorish behaviour, or so he guessed.

"So, okay, Sandra," he began with some urgency in his voice. "You wanted to tell me something about Aileen that you thought I should know. You said it was important. Lovely as you think this bar is I'd rather like to get up to Lindos By Night as soon as possible, if that's okay with you. So, what is it exactly?"

She was determined to be as evasive as possible, however, so as to keep him there with her for as long as possible. Her body language was definitely portraying that as she just remained staring ahead of her watching her cocktail being prepared, rather than turning her head to face him. Without looking at him she said, "I think it would be better if we waited until Callum brings my cocktail, Martin. It's not something I really want to start to tell you and then get interrupted halfway through, especially with what I fear may be your reaction. It is quite a private revelation"

Now he was even more intrigued, and getting very frustrated. What reaction, what sort of reaction? What could she possibly be going to tell him that she thought would make him react in a certain way? And a private revelation, what the hell could that be?

He wasn't waiting any longer though, or so he thought. "Look, Sandra, just bloody tell me will you. I'm not sure what you think my reaction will be but-"

He stopped dead as Callum placed her cocktail on the bar and told her, "My special, hope you enjoy it."

She took a quick sip through the straw, telling him while the barman lingered as she tasted it, "Hmm ... delicious, thank you." Martin was sure he saw her fluttering her eyelashes at the young barman as she added, "Yes, very special, indeed. All your own fabrication is it, or I suppose that should be concoction?"

"Yep, all my own work," Callum confirmed.

"And do you have any other specialities, Callum, drinks I mean?" she asked as she placed her cocktail down on the bar and leaned forward to place both her elbows on it, purposefully looking up into the young man's eyes.

Jesus Christ, Martin thought to himself, is she pissed? She's bloody flirting with Callum, who must be almost twenty years younger than her. In fact, Sandra wasn't pissed at all, and knew exactly what she was doing. It was a diversionary tactic, so as to stretch out and delay as long as possible what she certainly eventually intended to tell Martin about Aileen. The longer she could spin it out and delay him going up to Lindos By Night to meet Aileen the better, she figured. Aileen would be wondering where he'd got to, and no doubt Richard would be getting more and more amorous towards her.

Sandra had already heard Martin's phone in his short's pocket beep twice, no doubt with text messages from Aileen asking where he was; once outside Bar404 and the second time just after they got into Crazy Moon. He even went to reach into his pocket after the first one to get his phone and presumably reply, but Sandra grabbed his hand and told him, "Leave that for now, until I've told you what I want to tell you. You can always reply later."

Callum understood her innuendo perfectly, but he wasn't going to engage in that sort of banter with her. So, he merely replied, "Yes, there are plenty of other speciality drinks on the cocktail menu. Some are mine, but most of them are Marcos' creations." As he finished he handed her the cocktail menu again, and then added, "You can choose a different one next time. Go through the card if you want." Then he walked away to serve another couple of customers towards the far end of the bar.

No way, Martin thought. No way am I staying here while she tries to "go through the card" of cocktails, as Callum put it. So, he tried yet again to get her to actually tell him what she promised to tell him, but she continued to evade that and to so obviously flirt with Callum. Even though he was definitely not responding, not even to more of her fluttering eyelashes and the added continuous running of her fingers through her hair and brushing it back, she was not put off, wasn't stopping at all. Martin decided he'd had enough of her games when she actually asked Callum after he made her second cocktail, "Where do you go when you finish here, I mean to a club or something?"

Callum just replied, quite coldly, "To sleep," and then purposefully moved away to the other end of the bar once again.

Martin turned sideways on to her on his stool and told her, "Look, Sandra, I don't know what sort of sodding silly game you're playing here, apart from obviously trying to get off with a guy who is almost half your age I'm guessing, but either you tell me now what you wanted to tell me about Aileen or I'm leaving, right now."

She took a sip of her cocktail, placed it back on the bar, and then turned her whole body on the stool to face him in silence. She looked him straight in the eyes and then slowly, and quite deliberately said, "Aileen and Richard have been having an affair."

He looked completely stunned as he said, "What? When?"

"I only found out about it after we arrived here. I saw a text from him on her phone the first afternoon we were here on Pallas Beach. It came through while she was swimming and the stupid cow had left her phone switched on and on the small table between our sunbeds. It was almost like she wanted me to find out. Crazy!"

"Are you sure? Have you asked her about it, or him?" Martin asked, still shocked. "But they have been so antagonistic towards each other since he arrived here, not friendly at all."

She could hardly be any closer to him without falling off her stool as she continued to stare him straight in the face and told him, "I'm guessing it's because, just like me, the last thing she wanted was him turning up here, but he was adamant it seems. She knew it would be awkward. She's probably over compensating with the unfriendly bits between them, just so there's no chance I'll get suspicious. Anyway, that's what I reckon she thinks. And he's obviously so angry because he's turned up here to find she's been shagging you. He's angry with her, and obviously he's angry with you. From what I read in that text he sent to her it appeared he was coming here to tell her that he wanted to be with her, that he wanted them to be together. So, when he turns up and finds she's been fucking you here his ego has been well and truly really badly bruised. Believe me, Martin, Richard Weston is not a man who takes kindly to having his ego bruised, or even challenged, I know that from experience unfortunately. And it explains why he had such an argument with me before we left for our holiday. He was determined that he should come, and when I told him no, he wasn't happy at all. I reckon he was worried sick that while we were here together I would find out something about what had been going on between them, or that maybe she would let something slip out that would give me some hint. I didn't have any idea at all before we came away, although things haven't always been great between me and Richard over the past six months. I guess I know why now, although as you said earlier, he's not exactly an easy man to always get along with generally."

Martin had turned back towards the bar on his stool, and now just sat with his elbows resting firmly on the bar, staring straight ahead with his cheeks resting in his hands either side of them. He was speechless as Sandra continued. She was determined to unload the full details on him, or as much as she knew at least.

"I got a text from him on Tuesday saying he was coming, but I reckon the bitch knew he was coming much earlier. The text I saw on her phone on the beach that first afternoon was literally him pleading with her that he would be coming, and that he missed her, of course, the bastard! Mind you, his face was a picture when I told him about you and her, all the shagging, just after he turned up. He clearly had no idea. But then again, I don't suppose that's really the sort of thing you'd put in a text replying to your ex-lover if you want to stop them turning up on your holiday is it? 'Sorry dear, busy shagging someone else I met on the plane, so don't come.' Couldn't see that working out too well with anyone in general, and certainly not bloody Richard Weston with his huge ego."

As she finished she reached for her cocktail, took a last sip, and coldly, rather nonchalantly and bizarrely said, "Hmm ... yes, that is rather good. Time for another, I reckon. At least my telling him

185

about you and her as soon as he arrived got me a couple of shags with him straightaway. So, it's not all bad, I suppose."

He actually thought he heard her release slight, almost manic chuckle after that. He couldn't see as he still had his head in his hands staring forward vacantly towards the far end of the bar while he heard all her disturbing details, but she actually shrugged her shoulders and then tilted her head slightly to one side as she made that remark about it not being all bad.

She was in full flow, however, and was not stopping until she wrung the last drop of agony for him out of what she was telling him. She was enjoying it even more than she thought she would, although not merely because of his mounting agony and anger, but because she believed she was well and truly screwing over Aileen and any hope in her relationship with him.

"I knew he'd give in to my suggestion of that straightaway after I told him about you and her, a shag, I mean. His ego you see. His first thought once he heard about her and you was revenge, to get back at her, and what better way than a shag with me? He assumed that would piss her off good and proper."

She beckoned Callum over and ordered another, feeling very smug and self-satisfied inside that she had achieved precisely what she'd set out to do.

After Callum had gone off to make the cocktail Martin slowly lifted up his head from resting on his hands and elbows on the bar, visibly gulped, and asked, "How long?"

"How long what? How long has it been going on?" She knew exactly what he meant, but was even more determined to spin out his agony for as long as she could. She assumed that all the while Aileen would be wondering where the bloody hell he was, and suffering from Richard's no doubt overbearing attention at LBN. She figured that the longer she could detain Martin the more chance there was of Richard succeeding in persuading Aileen to go off somewhere with him so he could get into her knickers again.

"Yes, how long? Of course, how long has it been going on, Sandra? What do you think I bloody meant?" Now Martin's anger was growing. Perfect, she thought, exactly as planned.

"His text said they'd had four great months, but after what she said the other night about bumping into each other at their company Christmas party last December – you remember, when you asked about them working for the same company – well, I'm guessing it started then. As I pointed out in that conversation, he did stay over that night in the hotel in London where the party was. Plus, there have been a few other little things in conversations here between me and the two of them since he's been here, and when it was just me and her here, that have made me wonder."

Sandra was purposefully only telling him part of the truth of the situation. She deliberately never told Martin precisely, word for word, what the text said that she saw from Richard on Aileen's phone. She knew it exactly, word for word, but chose not to give him the whole thing, the whole picture. She never told him Richard actually wrote, "I know you said we should stop, and we did, but we had four great months and I can't, don't want to stop."

It clearly suggested that their affair was over, and that it was Aileen who stopped it, but that it was Richard who wanted to continue it again now, not Aileen. However, telling Martin that wasn't part of Sandra's plan of revenge. She preferred Martin to think that the affair was still going on.

Martin was shattered. He sat there in complete silence for a couple of minutes, staring blankly into space towards the wall at the far end of the bar, totally unfocused. What was rushing through his brain was had he been such a fool? Was all they had done just a holiday fling for Aileen? Something she'd embarked on because at the beginning of the holiday she had no idea at that time that her lover from back home was going to show up and make things awkward, especially with his wife there too.

Sandra let him stew. She was practiced at planting suspicions and doubt in an individual's mind in her MI6 work. This was more personal, but she knew she could employ the same skills. Just let him go over and over in his mind everything he'd done or said to Aileen since they'd met, as well as everything she'd done and said to him. She knew that was precisely what he'd be doing. Now she just had to sit there in silence, take another sip from her cocktail, and let him go over and over all that in his mind. Her revenge mission was complete, and almost perfectly successful, with the one solitary failure being the part of it of getting into his bed. She waited another few minutes in silence, wondering whether it was worth trying that part one last time again a bit later.

She was right about one thing though. She had been very successful with that part of her plan. As she suspected, he was, indeed, trying desperately to recall, going over and over, everything that Aileen and him had said to each other, and everything they'd done together since they met. As part of that he recalled what Aileen had told him outside Pal's on the second night of the holiday, When he asked her if there had been anyone else she'd met, a man, since her divorce, he remembered she told him, "Just one around the same age as me." But didn't she also say, "But that's all finished now, been like that for a while." Maybe she wasn't exactly telling him the truth, however. She was probably worried he might mention it again, 'the man around the same age' as her, when Sandra was with them, which would make her curious, because it seemed that as far as she knew then Aileen was not seeing any one.

One thing he certainly was able to decide there and then, however, was that he was definitely not going up to Lindos By Night tonight now to meet her, especially knowing Richard might still be there. Also, he wasn't going to Glow to meet her either. He guessed the two texts earlier were from her; the ones that Sandra prevented him from checking. So, he wasn't going to reply to them tonight either. He needed time to think this through before he spoke to her about it, or maybe even confront Richard as well?

Firstly, though he eventually ended his silence by asking Sandra, "Have you confronted them about it, either of them?"

"No, not yet, I've been biding my time, letting them sweat. As I said, I even shagged Richard a couple of times since he arrived just to piss her off, and made bloody sure she knew about it."

She was now trying to make Aileen the real focus of not only her anger but also his anger, the real bad person in all this. It was deliberate, through the words and phrases she was employing. That was the one she wanted to turn him against. She added, "I will though, before the end of the holiday, probably on the last day."

Once again he just stared straight ahead into space towards the far end of the bar. After another minute Sandra cynically chose her moment. "Fuck it, fuck them, and let's get pissed. Callum," she called out, "Two of your finest, strongest shots please, plus one for yourself, and more drinks for me and Martin here."

So, he stayed in Crazy Moon with Sandra. She was now so patently on a mission to get him drunk. She kept ordering more and more shots, while also continuing to blatantly flirt with Callum. The only time she diverted from focusing her attention towards the young barman was when, completely out of the blue, she decided to try just once more to get into Martin's bed, and complete the final part of the jigsaw of her revenge plan on Aileen.

"I expect you're really angry with her, Aileen I mean, over what I've told you, Martin. I know I would be if I was in your shoes," she started to say to him.

"Sort of, I guess, but I'm more surprised, stunned, than angry at the moment," he replied. "I just need to think things through, go over what she's told me since I met her. But surely you must be angry with Richard too, aren't you?"

"Of course, but this is not the first time. He has previous, if you know what I mean, and I doubt it'll be the last. The thing I can't get my head round is that Aileen knows he's done it to me before, and more than once. The last time, before Aileen, was with a young secretary at his previous job. I don't get why she would get involved with him when she knows that, because I told her all about it. She was my 'shoulder to cry on' when I found out about it. That is until I did something about it and confronted and embarrassed the woman at the place she worked."

"Really?" Martin interjected.

"Yep, and I was bloody good, totally destroyed her, and her employment. After I finished with her she had to leave the company straightaway."

Blimey, Martin thought, this is one tough, vindictive woman. While he was pondering that she moved into the final element of her plan.

189

"Not sure quite how to do that with Aileen, though, revenge I mean. Unless, of course, we kill two birds with one stone, so to speak; deal with both our anger with one perfect act of revenge."

While she had been building up to what she was going to suggest with her seemingly casual preamble about how she had dealt with Richard's past infidelities she avoided any eye contact with Martin. Instead, it was her turn now to stare blankly towards the far end of the bar as she spoke almost dispassionately about it.

Martin turned towards her with a confused look across his face at her 'we kill two birds with one stone' comment. "What do you mean by that?"

She turned towards him on her stool in order to look him straight in the eyes, deliberately placed her right hand on his shorts high up his left thigh, and then proceeded to tell him slowly, with as much sexuality oozing out of her mouth and in her body shape as she could muster, "You and me, your flat, your bed, remember. What I suggested earlier. It'd be fun, perfect revenge on her." She moved her hand even further up his thigh and squeezed it gently as she added, this time with her fluttering eyelashes so obviously aimed at him, "Call it a revenge fuck if you like, but it'd be a great way to pay her back, don't you think?"

He was shocked. He quickly grabbed her hand and removed it from his thigh as he told her, No, Sandra, I don't do revenge fucks, and I like to know all the facts before I do anything stupid. In fact, I don't really do revenge in any way, let alone what you're suggesting." His anger was now turning on her. What a bloody fine trio of people he'd met on holiday in these three, her, Richard, and even Aileen, he thought.

As he finished his refusal he looked away from her towards behind the bar and saw Callum raising his eyebrows and shaking his head slightly at what he'd obviously seen was happening. Not that Sandra saw him, but as Martin looked at him the young barman briefly raised his right hand to the side of his head and made a circular action with his index finger, indicating that he thought she was one crazy woman.

Sandra was quite drunk by now, but at least her growing inebriation had some calming effect of her ability to produce any sort of aggressive response, unlike the opposite effect it had on her husband, Richard.

She simply twisted on her stool back to face the bar and told Martin, "Okay, suit yourself, your loss, but I'll get my revenge on the bitch some other way eventually"

She had obviously lost all sense of what she was telling him. He was obviously going to relay to Aileen everything she'd told him that night, if only to get to her side of the story. Sandra seemed to have lost all comprehension that was what he was likely to do, of course. She'd gambled that he'd take up her revenge fuck offer, and having done so, that although he would obviously confront Aileen with what she'd told him about her and Richard's affair, Martin would have to keep some of what Sandra had told him to himself, especially her last remark about getting "revenge on the bitch some other way eventually."

Having been rejected by Martin, Sandra returned to focusing her attentions so obviously again on getting inside Callum's pants. There was very little chance of that happening though, Martin reckoned, given the increasing inebriated state of her. Generally, she wasn't an unattractive woman. However, in the state she had now reached - a mixture of the effect of the considerable amount of alcohol she'd consumed, particularly the numerous shots, together with her growing desperation for male company to console herself further – she was not exactly an attractive prospect to anyone, let alone a barman almost half her age,

Martin, on the other hand, had been more careful and circumspect with his alcohol intake, especially where the shots were concerned. He discreetly declined quite a few to Callum, or equally discreetly passed them back over the bar without Sandra realising. Consequently, he wasn't drunk, anyway not nearly as much as Sandra clearly was.

It was her state that concerned Callum most when Martin announced at one-thirty, "Okay, I'm off to my bed," adding quickly, "Alone," before Sandra could make her earlier suggestion once again.

In fact, she never responded at all, either because she was now angry with Martin also for not taking up her offer, or was just too drunk to bother. She was now slumped on the bar, with her head resting firmly in her hands supported by her elbows on the bar. Her lipstick, and even some of her mascara, was smudged. She was not exactly a vision of attraction.

Callum tried a desperate plea of, "What about your friend here, Martin, as he paid for his drinks?"

But Martin had had quite enough of Sandra for one night. He just replied, "Not my problem, mate. She's old enough to look after herself. Goodnight and good luck."

With that he lifted himself off his stool and headed for the door.

No sooner had Martin left than the now well pissed Sandra tried it on with Callum one final time. She took a deep breath and asked, "What time did you say you finish? Where do you go after?" Even then she still slurred her words.

Once again he declined, and even more resolutely this time. "As I told you before, to my bed, alone."

Meanwhile, Martin headed straight back to his flat nearby, increasingly confused and angry about what he'd heard about Aileen and Richard's affair. He was determined to stick to what he'd decided earlier and not go to Lindos By Night or Glow that night now. What he didn't know at the time was that Aileen never made it to Glow either.

As he lay in his bed alone at least he could console himself with the fact that he had resisted Sandra's advances and not succumbed to her blatant offers of sex. Even though he'd had a fair bit to drink, he was still aware enough to be actually alerted at the time to what she might be up to through his expertise and knowledge of Greek Mythology, and in that respect, by drawing parallels with the actions of the Goddess Hera, the wife of Zeus. Hera was the Queen of the ancient Greek Gods. She represented the ideal woman and was the Goddess of Marriage, but she was famous for her jealous and vengeful nature that was principally aimed against the lovers of her husband. Martin was pretty sure that Sandra's vengeful nature was aimed at ensuring she completely ruined any prospect of a relationship between him and Aileen. That is, if Aileen hadn't actually already done that enough herself through her supposed affair with Richard.

23

Saturday 2nd July, 2016: a quick disappearance

Martin woke with a headache at ten-thirty on the Saturday morning, part slight hangover and partly from what Sandra had told him the night before. When he turned on his phone there were now altogether five texts from Aileen, three from the night before he had ignored or Sandra had prevented him reading and replying to, and two on that morning. The final one the night before said she wasn't going to Glow and so wouldn't meet him there. She wrote that she was too tired after a very tiresome and draining evening with Sandra and Richard, so she was off to her bed.

He decoded he couldn't avoid the issue any longer, and certainly not perpetuate his anxiety over it for all the rest of that day. In any case, if he didn't respond to her texts she would surely wonder what had happened. Plus, of course, he definitely didn't relish the prospect of Sandra delighting in breaking it to Aileen that she had told him about Richard and her, or even fabricating some fairy tale along the lines that it was Martin who had tried to get her into bed, rather than the other way round. From what he'd seen of Sandra in action, God knows he wouldn't even put it past her to suggest, or even straight out say, to Aileen that they had actually slept together. He was determined to get his account of what had happened in first before Sandra had any chance to weave her fabrications, in addition to asking Aileen about her and Richard, of course.

Rather than just text, which can always be easily misinterpreted anyway he thought, he decided it would be best to firstly call Aileen and suggest they meet. He knew a call might be tricky as he wanted to speak to Aileen without somehow alerting Sandra, and if the two women happened to still be in the villa or already on the beach together that could be difficult.

"Hi, where are you?" he immediately asked after she answered.

"In the villa."

"Is Sandra there with you?"

"No, but why do you want to know that, Martin?" She was confused at his sudden interest in the whereabouts of her holiday companion.

"I'll explain later. So, she's not there in the villa?"

"No, there was a text from her on my phone when I woke up fifteen minutes ago telling me that she's gone to Rhodes Town for the day with Richard. She said he wanted to see it Can't imagine why, it's not usually his thing I think, history. He didn't seem very impressed when she started going on about the history of the island and all that the other night."

"Hardly," he agreed.

"She said in her text that she needed to talk to him alone about something, so maybe it is really more about that than the 'Street of the Knights' in Rhodes Town?"

Even though she thought she could probably hazard a pretty good guess at what it was that Sandra wanted to talk to Richard about alone – his affair with Aileen, and that she knew about it – she wasn't about to tell Martin that at that point. She even managed a small giggle down the phone after she made her flippant remark about the 'Street of the Knights'.

"Right, yes probably, you're probably right about Richard's lack of interest in history," he agreed.

"So?" she asked.

"So, what?"

"What's so important about whether Sandra's around, here, or not, Martin?"

However, he never answered her question directly. "Look, what about meeting for a late breakfast at Giorgos? I'll explain it all there, and I need some food inside me, a good English breakfast. In half-an-hour?"

"Sure, I could do with some food too," she agreed.

By the time they finished the call Aileen had already guessed what might be coming her way; what he was going to ask her about. She'd already picked up enough comments from Sandra to which double meaning could be attached to surmise that the secret of her and Richard's affair was no longer that, a secret. Although she didn't actually know at that point that Sandra had sought out Martin the evening before in order to deliberately tell him about it, she assumed that somehow she'd managed to let him know her suspicions. Aileen was smart enough to realise that ever since the volatile and unpredictable Richard had turned up something was bound to come out. She had been expecting and anticipating it, and had steeled and conditioned herself to deal with it in the way she knew best. Ultimately, she believed she was certainly experienced enough to do so.

When Aileen and Richard finally got back to the villa the night before Sandra was still in Crazy Moon drinking herself stupid, while trying unsuccessfully to get into Callum's bed. Aileen headed straight for her own bedroom, while Richard, in an almost similar state of inebriation as his wife at that time, headed for his and Sandra's bedroom. Aileen never checked, but she assumed that Sandra was already sound asleep in her bed, nursing her upset stomach. Richard, however, was initially surprised to find her not there. Before he could go to tell Aileen that though, he sat on the edge of the bed to remove his canvas deck shoes but simply slumped back onto the bed and into a deep sleep. Consequently, as she hadn't seen them the next morning before they departed for Rhodes Town, Aileen had no idea that Sandra hadn't actually gone back to the villa when she left her and Richard at LBN because of her supposed upset stomach.

Martin was already sat at one of the tables outside Giorgos in the shade from the baking hot approaching midday sun when Aileen arrived. This time she only very tentatively kissed him on the cheek as she bent down to say, "Hi." After she did so, and then sat down opposite him at the table, the owner, Tsamis, appeared and took their order of an English breakfast and coffee each.

There was clearly some tension in the air between them. Martin tried to ease it a little by telling her, "Sorry I didn't make it to Lindo By Night last night to help you out with Martin. Was he much of a pain? You didn't make it to Glow either you said in one of your texts?"

"No I didn't. Richard wore me down. He was extremely tiresome. The more he drank the worse he got. He got even worse after Sandra left. She had a stomach upset apparently. In the end I was really tired from it all, all his antics and rudeness. So, eventually I went to bed."

"Sandra never had a stomach upset, Aileen. It was just a lie to get away from you and Richard, and come and find me-"

She looked surprised, and confused, as she interrupted with, "Find you, why?"

He frowned as he went on, "She was determined to, I reckon, find me I mean. Not difficult as I was outside Bar404 drinking when she saw me, anybody would easily enough as they were walking by-"

Aileen interrupted again, "She knew you'd be there anyway. I told her earlier over dinner, well, her and Richard actually, that you were meeting those guys from England there that you knew."

"I see, well, she said she had something she needed to tell me," he continued.

Aileen definitely knew now what was coming. She waited in silence as he went on.

"But she wouldn't tell me at first, and then kept dragging it on without saying what it was. I thought it was all a load of bollocks at first, and that she just wanted to stop me coming to meet you at LBN for some reason, although I couldn't figure out why. Then she said she didn't want to stay outside 404, it was too public, and Richard or you might appear and see us there, which would be embarrassing. At that point I honestly had no idea what the hell she was going on about, what would be embarrassing for instance. But, to try to get her to eventually bloody tell me whatever it was she thought was so important so that I could then come and join you at LBN I suggested we went to Crazy Moon. We haven't been there yet. It's near to Bar404. Anyway, after more attempt at delay from her, and growing annoyance from me, eventually she-"

"Told you about me and Richard, our affair. I thought she'd found out, but she hasn't said anything directly to me." Aileen wasn't dragging it out any longer, and made it easier for him by interrupting.

He sighed heavily. Just at that point Tsamis brought their coffees. That produced a very awkward uncomfortable tense silence as they stopped talking while he placed them on the table. It was only broken after he walked away by Martin asking, with a mixture of incredulity and extreme disappointment in his voice, "So, it's true, you're having an affair?"

Now it was Aileen's turn to look confused. "Are? Are having an affair?" Her confused look changed into anger across her face at Sandra as she added, "Is that what the cow sodding told you?"

He was shocked at the vehemence of her response. "Well, yes, that was about it. She said outright that the two of you had been having an affair, and she clearly inferred it was it was still going on. That was what she led me to believe, anyway. She said she saw text from him on your phone the first day you were here, while the two of you were on Pallas Beach and you were in the sea swimming, which clearly suggested he was having an affair with you."

"So, she's been storing this up for over a week. That explains some of the snide remarks and innuendos then." She looked steely eyed at him across the table as she told him, "Had, Martin, it's had, not having." Then she reached into her bag for her phone, clicked on the text symbol, scrolled down, and told him, "Look, read the text for yourself."

In fact, although she was deliberately displaying to Martin visible anger at Sandra embellishing the truth in what she had told him, inside she was smugly pleased that her plan of leaving her phone for Sandra to see his message on the beach that day, and discover their affair, had succeeded perfectly. An hour before that, while Sandra was in the shower in the villa that morning, she'd sent Richard a purposefully provocative text saying, "Lovely place here. Sure I'll have a great time alone with Sandra. Good of you to agree not to come, as she wanted." She knew he'd respond at some point, and pretty soon that morning. He wouldn't be able to resist. It was just a matter of when, hopefully at an opportune moment for Sandra to spot the text. She'd deliberately left her phone on the small coffee table in the lounge of the villa while she was getting ready for the beach in her bedroom, but his response didn't come then. Instead, it came perfectly while she was swimming later. She'd seen it after she came back from her swim, but she wasn't sure, of course, whether or not Sandra had. From some of her barbed comments over the past week she thought she may have done. Now she was sure.

As she handed Martin the phone across the table she didn't wait for him to read it, but told him, "It says, 'I know you said we should stop, and we did, but we had four great months and I can't, don't want to stop'. That's what he wrote, and then bombarded me with texts for days saying he wanted to come here, wanted us to get back together, and all the rest of his shit. I ignored them all. Sure, I knew he was coming, but I never encouraged him. I told him not to plenty of times. But you've seen, he's pig-headed and just ignored them all."

"But you did actually have an affair, you and Richard then?" Martin asked.

At that point Tsamis brought their breakfasts, which produced another few seconds of awkward silence.

Eventually Aileen started to explain as she shifted uncomfortably in her chair. "What can I say, Martin? I wanted to tell you. Of course I did, and I was definitely going to, but I wanted to pick the right moment, and there never has been one with Sandra and Richard around most of the time."

He looked across the table at her blankly, not really knowing what to say. She reached over and grasped his hand as she continued, "It was stupid, a stupid thing to do, get involved with him. I realise that now, but I just lost my mind for a while. It's over now though, and has been for quite a while, but he won't take no for an answer. That's why I reacted the way I did when you asked if we 'are having an affair', rather than had an affair. Sandra knew exactly what she was doing when she led you to believe it was still going on, believe me. It was clear from that text she saw which I just showed you that it was finished. Sure, he keeps pestering me with texts, but I've ignored all of them. He's even tried it on a couple of times here, but I've told him to sod off, or words to that effect."

She was very convincing, and sounded sincere. She was good at it. However, she was being economical with the truth when she told him she'd lost her mind for a while in slipping into the affair with Richard. On the contrary, it was all part of the plan, and she knew exactly what she was doing then. Martin though, and meeting him and embarking on what they'd had in Lindos, certainly wasn't part of the plan at all.

He squeezed her hand encouragingly as she went on, "He was worried sick about me coming away on holiday with Sandra. He obviously thought something would come out. That's why he turned up here this week. Now I guess she knows anyway. As I said, she hasn't said anything to me yet. She's on some sort of revenge kick I reckon, and part of that is to drive a wedge between us. That's why she led you to believe the affair was still going on-"

Martin squeezed her hand once more as he interrupted, "That sounds about right, and obviously part of that was what she tried to get me to do last night. She even tried to get me to have sex with her last night. She was pissed, but twice she bluntly suggested we slept together, had sex, and in my bed in the flat."

"So you didn't?"

He was surprised she would even ask that and let go of her hand at that point.

"Of course not. She was a complete mess. As I said, pissed, and her lipstick was smudged all across her face, plus her mascara had run."

Aileen tried to lighten the mood a bit as she asked, with a cheeky grin, "So, you would have done if she wasn't pissed and a mess then?"

He realised she was joking and winding him up as he replied, "Stop it, no, certainly not. But when I turned her down flat twice she then proceeded to try it on with one of the young barmen, who I reckon was almost half her age."

She looked deadly serious again as she looked across the table straight into his face, and with as much sincerity in her voice as she could muster, said, "But it is over, Martin, I promise you. It's finished, and has been for months. It was stupid. You've seen what a prat he is. I can't imagine what I was thinking."

Once again, she wasn't exactly being truthful. She knew precisely what she was thinking when she started her affair with Richard. That was exactly what she'd planned. For emphasis, however, she added one more pleading, "It was stupid," and reached across to take his hand once more, continuing with another plea, "Don't let an idiot like him spoil this for us, please Martin."

Unlike their breakfasts, which remained untouched in front of them, he was still trying to digest all she had told him, plus what Sandra had the night before. After only a few seconds though, he surprised himself somewhat as he told her easily, "Okay, I see, of course not. We've all done stupid things at some point in our lives, I guess. Don't worry, I won't let him spoil it, we won't." He added, "Now, eat your breakfast before it gets too cold. I'm starving."

This time instead of reaching for his hand, she got up, walked around the table, bent down and kissed him intensely on the lips.

As she went back to sit and eat her breakfast he gave her a broad smile. Out of the corner of his eye he noticed Tsamis and the Slovak waitress, Sabine, grinning at him from inside the café through the open door.

As he tucked into his breakfast he asked, "So, what happened to Richard last night then?"

"I left him at Lindos By Night. He was well pissed. Who knows where he went after that?" she told him with a shrug of her shoulders and a straight face. Once again, she wasn't being truthful.

She watched him carefully out of the top of her eyes as they ate their breakfasts, trying to gauge his reaction, and if things were really okay between them. She waited a couple of minutes as they ate in silence. Then she put down her knife and fork and picked up her coffee. She took a sip, and with her other hand reached across the table, this time gripping his lower arm, as much to his surprise slowly and deliberately she said, "Fuck those two demented deranged maniacs. They well and truly deserve each other. Let's leave them to it, get out of here today. I bet we can find a flight to London today that we can get on, and just go. I've had just about enough of them now, Martin. Please say yes and let's just go?"

In fact, he was more than surprised. He looked totally bemused by her sudden decision and seemingly erratic spontaneous suggestion. As he hesitated before responding she wouldn't let it go, and pressed him, planting a tempting thought and offer in his mind.

"Come on, Martin, what do you say? I can be at your place with you, in your bed in London in trendy Highgate by ten tonight, I reckon, if we're lucky with the flights of course. Then we will be completely away from these two idiots and their games in their marriage. And you can do your writing, or whatever you have to do, just as easily in London can't you? I will try not to distract you too much."

As she finished she added a little side effect to her offer, raising her eyebrows slightly, tilting her head to one side, again slightly, and allowing a broad mischievous smile to spread across her lips. She was sure he couldn't resist that and refuse her suggestion.

"Err ..." despite her sexy charm offensive, and her inviting offer, he still hesitated, although only briefly. Within another ten seconds, as she now gazed intently across the table at him with those lovely brown eyes of hers, she was proved right. He couldn't resist and slowly, with still a degree of hesitation in his voice, agreed. "Okay ... err ... okay, yes ... yes, why not? ... Why not? ... As you said, fuck them!"

"Great!" She was bubbling again as she quickly added, "As I told you earlier, they've gone to Rhodes town for the day, so they're not around at the villa. She probably thinks that's one way to keep him, and her, out of my way today. She's bound to have presumed you'd see me to tell me what she told you last night. Anyway, I'll finish this, go back to the villa, throw all my stuff into my bag and come to your flat as quickly as possible. Then we can get on line and see about flights."

"Sounds good," he agreed, "I'll go back to my place and throw my stuff in my bag. But there's no internet in my flat. Tsamis has got wifi here though, so I'll look on my phone here for one now."

Within ten minutes he'd found a British Airways flight at four with spare seats and booked them on to it. He asked Tsamis for the bill. After they paid it Martin told her, "Okay Irish, let's go."

She took his hand, gave him a lovely cheeky irresistible smile, and said, "Irish? So, that's what you're gonna call me then? I like it." As she finished she kissed him, told him, "See you in half-an-hour at your place, hopefully less," and rushed off down the alley towards the villa through the Rhodes boatloads of daytime Lindos visitors.

By just after one o'clock they were climbing into a taxi in the Main Square to head to the airport and their flight.

It was gone seven when Sandra and Richard got back to the villa from their day in Rhodes Town. She had, indeed, confronted him while they were there over his affair with Aileen. She chose to do it over lunch, which turned into a very argumentative, nasty episode. She ended up screaming and shouting at him in a very embarrassing situation, such that at one point one of the Greek waiters came over to their table and asked them to quieten down, or rather her, as he just sat there in silence letting her vent her anger. He basically had no defence, and the most embarrassing moment came when her face totally contorted and she shouted at him, "You're just a useless, pathetic, conniving, deceitful piece of shit!"

That certainly attracted the attention of the rest of the customers sat outside the restaurant in the pretty Rhodes square, and plenty of the passers-by. It was at that point that the waiter approached asking them to quieten it down. It was fair to say that she got her point across to him very forcibly, although his non-reaction in any way didn't exactly demonstrate to her any remorse on his part. He never once offered even a paltry, "Sorry." Nevertheless, having vented her anger, determined to let him know she was fully aware of what he'd been up to with Aileen, the remainder of the day was spent wandering around the various historic sites in Rhodes Town in something of an awkward uneasy truce between them. It was only just before they were about to get a taxi back to Lindos that he dared to raise the subject again and ask if she had confronted Aileen about it.

She told him, in no uncertain terms, "No, not yet, but I will when we get back from here. Don't worry, that bitch is going to get hers. She's got plenty coming to her, more than she, or you, could know."

By the time they had got back to the villa, however, Aileen was long gone. Her and Martin's flight was within minutes of touching down at London's Gatwick airport at that time. Sandra went straight to Aileen's bedroom, knocked and, without waiting for any reply, simultaneously walked in. She was fired up to also give Aileen 'both barrels' of her verbal assault and condemnation, but she was disappointed of course.

Initially, she assumed that Aileen was still at the beach, or somewhere else in the village. That is until she noticed that her large bag was not in the room. She checked the small wardrobe and discovered that none of her clothes were there either. As she emerged from Aileen's room Richard asked, with some relief, "Not there? She must still be on the beach."

"All her clothes and her large bag have gone. I bet bloody Martin told her I knew what had been going on between you two," she said angrily as she began to walk back and forth across the lounge in an agitated fashion wondering what to do next.

"What? How did he-" Richard began to ask, but she never let him finish.

"I bloody told him all about it last night, all about you two, you prat. Of course I was going to do that wasn't I? Did you think I bloody wouldn't?"

Her anger was back, not that it had really completely gone away through the day. Like the hot sun, it had built up to its fiercest heat in the middle of the day when she confronted Richard over lunch. Then it subsided slightly subsequently during the rest of the day. This time, however, it was not just directed at Richard. Aileen was her target. She stopped walking back and forth, rubbed the back of her neck with her left hand as though she had an irritating neck ache, and eventually told him, "Maybe she's gone to stay with that shit, Martin. She's probably wound him around her little finger with her bloody innocent big brown eyes and her tight little arse. Spun him some alternative story and convinced him to believe her no doubt. Blinded by the brains in his dick he probably has done."

"Are you going to go there to confront her then," Richard asked tentatively, although he wasn't exactly sure why he was concerned at all about what Sandra was about to do any longer.

"Only one problem with that, Richard, I don't exactly know where his flat is. I know roughly what part of the village it's in, somewhere behind Bar404 and Yannis Bar, but where exactly down that alley, or even across the square off there, I haven't a clue. I can hardly go knocking on every door there till I find the right one can I?"

"Hardly," he agreed, hoping the impossibility of that idea would at least make her calm down for now. But Sandra wasn't giving up that easily, or calming down at all.

"It's a bloody village. Even if she's gone to stay with bloody Martin they can't hide in his flat for the rest of the holiday can they? She'll have to come out sometime, even if it's only to get the flight home."

Richard thought that was a logical assumption, but he decided the best course of action for him was to remain silent. So, he just sat down wearily from all the stress in one of the most comfortable armchairs in the lounge.

There wasn't much space for him to comment anyway as Sandra immediately pronounced, "Jack!"

Now Richard did ask, "Jack, what?"

"Jack Constantino. I bet he knows where Martin's flat is. Bound to, Martin's been coming here for years, remember, knows Jack well, he's sure to know."

She looked at her watch, saw it was now approaching seven-thirty, and told Richard, "I'm going to jump in the shower and then I'll go up to the Courtyard Bar and ask Jack where Martin's flat is, before it gets too busy up there for him to talk."

"What should I do? Shall I come with you?" Richard asked.

She merely gave him a look of total disdain and irrelevance as she headed towards her bedroom before the bathroom and her shower, eventually telling him, "You?" As she disappeared through the door to the bedroom her final disparaging shot to him was, "Who cares? This is all your fucking fault, not being able to keep your dick in your trousers yet again, and coming between friends! You can do what you usually do and go play with yourself. You're good at that. After all that's the only person you really care about isn't it!"

Sandra Weston was generally a hard headed, determined woman, but now over this she had gone into overdrive mode beyond even that.

By eight o'clock she was in the Courtyard Bar asking Jack Constantino if he knew the precise location of Martin's flat. Sandra told him that she'd promised to meet Aileen there as she hadn't seen her at all that day because she'd been in Rhodes Town all day. However, she explained that she hadn't realised she didn't quite know where Martin's flat was exactly, although she knew it was somewhere behind Bar404.

Jack told her that there was no number or name for Martin's flat, but he described just where it was in the alley that ran down from Bar404 and Yannis Bar, as far as he knew.

Sandra told him, "Thanks," and then lied further, explaining that she had to rush off as she'd arranged to meet Aileen there at eight, and was already late. "Be back in later no doubt," she added as she rushed out through one of the doors of the bar.

When she got to what she assumed from Jack's description was the door to the courtyard in which Martin's flat was located she banged the large metal door knocker soundly three times. At first no one responded, but when she tried again a guy who looked in his mid-twenties opened the door wearing a white vest and dark blue shorts. He looked as if he had been sleeping and her knocking had woken him.

"Martin, I'm looking for Martin," she informed him.

He wasn't a Brit or Greek and his English was limited. But he seemed to understand what she wanted, especially when she mentioned Martin by name. He turned slightly while he held the door open and pointed to the door to a flat across the courtyard, adding, "I there, Martin there."

There were two flats in the courtyard and she assumed he was indicating he lived in the other one. As she went to step through the door, however, he told her, "But Martin not here. Gone, left, lunchtime. I saw as I came back from work."

"Gone? Gone where?" she asked.

"England, he said me, England with woman."

"Shit!" Sandra exclaimed, telling him, "Thanks" as she stepped back out of the courtyard and into the alley. "Bloody cow" she muttered to herself as she set off hurriedly back to the villa to get her other phone.

When she reached the villa Richard was just appearing from the bathroom and a shower. He tentatively asked, "Find her?"

But she ignored him and rushed straight into their bedroom. He attempted to follow her, but she slammed the door in his face, telling him firmly, "Keep out!" She opened her suitcase and took out her other phone then immediately hit one of the buttons programmed for memory speed dial.

Within seconds a voice said, "What's up, Sandra?"

As quietly as possible, standing on the far side of the bedroom so that Richard would not be able to overhear, she replied, "She's bolted, Gill. She's bloody bolted, and he's gone with her. Back to England, his neighbour to his flat here told me. London I guess, but who knows. At least, I'm pretty sure that's what he said, the neighbour. His English wasn't great, an Albanian I think. Anyway, he seemed to be saying he saw them leave at lunchtime as he came back from work, and he definitely said Martin Cleverley told him they were going to England. It has to be London, that's where they both live. There are flights from here to all over the U.K., so it could be anywhere. Haven't had a chance to check yet where any late afternoon flights were going to in the U.K., guess you can do that anyway, but it has to be London, I'm sure."

What Sandra deliberately didn't tell her handler was the full series of events, and what may have prompted Aileen to bolt; what she'd told Martin the night before.

"Okay, Sandra, calm down. There's nothing you can do there now. If he's gone with her, and so suddenly, it leans toward substantiating the suspicions we, you, had about him, and that maybe she's been turned by him."

"Yep, seems like that could be," Sandra rather disingenuously agreed.

"We'll put out an alert for the airports and ports and pick them up if we can. Depends if they were able to get on a flight quickly, assuming they only decided and booked it today of course. Although they could have planned this well in advance and it was all a set up. Either way they may already have landed, be through passport control and away, if they left there at lunchtime. Anyway, leave it with me. I'll keep you updated. Enjoy the rest of your holiday, if you can."

"Thanks, but that's not going to be easy now, Gill, believe me. You have no idea." With that the line went dead.

Part Five: Brighton, first week of July, 2016

24

Thursday 7th July, 2016: confrontation Martin and Richard

Halfway through their flight back to London Aileen told him, "It seems such a shame to go straight back to steamy, stuffy London after being by the sea in Lindos, don't you think? I know Highgate is nice, and I know I said we could be in your bed there together by ten tonight, but it's not like being by the sea is it? It's London."

She knew precisely what she was doing, aimed to do. She was well aware that Sandra, as well as her Agency friends, knew exactly where she lived and would come looking for her once she got back to London. Sandra told her that bluntly after they left the Rainbird Bar in Lindos that day, after Sandra had been subjecting Martin to a virtual interrogation. She made it quite clear that Aileen would be pulled in by MI6 after she returned to London and quizzed on her relationship with Martin, in terms of what she may have told him. Probably Martin would be as well. She also knew they would check out Martin's place too, looking for them both.

As she'd figured out earlier in the week when she knew Richard was going to turn up in Lindos, she had to adjust to new circumstances. Now she was 'thinking on her feet', adjusting to new situations. Consequently, her adjusted plan now was to suggest as gently as possible that they go initially to somewhere other than his or her place.

"I know, why don't we go to Brighton for a few days, for the rest of our holiday, maybe till the end of the week?" she blurted out, trying to sound as spontaneous as possible.

"It's by the sea. It'll be nice, and we can get to know each other more without bloody Sandra or Richard being around, and all that stuff with him from the past. I booked time of work till the end of the week anyway. I'm sure we can find a flat to rent or a decent cheap hotel there online after we land, or even just go there on the train and find one when we get there? If necessary we could just stay in a hotel there tonight and then find a holiday flat tomorrow to rent till the end of the week. I'm sure there will be plenty of accommodation agencies we can go to and find one."

Yet again Martin was surprised by her apparently spontaneous suggestion, but he didn't take much persuading. He was being swept along by her charming attraction, and her apparent spontaneity with her suggestions only added to that. Why not, he thought to himself. He certainly had nothing to rush back to London for. He was supposed to be away for at least three weeks writing in Lindos, and there was nothing he had to go into the university for now that the semester had finished.

So, he readily agreed, and they went to Brighton by train after they landed at Gatwick at six U.K. time. They checked into a reasonable hotel for the night, deciding to look for a flat to rent till Friday in the morning. Over breakfast at Giorgos she'd tempted him with the suggestion that she could be in his bed with him by ten that night. In fact, it wasn't his bed, but one in a Brighton hotel instead, and it was almost a couple of hours earlier than ten, almost immediately after they got through the door of their fairly basic hotel room. After an hour in the double bed enjoying each other they showered, slipped out of the hotel briefly for pizza, then returned to the room, watched a movie on tv, and fell asleep in each other's arms on the bed.

They woke to a sunny Sunday morning by the sea in Brighton and checked out of the hotel after breakfast. They left their bags in a luggage room there while they went off to a nearby accommodation agency where they found a reasonably smart flat to rent for the week, one street back from the sea front in the centre of the city. They even went off shopping for food, milk, tea and coffee for the flat together in a nearby supermarket.

He was still somewhat bemused by the whirlwind train of spontaneous twists and turns she had put him through, or rather, that his growing affection for her had persuaded him to embark upon. It wasn't exactly usually in his character to act so spontaneously, but she had that effect on him. Nevertheless, he was very happy at that time, while she consoled herself with the belief that she was safe with him for the moment in Brighton. Why would anyone from the Agency find her there, including Sandra?

As they unpacked their bags in the flat on Sunday morning she realised she couldn't block out the recent past with Sandra and Richard completely and informed him, "Since we landed last night I've had a few texts from her, as well as from him, although I doubt that she knows he's still sending them. Obviously I'm not replying, and I've blocked calls from them, just in case you were wondering. They both sound bloody angry." she laughed as she told him that last part.

She knew that she needed to put off returning to her place, or even his, in London as long as possible. That would give her time to figure out her next move and avoid Sandra's MI6 friends turning up to cart her and Martin off somewhere unpleasant. She decided the way round it was to make yet another spontaneous suggestion to him. She was sure he wouldn't be able to resist, and that she would quite easily be able get him to agree to her proposal that they prolong their holiday a little more and go away for a spur of the moment weekend to Dublin at the end of their week in Brighton.

"Let's keep the holiday going for a bit longer. Please, please, Martin? I just don't want this to end now," she pleaded with him, using all the attributes of her sexuality, particularly her striking brown doe-eyed look. She knew he wouldn't be able to resist that as she added the pretext that she wanted them to get to know as much about each other as possible. That, of course, included showing him where she grew up in Dublin, she pointed out staring straight into his face. It was all too easy for her. She was right, he wasn't able to resist at all.

"Of course, good idea, Irish" he agreed. "I'll check out some flights online and you can decide what a good hotel is for us in Dublin."

She told him, "Thank you," added, "I love you," and planted a long, lingering intense kiss on his lips.

He was floating at her, "I love you," comment. He couldn't believe how quick and unreal it all seemed. It wasn't in his character at all these days to embark on such a journey emotionally, and so quickly. His practical side hadn't gone away completely, however, and it couldn't help kicking in. "We'll need to sort some clean clothes by the end of the week, or maybe sooner," he pointed out.

"We can just buy some here, can't we?" she told him casually.

"Or wash some we already have," he pointed out. "There is actually a washing machine and a dryer here in the flat, you know. I'm happy to show you how a washing machine works if you like," he joked.

She put both her arms around his waist and gave him a big hug, telling him with a smile, "I'm sure I can manage, thanks, and I can always try some of your clothes if I can't."

In fact, she did just that at times during the week, although not because she couldn't figure out how to operate the washing machine. Despite the fact that his t-shirts were clearly all too big and baggy for her she spent a considerable amount of time on a number of occasions wearing them in the flat during the week over just a pair of her knickers. If she wasn't in one of his t-shirts she would pull on one of his equally baggy on her polo shirts or short sleeved cotton shirts. He loved her wearing his clothes. He found it made her look even more sexy and irresistible, which he couldn't help but succumb to on a number of occasions. She knew precisely what she was doing, and what affect her dressing that way would have on him, of course. She loved it, and the sex that predictably followed.

He booked the Dublin flights online for Saturday morning, returning late Sunday night. She told him she'd booked them into the Jurys Inn hotel on Parnell Street for Saturday night, right in the centre of Dublin. She said it was a bit pricey, but she knew it, and it was excellent.

On the Tuesday morning he asked her, seemingly quite casually, "Is it going to be awkward when you go back to work next week, possibly bumping into him, Richard, I mean?"

"Highly unlikely," she replied. "He works at the company's offices in London Wall, in the city. Mine is in West London, South Ken. It's never happened before, except at that bloody Christmas party, of course. So, not likely to happen, unless he deliberately comes looking for me, I suppose. I reckon he's well and truly got the message now though. Anyway, I bloody hope so. That's for next week for me to worry about, if needs be, isn't it? I'm not supposed to be back at work until Monday, and we have a few more days here by the sea to enjoy, and each other, and then Dublin. So, let's not even think about all that for now, or especially him, please, Martin."

"Of course," he agreed as he kissed her, having got the information he wanted without alerting her to what he intended to do in a couple of days.

Later that afternoon he told her, "It's a bloody nuisance, but I have to go to London for a couple of hours on Thursday. I had an email from the Uni. There's a meeting about a possible case of plagiarism by one of my final year students that they want me to be at to give my opinion and background on the student. As far as they're concerned I could still be in Lindos I suppose, but I feel a bit guilty about it for the student if I don't go now I can because we're here."

She looked disappointed, but he attempted to suggest to her that it wasn't a big deal as he explained, "I know it's a pain, but the meeting is at eleven. I can get a train at around nine-thirty, get to the bloody thing, and it should only take an hour, so I should be back here by two, I guess. We'll still have that afternoon here together, as well as all day tomorrow."

She was silent, disappointment was still etched across her face.

"Look, you know I don't want to go, but I have to, and after this it will be the summer break and I'll be off for most of the rest of the summer until early September," he explained.

Her face brightened a little. Then she smiled in agreement, telling him, "Sure, it's okay, I understand, and, as you said, there's the rest of the summer to look forward to together. I'll amuse myself here, go shopping or something. I could do with some different clothes for the weekend."

Two days later on the Thursday Martin caught the nine-thirty train to London. However, he wasn't on his way to his university meeting. He'd assumed that Sandra and Richard had stuck to their original holiday plans and had only returned from Lindos that Wednesday, the day before. Assuming that Richard would have returned to work the next day, that Thursday, his plan was to go to Richard's office and confront him, warn him off Aileen. Having casually found out on Tuesday from Aileen what part of London the offices of her company in which Richard worked were located, he'd Googled the company and found the exact address in London Wall.

When he reached the offices he informed the receptionist who he was, adding, "I have an appointment to see Richard Weston."

He didn't, of course, but when she called Richard on the internal company phone system and told him Martin Cleverley had arrived for his appointment Richard never hesitated and replied instantly, "Really? Sure, send him to my office."

As soon as he entered the office Richard grabbed Martin by lapels of his jacket and forced him against the wall. "So, you two just up and pissed off then, just like that; like bloody scared rabbits. I had you figured as a scared runaway right from the first time I met you. You've got some bloody nerve coming here though. I'd say balls, but I don't think you've got any!"

"We-" Martin attempted to speak as Richard let go of his jacket lapels and walked away to behind his desk.

"We, it's bloody 'we' now is it?" Richard interrupted angrily.

"We couldn't put up with you and Sandra's bloody games any longer. You deserve each other," Martin told him as he straightened his jacket and went to sit down in the chair on the other side of the desk.

"Don't fucking sit down. You aren't stopping," Richard told him firmly. "And I wouldn't worry about whether we deserve each other or not. She's left me, or I prefer to say I left her, which is more

212

accurate. She's having some sort of sodding nervous breakdown it seems." He walked around the other side of the desk once more and again aggressively asked, "What the bloody hell do you want here anyway?"

"I want you to stay away from her. Leave her alone," Martin started to tell him. "She wants to be with me, not you. That's over, and has been for months she told me, but that you won't stop pestering her. Just leave her alone."

"Or what?" Richard glared into his face from a few inches away.

"I love her and she loves me," Martin blurted out suddenly. "She'll be happy with me."

"Boo hoo! How sad, you bloody wimp! You love her? After a week? You don't actually fucking know her at all do you? You might think you do after a week, but I can tell you that you don't, you bloody cretin!" Richard spat the words into his face, then backed off, turned his back and casually walked back to the other side of his desk once more.

As he sat down in his chair he said, in a very matter of fact manner, "So, when she told you she loves you did she tell you that before or after I fucked her in Lindos?"

"What? In Lindos?" Martin looked shocked.

"Yep, of course, on that Friday night before you two scuttled off back to London. Probably the reason she left, was afraid you might find out." Richard had a self-satisfied smirk on his face as he added. "I fucked her just for the fun of it, not even really for her or me to even enjoy it. It was more a case of doing it just to fuck you over."

"I don't believe you. It's not true. You'll bloody say anything to try and stop her being with me," Martin told him. Now it was him who was starting to get angry.

However, Richard wasn't backing off. Even though he remained sitting in the chair at his desk, and his voice was calm and controlled. He knew precisely what he was doing, or at least, trying to do.

"She loves it, sex. She's ravenous, can't resist it. Never turns it down, never could, even in Lindos with me. You can believe what you like wimp, but I know what happened. And at that Lindos By Night bar after Sandra left us that night she told me all about you. She loves to talk about it too you see, sex I mean, compare it."

213

"But, she-" Martin attempted to interrupt him.

"What, she never talked about it with you? Is that what you're going to say? Really, well I can tell you she loves to, believe me. Of course, you won't though will you, believe me? You don't bloody want to do you? Doesn't fit your nice, cosy, little sodding fairy tale world does it? Well, maybe this will convince you."

He stood up out of his chair and his voice got louder again as he stayed behind his desk. With an increasingly aggressive, nasty, mocking edge to it he added, "She told me she thought you were pathetic. She said you had your eyes closed while she was fucking you. What were you thinking about then you pervert? Your mummy was it? It's okay though. You shouldn't feel embarrassed, you creep. I can tell you from experience, plenty of experience, that you don't fuck Aileen, she fucks you, well and truly. That's the way she is, the way she likes it, to be in control all the time. That's what she was on that Friday night in that alley in Lindos, in control. She wanted it alright, there and then, and she was going to make bloody sure she got it. And she did, well and truly, believe me. She likes the danger too, the danger of possibly getting caught, being seen by someone in that alley that night. When she's in control she makes sure she always gets what she wants."

He deliberately changed his tone completely once more as he sat back down and continued in a very matter of fact, pitiful, softer voice, just like he was giving a boring report to a business meeting. "So, basically, she told me at Lindos By Night that evening that she just took pity on you. That she'd really just given you a sympathy fuck. All that enough to convince you, you wanker?"

"No, that's all bloody lies. I don't believe you. I know she loves me. She told me," Martin attempted to dismiss what he didn't want to hear.

"Oh yeah? Really? You think so? Is that what she actually told you, because she definitely wasn't saying that in that in that alley in Lindos on that Friday night." Richard was smirking once more as he added, "She definitely wasn't saying 'oh, but I love Martin'. Actually she wasn't saying anything, just moaning in pleasure in that alley along from that Courtyard Bar. Don't worry, she was enjoying it for sure; loved it. I could tell from her reactions that she was definitely enjoying herself I'd say, old boy."

He finished with a patronising condescending grin across his face.

"I don't believe-" Martin tried once again to interrupt, but as he got up and walked around from behind the desk aggressively towards him once more, Richard was determined to spew out everything at him.

He stopped and glared straight into Martin's face from around only six inches away. His face was now once again contorted and bright red with rage as he spat out at him, "That was all happening that night in Lindos while you were engaged in my wife's little revenge fuck, weren't you? She told me all about it, not that there was much to tell about the actual fuck though, she said; all a bit disappointing apparently."

Martin could only react to Richard's barrage with another incredulous, "What?" followed quickly with, "No, what revenge fuck? That's even more lies and absolute rubbish. It never happened. She tried it on, but I turned her down, twice."

"That's not the way she describes what happened, matey." Richard had stepped back a couple of paces, turned around and headed back behind his desk as he almost nonchalantly told Martin that.

"It's not bloody true, not at all. She's lying, or else you're lying again and she never told you that at all. But it never happened." Now Martin was pacing back and forth across Richard's office with his head down, getting increasingly angry and frustrated. Richard had completely screwed him up, and had deliberately planted a whole minefield of doubt in his mind about Aileen. It was no contest, and Martin was really thinking now that this was a terrible idea, coming to see him.

Meanwhile, Richard had achieved precisely what he set out to do, although he still had more fuel to throw on the fire of Martin's anger and frustration – a killer blow.

"Sure it is, of course you'd say that's a lie. You bloody screwed my wife! People don't screw my wife! Did you tell Aileen about that when she told you she loved you, or when you told her you loved her, perhaps? No, of course you didn't did you, you bloody liar! I bet she'd love to know that, don't you think?"

Now he was really taunting Martin, who just reacted with the same phrase over and over, gradually raising his voice. "It's all lies. You're full of bullshit! Sandra never told you I fucked her that night, because I never did. Or, at least, if she told you that then she was lying, because it never happened. And you and Aileen in that Lindos alley; that never happened either; I know it didn't. I'm sure it didn't. It's all just part of your bloody mind games."

Richard was right in Martin's face once more as he taunted him again, with his voice full of contempt and bile, "Really? You think so? Well, just ask her, ask Aileen then you fucking wimp! You're too afraid of the bloody answer though, aren't you?"

Martin could only react with a pleading, almost pitiful, "But, I love her, you don't. You just want her as a convenient fuck."

Still right in his face Richard responded by mocking him yet again with, "Well Boo hoo! Do you! Where are we, in the bloody school playground you prat?"

He turned and moved away to return to sit in the chair behind his desk. As he lowered himself into the chair he added, in a much more measured tone, again deliberately almost matter of fact, "That's what she is, isn't she, convenient, and a bloody good fuck too? I told you, she loves it. She's a good screw don't you agree? Of course you do."

He was grinning across at Martin once more, a self-satisfied grin as he continued, "But you have to go and confuse that with love though, because that's what you are; a bloody airy fairy liberal romantic. You fucking cretin! Anyway, she'll never settle for anyone now. Can't you bloody see that? She's too damaged, but you never will see that will you, never accept that? You bloody idiot!"

While he told Martin that Richard was moving the mouse to his laptop around on his desk as he peered at the screen. He finished speaking with a dismissive, firm, aggressive, "Now just piss off, I've got work to do!"

Martin turned towards the door to leave, realising and accepting that there was absolutely no point in trying to reason with him anymore. Just as he got there and reached for the handle, Richard looked away from the computer screen and told him, again in a

216

deliberate, completely different softer tone of voice, "No, no, that's not fair, old boy, You were right. I didn't fuck her in that alley in Lindos on that Friday night."

Martin half-turned around to look back across the office, where he saw a grinning Richard, staring across at him. He simply said pathetically, pitifully, with the sound of massive relief in his voice, "Oh, right, thanks, I thought not."

As Martin turned the door handle and began to open the door Richard returned to peer at the screen of his laptop, seemingly disinterested. But, accompanied by what had now turned into a complacent, smug smile on his face, he couldn't resist adding nonchalantly, "Ha ha! No, I lied just then. Of course, I fucked her then, or to be more accurate, she fucked me. She couldn't get enough of me in that alley. I told you, she loves the excitement, the danger of it, of possibly getting caught. Now just bloody get out of my office and my life, you creep."

Martin left, shattered, confused, in turmoil, and emotionally drained, just as Richard intended. As he sat on his train back to Brighton he really had no idea what to believe; whether what Richard had told him was just a malicious pack of lies or not. He'd only met him a very few times, but he'd soon come to the conclusion that Richard Weston was a nasty piece of work, who loved nothing more than to play games with people's lives, their minds, and their emotions. That was the one thing he did know for sure, along with the fact that he was going to have to pretty soon face Aileen, tell her what Richard had said, and ask her whether or not any of it was true. And hopefully sound convincing enough that he actually didn't believe any of it.

217

25

Friday 8th July, 2016: trust and faith

Throughout his train journey back to Brighton, as well as all through Thursday evening, Martin tussled with his dilemma of whether, when, and then how, to tell Aileen what Richard claimed had happened between him and her in the alley in Lindos. He didn't know what to believe. What if it was all just a lie; a trick by Richard to drive them apart? If, as he believed and hoped, it wasn't true but he gave her any indication whatsoever that he thought it might be, doubted her in even in the slightest way, then that could certainly drive a wedge between them, just as Richard no doubt wanted.

Finally, Martin decided he had to tell her. He would do it on Friday morning. He would be very careful not to sound like he was confronting her as such. He would just tell her, but preface it by firstly telling her that he knew it was all a lie and it was obviously Richard playing games.

However, his agonising wasn't resolved by any means on the Friday morning. He never expected or anticipated her response at all. He assumed she would deny it and, indeed, insist it was all a pack of lies; that Richard was playing games. That was what he hoped her response would be; an adamant denial. He presumed that her only other possible response would be to confirm it had happened, as Richard suggested, but he couldn't countenance that for one moment – not only that it had happened, but also that she would confirm it had.

Instead, however, she said next to nothing in response. They were walking on Brighton seafront in the warm sunshine just after midday, holding hands and stopping to look out at the sea occasionally, as well as exchanging the odd kiss. She obviously sensed his unease as

218

eventually she asked, "Is something wrong, Martin? You seem a bit distracted."

"I have to ask you something, and I'm not sure where to start," he replied, as they stopped walking.

"Just ask then, it can't be that big a problem, can it?"

He stopped walking, turned to look straight into her face, took a deep breath, and told her, "Okay. I didn't go into the Uni in London yesterday. I went to see Richard and-"

She frowned and looked stunned as she interrupted with, "What? Why? Why go and see that prat?"

"You said he was still trying to contact you, calls and texts, so I just wanted to tell him to stop, back off."

"And how did he respond to that?" Her voice had a clear strand of slight anger in it at what he had done.

"I think he got the message, well, eventually I think he did. I think he will back off, but that was not all of it. He told me something more that he claimed happened in Lindos between you two."

She remained silent while Martin continued, stuttering a little over what he had to tell her. He never actually did what he'd decided, never prefaced what he said by telling her first that he knew it was all a lie. He clean forgot to do that unfortunately.

"He claimed … he claimed …" He stopped and took another deep breath. "He claimed that … that you and him had sex in the alley behind the Courtyard bar on that Friday night that Sandra left the two of you alone at Lindos By Night. He put it more graphically, and he even taunted me to ask you if I didn't believe him, which I didn't of course. I told him he was a bloody liar."

"Well, he obviously is then, if that's what you believe, if that's what you think, Martin," she told him in what was a very surprising, confusing noncommittal response, which he never anticipated at all. He couldn't work out from it if she was saying they didn't or they did. He was hoping for a much clearer and stronger denial, but he wasn't about to get it.

"He started to say, "So, It's not-"

Before he could complete what he was going to ask, she turned around and began to continue to stroll along the seafront, telling him,

219

"Come on, let's get some lunch and a drink. I'm starving." He was bemused. Was that a denial or not?

He followed, caught her up, and they went for a pub lunch. As they finished their drinks he tried to ask her about it again, but once more she dismissed it, simply telling him forcibly, "I don't want to talk about him. If you want to believe it, believe him, then you can."

He decided to leave it for the moment. Nevertheless, he wasn't at all sure that he could merely ignore it. His character meant he was bound to let it gnaw away at him. Perhaps it was the academic in him, but he was someone who couldn't just let something drop without getting to the bottom of it. By seven o'clock that night it had been eating away at him for over a day since Richard told him, so he decided to try again before they went out for dinner on their final night in Brighton. However, Brexit, politics in the shape of Irish nationalism, and his degree of insecurity about her feelings for him, got in the way first.

He was lying on the bed in the flat in a polo shirt and jeans watching the television news as she emerged from the shower with a towel wrapped around her. As she proceeded to remove the towel and pull on her own jeans she told him, "Hadn't you better pack your bag for tomorrow yet, Martin, instead of just lying there watching the sodding news? I've virtually done mine, except for a few things in the morning. What's new on there, anyway? Nothing, I'm guessing?"

"Just bloody Brexit. It's all over the news. There must be some other things going on in the world surely," he told her.

"Don't worry, this Brexit shit is going to go on for years yet. It's not as simple as they would have people believe," she commented forcibly.

He'd never heard her comment on anything political before, so that came as a surprise, as did what she told him next as she pulled a white t-shirt over her head..

"You know what, they haven't even considered what's going to happen with my country from Brexit, with the border and the peace agreement. Not given it a thought at all and there was nothing about it in the campaign on either side, leave or remain. It's like we don't exist, but then you Brits, or I should say the bloody English, have always treated Ireland and us Irish like that. Arrogant bastards! The only good thing about Brexit is that I really do think it could come back to bite you English on the bum and result in a reunited independent Ireland thankfully."

Now not only had he never heard her comment on anything political before, but never heard her make any comment like that fervently in support of Irish nationalism. He decided it would be best to try and lighten the moment a little in advance of the serious subject he wanted to raise once more, what Richard had told him. So, he said, "I hope you don't think all the English are arrogant bastards, not this particular one anyway?"

That at least brought a smile to her lips as she climbed onto the bed alongside him, then rolled over on top of him and kissed him. As she lay on top of him staring into his face for a silent minute with the smile back on her lips, she eventually told him, "Although I might have to actually bite you on the bum English if you don't behave yourself, if you aren't good to me."

He just stared back into her mesmerising brown eyes, returned her smile, and kissed her strongly.

Still on top of him she asked, "What time do we have to leave in the morning? Not too early I hope?"

"Afraid so, Irish, we need to get the train at six-thirty, that means Gatwick by seven-thirty for nine-thirty flight."

"Ouch, bloody early then," she commented as she got off of him and up from the bed. "Still, I suppose having an early flight means at least I get most of Saturday out of our short weekend to show you my Dublin."

"Okay, so it's only a short two days there, but it's your home, place of your birth, and I want it to all be special. Not only our first weekend away together, but it's about me finding out more about you, who you are, where you're from. It was all your idea initially remember. I know it's all still really new between us, but I wanted to do this. I want to know everything about you, and then I want you to know everything about me when we get back to my place in Highgate. That's what love is, isn't it, that and complete trust? Of course, I'd like Dublin to be longer, but you have to be in work first thing Monday morning anyway, I guess."

As she stood in front of the wardrobe mirror and brushed her hair she hesitated a slightly. "Err ... hmm ... yes, I suppose that is what love is, knowing everything and trust, and yes I do have to be in work on Monday."

He got up from the bed and walked over to place his arms around her waist from behind, giving her a small hug. While he looked at her in the mirror from over her shoulder completely enraptured he asked, "So, tell me again how much you love me. I want to hear it from you over and over again. You know how much I love you already. You do don't you, love me still, I mean? I know that today at times I could seem a bit fucked up, insecure, but that's because ... because ... well, because of not knowing about ... you know ..."

His voice tailed off and he stopped speaking as he removed his arms from around her waist and she turned to face him. She looked him in the eyes for another full silent minute as neither of them spoke. Then she turned away from him and walked over to lay back down on the bed, with her head propped up by a pillow.

While he stood there motionless in front of the wardrobe looking across at her laying on the bed she eventually replied, "Well, I haven't really known you that long of course, but it seems to me that you do get a little moody sometimes. I think that's because you like to write. People who like to write are always a little fucked up. They are always busy watching everything, everybody, people and their characteristics. They think everything is in a novel, or could be, so they analyse everything they see and hear down to the minutest detail. You analyse everything, want to know every little bit of everything, so you can analyse it to death. It's like you're constantly character building, building an image of the characters you're going to write about."

"Really? You think so? Is that what I seem to you really?" He asked as he walked over to sit on the edge of the bed next to her.

She laughed and then told him, "See, you're doing it right now, analysing to death what I just told you. I bet it's really whirring around in your brain right this second."

She grabbed a handful of his polo shirt, pulled her into him and kissed him intensely. As she let go of his shirt and pulled back from the kiss she told him, "Every time you look at me that way, in the way you just did in that mirror over there, I can see there is total and complete romance in your eyes. So, of course I still love you, you fucked up English writer."

She let a broad smile spread across her lips as she finished telling him that. Her eyes were sparkling as she kissed him passionately once more and then told him, "Now get in the shower or we'll be late for that dinner at eight."

He got up off the bed, pulled off his polo shirt, and began unfastening his jeans as he headed towards the bathroom and his shower. As he reached the bathroom door he stopped, turned back to face her, and decided he really couldn't put it off any longer; this was the moment to try to ask her once again.

He didn't even need to be specific and simply asked, "But why won't you just tell me? Just tell me one way or the other." He was now practically pleading.

She knew exactly what he was referring to, and had been fully expecting him to raise it again at some point. She looked up at him from the bed with her face filled with exasperation. "Why is it so important? Don't you trust me? If you trust me why would I need to answer that? If you trust me why would you even ask? Anyway, what does it matter one way or the other? That prat is in the past-"

"But, I just-" he tried to interrupt, but she wouldn't let him finish.

"Don't you know that the only way to find out if you can trust someone is to actually trust them, Martin? That's Hemingway. That's what he believed. I thought you, of all people, would know that. I just don't understand why you have this incessant obsession, need to know."

He stood in the bathroom doorway with the top of his jeans unfastened, his voice getting louder and straining with emotion, pleading with her. "Precisely because I want to know, precisely because I do need to know."

He walked across to the bed and sat down on the edge of it beside her. Then he took hold of her hand and told her tenderly, "Look, Aileen, when you're already in a relationship, or even only just embarking on a relationship with another individual, there's a moment, there's always a moment when it comes to the opportunity of sex with another, different, person. That's when a person has to decide I can do this, I can give in to this, or I can resist it. I don't know when your moment was, but I bet there was one. I know there was. There must have been. Just tell me, please, just tell me the truth now and it'll all be in the past. I won't ask again."

She removed her hand from his, but coldly and dispassionately asked again, "Why? I don't understand why you need to know, why it is so important. It's not to me. It wouldn't be to me if I was you. It's in the past. Richard Weston is a prat, a pompous prat. I made a huge mistake and had an affair with him in the past. I can't understand why it is so important to you whether he is telling the truth or not? He's not important to us at all is he? He's irrelevant, and that's the way I prefer to leave him, leave it."

Now he was not only getting frustrated, but also increasingly angry once more as he got up from the bed and slowly wandered across the room again towards the bathroom door, shaking his head slowly from side to side as he went. He just couldn't understand why she couldn't merely tell him the truth, deny it. Eventually everything that had been festering for over a day, built up inside him over it, exploded. He raised his voice and told her, "Because I'm bloody addicted to it, the sodding truth. That's why I can't leave it."

"Maybe you should just have a bit more faith in me, Martin," she told him as she looked across to him with an element of despair in her eyes. "That's what I don't like, don't understand. That you could even think to believe even the minutest part of what someone like him tells you about me. That you even need me to deny it before you would believe it's not true. That's what really hurts." She repeated, "You should have more faith, Martin. Trust between two people in a relationship has to be based on faith in each other doesn't it, or it is nothing."

Unfortunately he didn't help himself at that point by reverting to his academic self, standing in the doorway with his jeans half undone. "Yes, Aileen, trust is a fine thing, but blind faith is not a fine thing. Socrates wrote that, and therefore trust can't be based on faith, he argued. Knowing everything about each other and complete trust, that's what I said love was earlier, didn't I? And you agreed."

She looked across at him from the bed. Now it wasn't doe-eyes of hers that were gazing up at him in a fixed stare, but eyes filled with a piercing mixture of growing anger, frustration, disappointment, and even a hint of a tear, he thought. There was an awkward silence of a minute or so as she looked away from him towards the far wall and he stood frozen in the bathroom doorway wondering what to say next as she hadn't responded at all to his last comment.

Eventually, at the end of that time, to his utter total shock she turned her head back towards him, brushed a couple of strands of her hair off her face with her right hand, and simply told him dispassionately, "Trust, not faith you say, okay trust wins, Martin. Then I don't love you anymore."

He was stunned. It felt like he had been hit by a very large truck. His face betrayed his total incredulity for half-a-minute, which felt like an hour to him while he stood there in silence trying to comprehend what had just happened. What had started out as a seemingly straightforward issue about Richard Weston's lies over sex, infidelity, and the truth, had metamorphosed into an uncontrollable alien beast between them, of jealousy, trust and faith.

"What? Since when? Since … since … since when … since when don't you love me anymore?" he eventually asked in a faltering voice as he quickly walked back over towards the bed still reeling from her outburst..

"Now, just now. You want trust, not faith, you believe in trust, but not in having faith in someone. I trusted someone before, my ex-husband. But I also had faith in him, faith that he loved me, and ultimately he abused that faith and let me down. That's why faith is more important to me, Martin, faith in each other, faith in my beliefs, faith in what I value, more than you'll ever know. But clearly, the fact that you even felt you had to ask me about what Richard claimed happened between us on that Friday night in Lindos means you don't have any faith in me, no faith in me not betraying you. Yes, trust is important, but without faith in each other, unquestioning faith, call it blind faith as your Greek philosopher Socrates did if you want, without that there can be no love and all this is pointless."

She stopped speaking, hesitated for a brief moment as she looked down at the duvet, then looked back up at him, and without any sign of emotion at all in her voice told him, "So ... it's over, and that's why."

He panicked from the shock of what she'd told him, what had just happened, and desperately tried to retrieve the rapidly deteriorating situation between them as he now stood by the bed, next to her.

"No, no, no, how can you say that so easily? I know you don't mean that. Don't do this, please, not just like that. Let's talk about it more, bloody trust and faith, or whatever you want. Please, I promise I won't ask you anymore about Lindos and you and him. That's all in the past, just like you said."

She looked up at him once more in silence for almost a minute as he stood rooted to the spot by the bed. She let out a heavy sigh, which he took to be a good sign that she was obviously reconsidering, realising what she'd done.

He reached down and took her hand again as he told her, "Let's not do anything foolish from arguing over nothing, and certainly not over Richard bloody Weston and his lies."

She looked up at him out of the top part of her now once again smouldering deep brown eyes as he added, "I love you, you know that. Let's not lose what we have."

He thought he detected a very slight nod of agreement from her, and a tear or two now in her eyes. In any case, he couldn't mistake that she definitely smiled up at him slightly as she told him, "Just take your shower, English. The table for dinner is booked for eight remember."

Her apparent quick mood swing once again surprised him; the ease at which she seemed to give in to his plea to not lose what they had and her seeming willingness to just carry on with their planned evening. He was certainly concerned over how she could change so quickly, swing from one decision to another. Nevertheless, he was just pleased that she had apparently retreated from ending their relationship just like that.

"Okay, of course," he told her as. he headed once more towards the bathroom door and his shower. This time he felt relieved, and much happier than he had done over the past half-an-hour or so. In fact, he had no idea whatsoever about what she had just done; no clue about the argument she had just deliberately contrived and manipulated.

She had concluded some considerable time ago, soon after her divorce, that she didn't want to be defined by whether she was with one man or another. If her divorce had shown her anything, it was that she should be her own person, and not whatever person some man or other wanted and preferred her to be. Alongside that she'd soon realised and learned that she could easily be fulfilled by appealing merely to men's lust, and not unnecessarily their love. Not only was that realisation a useful tool in trying to achieve her reawakened and revived political beliefs, but together with those beliefs it had helped reinforce confidence in herself as her own person. Consequently, now she always did what she needed to do when and how she wanted to do it.

She'd reached that conclusion long before she even met Martin Cleverley. Although he didn't know it at that time as he took his shower relieved, he was about to experience the full consequences of that philosophy within her, and by which she now lived her life.

227

26

Gone: another disappearance

When Martin emerged from the shower with a towel wrapped around his waist Aileen was no longer in the bedroom. Presuming she was in the lounge waiting for him to get ready he called out to her, but as he walked across towards the bedroom door he spotted a hand-written note on one of the pillows on the bed. He picked it up and read, "The secrets and lies that haunt us, and the truth that sets us free. Take care, Martin. x".

Once again he was shocked, stunned by what he read. "No, no, don't do this," he said aloud. He called out her name frantically and rushed into the lounge, but she wasn't there. He dashed back into the bedroom and checked the wardrobe. Her bag and all her clothes were gone. He was distraught. He couldn't comprehend what had just happened. Even as he was going into the shower he thought everything was now okay, sorted out, cleared up. Obviously, he was wrong. He quickly grabbed his jeans, pulled on the polo shirt he'd taken off to go in the shower and his trainers. He had no idea where he was going, but he rushed out into the street outside the flat. Bewildered, he ran to one end of the street and then the other. He looked down each of the streets that ran off the one the flat was in, more in hope than expectation; hope that she was just trying to frighten him, or maybe had changed her mind and would be waiting in one of those streets or making her way back to the flat. At each end of the street was a pub. He charged into them, frantically checking each bar looking for her.

There was no sign of her anywhere. Eventually, he gave up and wandered slowly back to the flat, where he picked up his phone and called her. He was stunned once more, and even more confused, when an obviously pre-recorded information voice message told him, "That number is unobtainable." He couldn't believe it, so he frantically tried it five more times and got the same message.

As he wandered the streets of Brighton aimlessly all that evening, hoping to find her, he tried her phone constantly, but always got the same message. At one point he thought that perhaps she would turn up at Gatwick airport for their flight to Dublin on Saturday morning, once again in the vague hope that she may have changed her mind and decided to come back to him. He'd go there in the morning anyway, just in case, he convinced himself. So, he did. He got up early, not that he'd slept much. The bed felt empty and cold without her. As they'd planned he caught the six-thirty train to Gatwick. All the while he was looking around on every part of the journey, just in case he would spot her. At Brighton station, on the train, and finally in the terminal building and check-in at Gatwick airport. Nothing, there was nothing, no sign of her whatsoever.

In the end he decided there was absolutely no point in him going to Dublin alone. He had both their flight tickets so there was no way she could get on the flight without him. In despair he headed back to his flat in Highgate, constantly checking his phone on the way just in case there was a text message or a voice message from her, but there was nothing. It was as if she'd disappeared off the face of the earth. Once he got to his flat he even tried calling the Jurys Inn hotel in Dublin she'd booked them into, or said she had, he hadn't actually got the booking confirmation, she had that he presumed. He only knew the name of it. Maybe he could check with them to see if she'd actually checked-in there. However, when he called them not only had she not booked in, but they had no record of any booking in her name or his.

Now he really was even more confused, bewildered, and was experiencing a whole range of crazy emotions, going through a mass of scenarios in his head. He continued to try her number all over that weekend, but simply got the same "number unobtainable" message. He spent an uncomfortable, uneasy, distressing and tiring weekend in his flat going over and over in his head every detail of their time in Lindos together. Going over and over what he actually knew about her, which he quickly realised wasn't actually a great deal.

By Sunday afternoon he was exhausted with it all and the lack of sleep. He even began to think he might be imagining things. On early Saturday evening as he returned to his flat from a quick trip to the local supermarket he thought briefly that someone was following him. Then later, as he looked out through the flat's curtains he was sure he noticed a car with two people sat in it near the flat which had been there for quite a few hours with its occupants. However, he dismissed his paranoia as being down to his overwhelming weariness.

There was one last chance to find her, one more possibility; a good one surely. He'd go to her company offices on Monday morning. He knew the company's name. She worked for the same one as Richard, but in South Kensington she'd told him. He got online, found the company's website and then the address of their offices in South Kensington.

Now finally he relaxed a little. He knew she was going to be back at work the next day. She'd told him that when they'd decided to go to Dublin. Yes, she had to be back at work on Monday morning, she'd said in answer to his question. He definitely remembered her saying that. So, he'd go there in the morning. Not too early though. He didn't want to turn up there causing a fuss or a scene the minute she'd arrived back from holiday. He'd aim for around eleven.

On the Monday morning he took the tube to South Kensington station and headed from there towards Cromwell Road and her company's offices. It was only a few minutes' walk from the station to the small square in which the offices were located. He walked quickly, determined to finally find her. At ten past eleven he entered the building and found the name of her company on the board in the lobby listing those in the building. The company's reception was located on the third floor the board indicated, so he headed for the lift.

Immediately ahead of him as he emerged from the lift was a reception area with a young blonde haired woman sat behind a counter. He approached it and saw from her badge that her name was Sylvia. She looked up as he reached the counter and said, "Good morning. Can I help you?"

In all his stunned confusion he hadn't actually thought through just how he was going to play this, so he hesitated slightly, not sure quite what to say first. In the end he simply blurted out her name nervously, and nothing else, "Err …Aileen Regan."

Sylvia looked confused, obviously having no idea quite what he wanted, although she did give him a small polite smile as she replied, "Sorry, sir."

He took a deep breath and tried to control his nervousness, before he got himself together a bit more and then asked, "Oh, sorry, yes, Aileen Regan, can I see her please?"

"Which department is she in, sir?" Sylvia asked as she clicked the mouse on her computer to bring up on the screen the list of the company's departments, employees, and their extensions."

"Ermm …" he hesitated once again as Sylvia now peered up at him from her chair behind the reception counter. He hadn't thought about that, hadn't thought this through at all. Maybe it was the effect of the lack of sleep on him.

"Ermm …," he tried again, "Ermm … not really sure, but I know she's at P.A. Yes, that's right, a P.A. for an Advertising Executive."

"We are an Advertising Agency, sir. We have a lot of Advertising Executives," the receptionist informed him quite sharply. "Have you any idea which one?"

"Not really, well, not at all actually," he told her. "I just know she works here, works for your company."

"I'll check the staff directory, sir," Sylvia told him as she clicked on her mouse once more. "Regan was it, Aileen Regan? Is that Regan with only one 'e' and no 'a'?"

"Yes, that's right."

As she scrolled down the screen through the staff directory Sylvia muttered, "Radford, Rawlings, Rawlingson, Redford, Roberts." She looked up at him from the screen and told him, "No, there's no Aileen Regan, no Regan at all in fact, sir. Sorry."

A mixture of confusion and disappointment spread across his face. He said nothing for almost half-a-minute, and then scratched his head and told her, "But there must be. She told me this is where she worked."

"No, sorry, sir, there's definitely no one of that name working here," the receptionist told him once more.

He turned away and started to walk forlornly towards the lift. Just before he was about to press the button to call it one last desperate thought jumped into his head. He turned around and walked quickly back to the reception desk and Sylvia behind it.

"She's been on holiday, on holiday for the past three weeks, so …" Even as he got halfway through what he was about to suggest he realised it was a stupid, futile thing to ask; whether she wasn't in the staff directory because she'd been on holiday? Stupid and crazy, he thought. He was losing his mind.

However, Sylvia must have recognised the growing despair on his face and took pity on him by suggesting, "Look, sir, I can get someone from HR to come and see you. Maybe they will be able to help you? Perhaps this Aileen Regan you are looking for did work here in the past, but doesn't anymore. I've only been here six months, so if they worked here before I wouldn't know, but HR may be able to check their records for you. Although, if she did work here and left they wouldn't be allowed to tell you anything more than that I expect."

"Thanks, that might help," he told her. He was grasping at straws as he was sure that Aileen told him she was still working there, not that she had worked there previously.

"Take a seat while I tell HR what this is all about and get someone to come and talk to you please, sir," Sylvia suggested as she picked up her phone and called HR. She told them what Martin wanted, or rather who he was looking for, and the woman in HR said she would check the company employee records and then come down to reception to let Martin know what she'd found, if anything. However, she emphasised to the receptionist that she should inform him that HR would only be allowed to confirm whether or not Aileen Regan had ever worked for the company, but nothing more.

Fifteen minutes later the woman from HR emerged from the lift and the receptionist pointed in the direction of Martin, who was sitting on one of the pale green reception couches, becoming increasingly frustrated. Before she could go across to him he anticipated who she was and jumped up to walk over to her at the reception counter. However, his frustration wasn't removed, or even reduced in any way, by what she told him immediately.

"As our receptionist told you, sir, no one of that name works here now, nor, according to our records has anyone called Aileen Regan ever worked for the company."

He frowned, and briefly slowly shook his head from side to side, saying nothing in response for half-a-minute or so as he merely stared blankly into space towards the pale green wall behind the reception counter. Eventually he lowered his head and covered his face with his hands in obvious despair.

"Sir?" the HR woman asked, "Are you okay? I'm sorry we can't be of more help to you, but I can certainly assure you that no one called Aileen Regan works here or has ever done so," she repeated.

He lifted his head out of his hands and straightened up, telling her as he did so, "That's okay, I see, thank you for your help." He tried to explain, in a vague assumption that it might help. "I just don't understand, you see. I only met her a few weeks ago on holiday, but I'm certain she told me she worked here. I'm certain, a hundred per cent sure, but I just don't understand why she would lie about that."

He was clutching at one final straw as he asked, "Maybe in another of your offices, perhaps she works in another of your offices? I know that you have a few in London, for different departments of the company?"

"The record of all the company's employees is kept here in our HR department, sir," the woman started to explain. "We only have the one for all of the company offices, and all employees, not just in London, but all across the country. If anyone called Aileen Regan worked for the company anywhere in the U.K., not just in London, they would be on our employee records here in my department."

He was shaking his head from side to side once again, now becoming a little distraught once again at the frustration and confusion of it all. Weariness from a mixture of lack of sleep over the weekend, and from puzzling over and over about the mystery of the disappearing Aileen, began to sweep over him. His legs suddenly felt like lead and any remaining colour was rapidly draining from his face.

The woman from HR asked once more if he was okay and the receptionist offered him some water from the nearby water cooler.

As she went to get it the woman from HR guided him back to one of the reception couches, suggesting he sit down for a few minutes.

As he took the plastic beaker of water from the receptionist and thanked her he again said, "I just don't understand. This is crazy. Why would she do this? Why play bloody silly games? I know we only met on holiday, and I've only known her for a couple of weeks, so obviously didn't know that much about her, but we got on so well, even came back and went to Brighton for the week. We were supposed to go to Dublin for the weekend on Saturday morning, but …" His voice faltered, so he took a sip of the water and then continued, "but then she just disappeared on Friday night. Just left the flat we were renting in Brighton. Walked out while I was in the shower, and when I came out she was gone, and all her clothes and stuff."

The two women were now sat either side of him. As he recounted what happened he had leaned forward to place his elbows on his knees and rest his hands on his cheeks. Again, he was vacantly staring ahead into space. The two women looked across at each other behind his bent back. Their faces, and the looks they exchanged, showed that they were both obviously increasingly uncomfortable with being stuck with this stranger who had wandered into their offices looking for someone that didn't exist, at least not in terms of working for their company. Just as the HR woman was about to say something to the effect that they really should get back to work in order to try and extricate the two women from what had become an awkward situation, Martin reached inside his jacket for his phone.

He clicked onto his photos, pulled up one of him and Aileen, and then showed it to the two women as he said, "Look, look, this is us in Rhodes just over a week ago. Doesn't that look like someone who is happy? Why would she disappear?"

The two women were now increasingly concerned at the possibility of being stuck with this strange guy while he showed them his holiday snaps. So, initially they both showed a distinct lack of interest, but then the receptionist started to stare more intently at the photo without moving her head at all. She reached to take the phone out of Martin's hand and moved it closer to her face as she peered at the photo for a few seconds more. She looked up from the phone and then across at the woman from HR. A frown now spread across her face and she said in a surprised, incredulous voice, "But that's Kathleen O'Mara. She left over three weeks ago."

The woman from HR took the phone from her, looked at the photo closely and agreed. "Yes, it is, that Kathleen. She gave a month's notice, but she took the three weeks of holiday she was owed as part of her resignation notice. She left on the seventeenth of June. Some of us even went to the pub across the square with her that lunchtime for a leaving drink. Not that many people here really knew her that well, but, well, it's just something we do. Any excuse for a lunchtime drink on a Friday, if you know what I mean."

Martin's confusion wasn't abating at all now, if anything it was obviously increasing rapidly and getting considerably worse. His head was spinning, although he did actually manage a mumbled, "Yes, I see," to the woman's "any excuse for a lunchtime drink comment." As she handed him back his phone he took a deep breath and asked, "Are you sure? Kathleen O'Mara? That was, is, her name? And that's definitely her?"

"Yes, that's Kathleen for sure, and that's definitely the name she used when she worked here. We had National Insurance and tax details for her in that name in HR."

"Phew!" he said and he puffed out his cheeks. As he then rubbed the back of his neck with the palm of his left hand he asked, "So, did either of you get any idea where she was going to work after she quit here by any chance?"

The receptionist told him, "No, not at all really. She did tell us at the pub that she was going on holiday to Greece the week after she left, but I don't think she told anyone what she was going to do for a job after that. At least, I didn't hear her say in the pub. She never mentioned it. I asked her a couple of times after she gave in her notice, but she just said 'something will come up' and that she 'wanted a break'."

"I don't think she had anywhere, any other job lined up. I'm sure we've never had any request for a reference for her from any other company. I would've thought we would have had if she had another job to go into. That's usual," the HR woman told him. She quickly added, "Although, strictly speaking I shouldn't even be telling you that."

As she once more looked at Sylvia she told him, "I'm sorry, but we really should be getting back to work now. I'm sure Sylvia has got calls to deal with, and I've got things to deal with in the HR department. I'm sorry we couldn't be of more help. As I said, I've probably told you more than I should have anyway, about not having a reference request for her I mean. Hope you find her."

With that the two women got up and left him sitting on the couch bewildered in a complete daze. He sat there for two full minutes and only managed to drag himself off to the lift when he felt the still concerned gaze of the receptionist on him.

After he emerged from the building he meandered slowly into the small park opposite in the square in which the offices were located, still stunned and numb. He slumped onto a green ornate metal bench just as he entered the park. In his continuing bewildered and confused state he tried to go over and over in his mind everything she told him about herself. Obviously she wasn't who she said she was at all. He eventually came to the conclusion that no wonder she was spooked by him saying he wanted to find out all about her and her past, and where she grew up. That only confused him even more however, as he recalled it was actually her suggestion that they go to Dublin.

Part Six: Boston Logan International Airport

27

Tuesday 12th July, 2016: Kathleen O'Mara

A middle-aged woman with short dyed blonde hair approached the Boston airport passport control booth and placed her American passport on the counter for the officer to check. After a few minutes checking he returned it to her saying, "Welcome home."

As she came through the automatic sliding doors into the Arrivals Hall she scanned the waiting group of disparate individuals, mostly drivers waiting for their pick-ups. She quickly spotted and recognised hers, a short, stocky, dark haired man in his early thirties, wearing a thin dark blue anorak and jeans, and sporting a couple of days, obviously attempted, designer stubble. She made eye contact and gave him a slight nod of recognition, which he returned, equally slightly. Without speaking they turned together and headed out through the exit of the Arrivals Hall and towards the airport car park. They took the lift to the third floor and as they walked out of the lift the man spoke for the first time, pointing to his right and telling her, "It's over here, the next row back."

When they reached the black limousine he held open one of the doors for her to slide into the leather back seat, telling him as she did so, "Thank you, Patrick."

"Welcome home, Kathleen," he said before closing the door and putting her bag in the boot of the car. After he lowered himself into the driver's seat he asked, "The usual place, your flat on the harbour?"

"Yes, I definitely need my own bed for a while."

As soon as they drove off her phone rang. Recognising the caller's name on the screen, as she answered she told them immediately, "Wait a second," without allowing them to speak. Even before she could instruct Patrick he automatically pressed the switch on the dashboard to raise the soundproof screen between him and the back seats of the car.

Once the screen was fully deployed she told the caller, "Okay, go ahead, Michael."

The voice on the other end of the phone told her, "Another good job well done, Kathleen. The Bhoys are well satisfied. You fucked her over good and proper. And to think that over all those years she's never suspected a thing about you, actually thought she was in control. Her marriage is well and truly knackered now apparently don't you know, and so is her bloody MI6 career too. Our informants tell us she's virtually had a nervous breakdown since you disappeared. Her marriage, and then her career, all went tits up within a few days, especially when MI6 were shitting themselves over what they thought she may have disclosed to you. Revenge is sweet don't you think, especially when served cold as they say? It took a while, quite a few years, but I knew we'd get the bastard in the end, that you'd get her in the end, Kathleen. Payback for all that shit and grief she's caused us over the years."

"Yep, it all went relatively smoothly, just as we planned, Michael. They've never suspected at all that I was a plant, right from the time I pretended to innocently let her recruit me at Uni. All this time she never had a clue, the dull cow. She thought she was so bloody clever. My cover's blown now though, but at least I'm free of all that pretence of being her sodding friend. As you said, it's payback for all the grief she's caused the organisation over the years. Personally though, most of all it's payback for what she bloody did to my father for the sodding English and their Secret Service all those years ago. Thanks to that false identity and legend the Bhoys manufactured for me all those years ago she didn't have a clue that he was my father. Good old Aileen Regan, eh Michael?"

239

She laughed down the phone line in response to his reply of, "Aye, she's a fine girl is Aileen, to be sure, Kathleen."

Her voice changed. There was audible anger and a vindictive edge to it as she continued, "Bloody Sandra Weston knew exactly what she was doing for them when she set up my father. They had to have a sacrificial lamb, even when he was nowhere near the bombing. They bloody knew that, she bloody knew it too. She must have done. The evidence and his alibi was there plainly for them to see, but they hid it, and then let loose one of their death squads on him, even though it was five sodding years after the Good Friday peace agreement. Because of that it was all hush hush. Even though I was working for them, or at least they thought I was, it was all kept so tight security-wise that I never even got a sniff of it, and nor did many people at all, except for that cow. She was right at the heart of it, coordinated it all, so the Bhoys informed me when they discovered that a couple of years later. Of course, she never knew he was my father, but because of the sensitivity of it being well after the peace agreement she kept it all to herself and her tight small team anyway. At least it's settled now, for my father. And a nervous breakdown you say, Michael? That doesn't surprise me at all. She always was highly strung; even way back when she thought she was recruiting me. Then later there was that Tehran balls up she was involved in. The way she went on to me about it afterwards, she almost had a nervous breakdown over that shit then I can tell you. When the asset she was supposed to be getting out of Iran got banged up by the Iranians she fucked up good and proper. She went on about it to me for weeks."

She stopped speaking momentarily, and her voice change once more to a much softer tone as she asked, "But Cleverley, what about him since I disappeared? Anything? Have you picked up anything?"

"You gone a bit soft over him, Kathleen? There's something in your voice that suggests you might have. Have you?"

"Don't be stupid, Michael, and don't get above yourself and try to play silly games with me." The tone of her voice had immediately changed distinctly again, and she added, "You'd lose. Just remember that."

His voice changed back to a much more serious business-like tone, focused back on the subject. "Sure, Kathleen, I'll remember that, of course I will. Anyway, Cleverley has been looking everywhere for you, not that he's ever going to find you now of course. Our contact person inside the company who got you the job there so you could eventually get access to Richard Weston told us he even turned up there yesterday looking for you. Apparently he did discover your real name though after he showed a holiday photo of the two of you and they recognised you."

"Yeah, that was a mistake in Lindos; a stupid mistake. I'm not usually so careless, but he was so insistent on a bloody photo of the two of us together. That was difficult to avoid on a holiday, I suppose, but I won't make that mistake again. Anyway, I ditched the phone he had the number for straight after I walked out on him in Brighton, so he's not going to find me that way. Getting me into Richard Weston's company, getting me a job there, was a good move, as was making it in a different division of the company location-wise. That enabled me to keep my distance from that dickhead Weston until I was ready to make my move, and use my two different identities. It was always quite a risk that all that dual identity stuff might backfire there at the Christmas party when I pretended to accidentally bump into him. Probably the most risky part of the whole operation, him knowing me by one name and me being known by another in that division of the company I worked in. I knew he'd be there though, and pissed. So, it was always going to be the most opportune moment for making contact with him without her being around, and then getting into his pants. I simply made sure I was alone at the bar when I accidentally bumped into him, and then I isolated the two of us from the rest of the people there as quickly as possible. He's such a pompous, egotistical prat that I think he thought he was moving in on me, approached me, and was chatting me up. I knew it wouldn't be difficult at all to reel him in. From all that background stuff you did on him and fed me about his drinking and womanising I knew he was bound to be pissed, and there was no way he was going to be able to keep his dick in his trousers that night, not the way I looked, the way I was dressed. The idiot even made a point of going on about it, and complimenting me endlessly. I assume that was his technique for getting into my knickers, or so he thought. Little did he know that he didn't really need to try that hard. It was going to happen anyway if I had my way. I made sure of that, believe me, Michael. I'm good at it."

She let out a small laugh after she said that and then continued, "It was almost too easy. Anyway, it was a perfect way to get at her through her life outside MI6; a masterstroke, causing chaos in her private life and using it to help destroy her. So, in the end all that research you did on him, particularly the stuff identifying him as a target who couldn't keep his dick in his trousers, all that made it so easy to hook him and then use him to get at her. A job well done, Michael."

"Blimey! That's praise indeed coming from you Kathleen. Not something that happens too often. To finish what I was telling you about Cleverley though, my guess is that eventually he'll give up looking for you soon, and just settle for his life as a wimp of a Professor."

She responded initially with a cynical laugh down the phone line, before agreeing, "You're probably right. He was a just a useful prop, a useful convenient cover that I happened across on the Rhodes flight, as well as a nice bit of fun of course. A not unpleasant diversion to keep the target, Weston, confused while I finished her off. Much better that way initially than a bullet - a nervous breakdown and the loss of her MI6 stuff, as well as the end of her marriage. Bloody brilliant. Slower, but ultimately more psychologically agonising and painful. Passion is a dangerous and sometimes lethal weapon in the right hands, Michael. Used for a person or an organisation's own ends it can produce and achieve the ultimate desired results, even without bloodshed if you can just mind fuck someone initially instead. I always find that's quite good fun. Yep, I always enjoy that a lot."

"Jesus, Kathleen, you really are one cold bitch. The Bhoys always say you are, but I never really believed you could be as tough as they said. What is it that keeps you going after all this time? You don't need to now surely do you, especially now your cover has been blown? This was ultimately the one job you wanted to complete, wasn't it? So, why not stop now?"

"You wouldn't understand, Michael, not unless you've done it, been part of it, been right in the middle of it. Strangely, it's actually the heady addictive allure of constant duplicity and deception that I love. That is what keeps me doing it; all that lying and cheating, and being someone you're not. I love all of it. I love the game, and all that's connected with it. It's like a drug, which is why I can't stop, and I'm sure there'll be plenty to keep me going, keep me busy for a while yet."

"Well, you're right about that, there's plenty going on at the moment, for sure. Although the Bhoys at the top are a bit distracted at present trying to get their head around the bloody Brits and all this Brexit shit after the referendum result. It's clear that none of the Brit politicians, or the people voting for Brexit, has given any thought whatsoever about the border, not given a shit over it."

"They will, Michael, they will, believe me they'll have to. They'll wake up and realise it eventually, the bloody idiots! But I'm sure the Brits will have plenty more to worry about from the global economy generally as well over the next few years, on top of Brexit."

For no obvious reason, right off the top of her head she bizarrely rattled off down the phone line a potted, succinct analysis of the world economic system. "Besides Brexit there'll be, let me see, a shock to global trade, financial instability in China, global monetary tightening with rising interest rates and the end of quantitative easing, rising private debt in the developed world, and of course, the unresolved ongoing Eurozone crisis. So, from all that on top of Brexit, the U.K. will be well and truly stuffed by another recession towards the end of 2019 or in 2020, just like after 2008. I'd say that given all that, from our point of view we'll pretty soon be looking at a reunited Ireland at last, Michael. Something good will come out of the shit of Brexit anyway then."

"Phew, you're not just a cold bitch then, Kathleen, but a bloody clever one too. Quite a dangerous explosive cocktail, I'd say."

He couldn't see it from the other end of the line, but a self-satisfied grin of pleasure was etched across her lips as she agreed, "Hmm ... if you say so, Michael. Anyway, I like to think so."

"What about, Richard Weston, Kathleen?" he asked, changing the subject slightly, away from her favourite subject, herself. "Don't you want to know what's happened to him since you also fucked him over, just to tie things up?"

"Can't say I do, Michael, not really. He was, is, just an arrogant prat, a useful one for us, but a prat's a prat. Who cares?"

"Right, useful, yes I guess he was, to get at her through him."

"You know, Michael, when men talk about the agony of being men, they can never quite get away from the recurrent theme of self-pity. That sums up Richard Weston as far as I'm concerned, from my experience of having to spend so much time in his bloody company, in bed with him for the sake of the operation. It could also definitely apply to Martin Cleverley, the self-pity, along with his insecurities where women are concerned I'd say. But when some women talk about being women, they can never quite get away from the recurrent theme of blaming men, and that about sums up Sandra Weston too. Anyway, there's a little bit of philosophy to end this conversation with, for you to dwell on as a man, Michael. It's been fun once again. Till the next one. Meanwhile I'm going to enjoy the delights of Boston, some good lobster and a glass or two of Sam Adams for a bit. Bye."

"Err … yes, thanks for that little gem for me to dwell on, Kathleen. And yep, till the next one, we'll be in touch. Just to let you know before you go though, the Bhoys wanted me to inform you that it's been decided to finish her off completely anyway, Weston. As I said, she's had something of a breakdown and she's well and truly broken. However, it seems that's not enough for some of the Bhoys at the top. They want their complete revenge, want her eliminated and-."

She didn't let him finish, and interrupted eagerly with, "Let me do it? Tell them I'll do it, I want to do it."

"That's what the Bhoys at the top said you'd say. They told me that if you did then we should let you do it. So, okay, I'll send you the details of where and when through the usual channels, set it all up for you with a team of two others to sort logistics and the rest of the stuff. It'll be in the U.K. though, which could be tricky for you now, but if you really want to do it we'll set you up with another passport and a new identity. But it'll have to be a short and sharp operation, because it'll be high risk for you now. So, we'll check out some stuff about her movements and sort a good day for it. We'll arrange it so you can just fly into the U.K and be met by one of the team late one afternoon, do it the next day, and then fly out again later that day or evening. We'll sort a scenario that makes it look like suicide. I'm sure you and the team can fix that, and after her nervous breakdown her people at MI6 should be easily convinced that's what happened."

"That sounds fine, sounds good, can't wait, Michael. Looking forward to it, been waiting a lot of years for this."

"God, you really are one cynical, callousness woman, Kathleen. I hope I never cross you."

"Then you'd better not, had you, Michael. That's me though, but maybe it'll not be Kathleen for much longer, eh? I'll message you a photo for the new passport. Looking forward to another new me to go with my new hairstyle and colour." She laughed down the line, and then added, "As I said before, it's been fun, Michael. I'll look forward to the details soon of that next little job you've got for me. Make it soon. Bye, be safe."

Meanwhile, back in London Martin Cleverley had all but given up trying to find the woman he knew as Aileen Regan. He had completely run out of ideas about where to look for her and who to possibly contact. For a fleeting few moments he thought about trying to find, contact, or see Sandra Weston, but concluded that she almost certainly wouldn't be forthcoming with much help given what happened between her husband and Aileen. And there definitely wouldn't be any point in trying to see him again after what had happened last time. Not that Martin actually thought there was much of a possibility that he would know where Aileen was anyway. It had been four days since she disappeared, walked out on him, and as far as he could see, she had completely vanished of the face of the earth.

He recalled what had crossed his mind as he sat relaxed in the Lindos sunshine outside Giorgos café bar with his small beer almost three weeks before, just after he'd met her. Just what was that something that sparked between two people, particularly middle-aged ones and in his case a man and a woman, which drew them together in a moment of uncanny recognition? What usually followed as a relationship between two people developed was certainly a Greek labyrinth to be unlocked – the code of attraction, and ultimately love, were necessary if the clear correct path out of the labyrinth was to be discovered.

The relationship labyrinth was something most people could not help, or avoid entering at some point in their life. Once inside they could feel lost, with no clear sense of direction regarding the relationship. Stuck in the labyrinthine maze of minute disparate, often contradictory events and feelings they would increasingly never be able to see the whole design of the labyrinth, the bigger whole picture, the benefits and connections to the heart or centre of the relationship.

The labyrinth in Greek mythology held terror within it, but ultimately there was also love. Although not involving actual terrors, perhaps the labyrinth of Greek mythology was a pretty good analogy for his relationship experiences with Aileen. The centre and heart of relationships may not always be where you think it is or where you want it to be. Mostly people in relationships desire a clear pattern, shape and design to them – an understandable clarity and meaning. He knew he did. He now realised that in the labyrinth that was his brief relationship with Aileen he had, indeed, never seen its whole design, the bigger whole picture, not least because of the maze of minute disparate, often contradictory, events and feelings over that whirlwind couple of weeks with her, particularly in Lindos. He certainly now never had any clarity at all about it, or any understandable meaning to it, especially when it came to issues of faith or trust. Ultimately, he had found his way out of his own Greek relationship labyrinth, but definitely did not arrive at his hoped for destination.

CPSIA information can be obtained
at www.ICGtesting.com
Printed in the USA
BVHW081236120819
555664BV00025B/2520/P